SUSPECT PASSIONS

by

VK Powell

2009

SUSPECT PASSIONS

ISBN 10: 1-60282-053-8
ISBN 13: 978-1-60282-053-1

This Trade Paperback Original Is Published By
Bold Strokes Books, Inc.
P.O. Box 249
Valley Falls, NY 12185

First Edition: March 2009

CREDITS

EDITORS: JENNIFER KNIGHT AND SHELLEY THRASHER
PRODUCTION DESIGN: STACIA SEAMAN
COVER DESIGN BY SHERI (GRAPHICARTIST2020@HOTMAIL.COM)

Acknowledgments

It would not be possible to do the work I love without the support and encouragement of amazing friends. Thank you for your understanding when I hide away for days to create a new character, write another chapter, or struggle with edits. Thank you for insisting that I come up for air occasionally so I can appreciate how wonderful you all are.

To Radclyffe and Bold Strokes Books, deep appreciation for allowing me to do what makes my heart sing. I thank Jennifer Knight for her wisdom, guidance, and humor and for helping me become a better writer with each project. My gratitude also goes to Shelley Thrasher and Stacia Seaman for their attention to detail when most of us are ready to move on to something new. And to Sheri, many thanks for bringing my words to life in graphic form. The cover is wonderful.

To all the readers who support and encourage my writing, thank you for buying my work, visiting my Web site (www.powellvk.com), sending e-mails, and showing up for signings. You make my "job" so much fun!

Dedication

For Lyn, beloved friend near or far. AIRTIC

CHAPTER ONE

A beautiful mocha-skinned woman was standing against the back wall of the restroom when Sydney Cabot entered. She wore a red leather bodysuit unzipped past her navel, revealing full breasts and a tuft of dark hair between her legs. As Syd approached, the woman slid her hand inside the shiny material and stroked one breast in a circular motion. "Are you watching or participating tonight?"

"Do I know you?" Syd couldn't believe the woman's audacity.

"You certainly do, in the biblical sense, right here in this very place." The woman's smile was bold and suggestive of someone skilled in the art of conquest. "You refused to go home with me."

The attractive African-American looked familiar but Syd couldn't come up with a name. She should've been unforgettable—Amazon came to mind, large and muscular, but all woman. Her short hair clung to her head in light waves. Her eyes were almost catlike, their hue a brownish gold. "Ah, yes. You're…"

"Lacy," the woman supplied. "At least, that's the name you seemed to prefer last time."

"Sure, I remember," Syd lied smoothly. A scramble of indistinct memories converged in the back of her mind. Her tactile senses said she'd touched that provocative body before, but she could not remember when or where. "Hey, good to see you again."

Lacy passed on the opportunity for small talk. She held the last stall door open. "Well?"

Syd inhaled a blend of scents, disinfectant pine and various women's perfumes, the lingering traces of patrons who'd passed through this room tonight. "Look, Lacy, I'm sorry but there's been a big mistake. I have a girlfriend and—" Syd stopped, realizing that was no longer true.

"Yes, you told me all about your little vanilla lover." Lacy pushed her jumpsuit to the floor and stepped out of it. "You're nothing if not honest, darling. But I satisfy your *other* needs."

She seductively stroked her breasts. Her body was a vision of perfectly toned muscles, which seemed to quiver with sexual energy.

"I don't know what you're talking about," Syd said. "What other needs?"

"The new tastes you've developed lately. Come here, lover, and I'll show you."

Lacy grabbed the front of Syd's silk blouse, pulled their bodies together with surprising force, and covered her mouth with a searing kiss. With practiced precision she turned their joined bodies into the small booth and pinned Syd against the wall, leaving the door open.

Syd struggled, but her arms were trapped at her sides by the more powerful woman. Lacy's firm body rubbed against hers with increasing intensity. Syd gazed into the single naked lightbulb that hung overhead, blinded to everything except its harsh glow and the severe ache building inside her. She clamped her legs together to block Lacy's groping hands. But the more she resisted, the more excited she became. She wanted to be taken, and this woman knew it.

"That's right, baby, fight me. It makes you feel alive, doesn't it?" Lacy chuckled, opened the zipper of Syd's trousers, pushed them to the floor, and off. She smiled at the absence of panties and raised Syd's left leg onto the toilet seat. Lacy kissed Syd again, then replaced her tongue with her index finger. Sliding her wet finger down Syd's chest and abdomen, she dipped into the silky moisture between her legs.

No, it doesn't make me feel alive, Syd thought, *I want to get away from you!* But even as she looked toward the door, her body betrayed her and she was gripped by a wave of raging desire. She buried her face in the voluptuous breasts pressed against her and breathed in the aphrodisiac of sweat and sex. Simultaneously she closed her fingers in the tight curls at the base of Lacy's stomach and tugged.

"Oh yeah, baby, do it. Pull it. Bite my tits," Lacy begged, in labored breaths. She placed her fingers against the bony mound between Syd's legs, entered her roughly one at a time, and then plunged deep inside.

"Fuck me harder!" Syd urged. "Make me feel it!" It was as though someone else was in her body, willing this woman to take her, to make her feel something—anything. Even pain was better than the numbness she wore like a cloak since the shooting.

"You don't do things the easy way, do you, lover?" Lacy purred.

Syd felt like her insides were being ripped out as Lacy's sudden withdrawal created a vacuum where Syd wanted fast, hot pain. "Just fuck me, now," she begged.

Intense pressure replaced the void as Lacy forced her fingers back inside all at once and closed them into a ball. She hammered her clenched fist deeper into Syd time after time, using her free hand to pinch and twist her exposed clit. Syd felt as if she was splitting open from the girth and force of the thrusts, but the pain only heightened her excitement.

Her mouth covered Lacy's nipple and she sucked harder, in time with the pumping inside her. There was no tenderness, only the need to be completely possessed, totally fucked by a stranger who asked nothing more than that and to whom she owed no explanation.

Syd's body shuddered with tremors as she felt herself tighten around the hand that occupied her centermost cavity. She opened her eyes and waited as lust shrouded her vision. Her back arched and a rasping scream rose in her parched throat. Wave after wave of hot juices drained from her. She clutched Lacy to her and convulsed as whimpering cries of pleasure and agony forced their way up her throat and out into the heavy air. The climax ripped through her with an energy she didn't recognize, dissolving all thought and providing the physical release she craved. Then, afterward, there was only an emptiness of unfathomable depths.

Lacy pulled Syd's right leg between her own and rubbed herself along the length of the shapely thigh, her fist still buried inside Syd's convulsing body. After a few long, unhurried strokes, Lacy collapsed against her. "My God, woman, you just keep getting better," she breathed onto Syd's neck.

Syd pushed back and looked at the clinging woman, unable to believe what she'd just done. Lacy's body shimmered with perspiration and the flush of satisfaction. Their bodies were still joined and their panting breaths filled the room with heat and a strange echo.

Just over Lacy's shoulder Syd caught a flash of something. She blinked to focus. A woman, still as death, was staring into their stall. A bright red flush roared up from the woman's shirt collar, over her face, and sparked fire in her cobalt blue eyes. Her intense gaze lingered on their bodies as if committing the image to memory. The tight press of her lips told Syd all she needed to know—prude. The woman smoothed her closely cropped honey blond hair in a fidgety gesture of embarrassment, then spun on her heel and walked quickly toward the door, mumbling something about consideration for others.

Her mood destroyed, Syd disentangled herself from Lacy, gathered her clothing, and dressed again.

"What are you doing?" Lacy asked.

"Thanking you for a great time and leaving." With a perfunctory wave, Syd exited the restroom and the club. She stepped out into the crisp April air just as a gray Acura, driven by the disapproving blonde, spun out of the parking lot.

Syd wasn't sure why she'd bothered to rush out here. Granted, the blonde was attractive and tall, with a firm body, great ass, and a swagger that would make any woman swoon, but she was a puritan nonetheless. Her condemnation was broadcast in that critical icy glare; you'd think she'd never seen two women having sex.

She probably never got any, Syd concluded, but why did some women find it necessary to judge each other's lives? Didn't we get enough of that shit from everybody else? The entire lesbian nation should celebrate with cheers and catcalls every time another sister had an orgasm.

Regan Desanto ramped down on the accelerator and spun her vehicle out of the Cop Out parking lot. The muscles in her legs ached from the restraint she'd imposed by strolling away from that restroom when she'd really wanted to run. But one thing life had taught her was control. No one would ever see her lose it again. So, anyone watching her walk to the Acura would have seen a woman unaffected by the increased pounding of her heart and the heat surging beneath her skin.

She wondered why she'd gone to Cop Out in the first place. She never found anything she wanted in bars or brothels, and she'd tried several times. But after only a year in High Point, North Carolina, her adjustment was proving more difficult than she imagined. Her intuition had begun to atrophy and her emotions to transform into lumps of home décor in this furniture capital of the world. She knew it really wasn't the place as much as the disassembly of her life and her relocation hundreds of miles away from everything familiar.

Martha, her fifteen-year partner, had been the essence of her life since they were in college. But last year Regan had been exiled from their relationship like a pile of putrid garbage. Now she was in a strange place with no real friends, an aging grandmother, and no life beyond work. The club had sounded like a good idea earlier, an attempt to begin a social life and maybe even make a few friends. But she didn't need or want friends who thought sex in a public restroom was fun or acceptable. Regan shivered at the recurring vision and concentrated on where she was going, which seemed to be her grandmother's assisted-living facility. She parked carelessly outside the building. Her legs shook slightly as she got out of the car.

She took a deep breath to calm the uncustomary pounding of her heart before she tapped lightly at Isadora Pearce's room. Her grandmother could always tell when she was upset or worried and she didn't want to alarm her, especially when she wasn't sure herself why she was so out of sorts.

Her grandmother's soft voice invited her into the small room that had taken the place of her three-thousand-square-foot home. Inside, the space had been converted into a memory bank filled with anything that evoked a happy story or recollection. She noticed with a pang of guilt that her grandmother was already in bed.

"Hi, Gram. How're you feeling?" Regan kissed her on the head and slumped into the cushioned rocker beside her.

Izzy Pearce looked surprisingly good for a woman who'd had three heart surgeries in the past five years. Her fiery red hair had been invaded by silver and the result was striking. At seventy-five, her once-flawless facial features had headed south and filled with wrinkles, but her sparkling blue eyes hinted at her astute mind and clever wit.

"Hi, honey. I'm doing great." Izzy glanced at the large wall clock. "I didn't expect to see you tonight."

"I'm sorry it's so late. I was out riding around. Guess I lost track of time."

Regan loved Izzy and hated lying to her. She'd been the only person in Regan's family who helped her in any way, taking her in after high school and helping her get a scholarship to attend Xavier University to study law. Izzy treated her like she mattered. That's why she'd moved to this small town next to nowhere in the first place; not because Izzy needed *her* but because Regan needed to be close to the one person who thought she was special.

"Don't ever apologize for coming to visit. But it *is* Friday night. I hoped you were on a date with some hot woman." Izzy studied her. "You look a little flushed. Maybe you already had the date?"

Regan knew Izzy meant well, but the questions about her personal life always caused a pinch of embarrassment and too much pain. "No, Gram, no date."

"Then why is your color so high? And you have those little crinkle lines around your eyes that usually mean you're thinking about something."

Izzy knew her entirely too well, and her capacity for listening was like being surrounded by a warm blanket. Regan had never been able to resist her invitations to confide, subtle or otherwise. "Okay, I went to a club tonight but it turned out to be a bad idea." The couple in the ladies' room flashed through her mind again.

At first, she couldn't believe anyone would be having sex in such an impersonal, public area. But the moans reverberating off the walls of the cramped space were distinctively sexual, and she was drawn involuntarily toward them. A stall door was open and the scene inside paralyzed her. With her muscles locked, she'd been torn between an urge to run, a compulsion to launch into a legal sermon, and a voyeuristic yearning to watch.

The two women were entwined like braided coils of rope, strong and tight. The contrasts of their bodies, black and white, large and small, dominant and submissive, conjured up unfamiliar desires in Regan that twisted her insides with longing and clouded her mind. Muscles rippled in the stronger woman's naked back, buttocks, and legs as she manipulated the smaller woman against the stall and rubbed their pelvises together. Throaty pleas from the brunette belied her feeble attempts at physical resistance. Her moans bounced off the tiled walls and plucked at a frayed nerve threatening to unravel inside Regan.

The distinctive smell of arousal mingled with moist air in the confined space and settled over Regan like a second skin. She tried to look away from the intimate exchange but felt as if she'd become an unwilling participant, ensnared in the sights, sounds, and scents of their spiraling sexual serenade.

The dominant woman raised the brunette's left leg onto the toilet seat, opening and exposing her, stroking and licking her, while she begged for more. Then she entered the smaller woman and plunged her fist deep inside. The power with which she claimed her surprised Regan and forced a gasp from her aching chest. But the brunette's response was anything but pained.

Her shapely body stiffened. The bronze color of her tanned skin deepened. Preorgasmic tremors twitched and rippled the surface of her skin. Low, husky moans magnified into sharp, needy pants. Then she opened her eyes and looked directly at Regan as the tall woman pistoned her fist in and out of her convulsing frame. Regan shivered. She wasn't sure if it was from her own arousal or the unseeing emerald green eyes that looked through her.

The brunette's entire body humped, thrashed as she rode her lover through wave after wave of orgasm. Regan had never seen a woman so fully engaged in sex that she was oblivious to her surroundings. This woman appeared to not only love sex but to crave it for some reason beyond physical pleasure. As her body reveled in the sensations, she stared, unseeing. Regan detected a void in the lust-clouded depths of the woman's eyes, the absence of something vital. She wondered what could sever the connection between the physical and the emotional in a woman so beautiful and vibrant.

When the brunette finally registered her presence, Regan knew she had to get out before she launched into a diatribe about the inappropriateness of their behavior in public.

"Honey, are you all right? You look all flushed again. What's going on?" Grandma Izzy was staring at her with those Irish eyes that knew when she was lied to.

"I walked in on a couple having sex in the ladies' room at this club. Just surprised me."

Izzy took her hand and gave it a comforting squeeze. "Honey, it wouldn't do you any harm to have a little sex. It's been a year since Martha. Get on with your life while you're still young enough to enjoy it."

"Please don't start, Gram. I'm just not ready. All I want is to spend time with you and get more established in my job." Regan rose from the recliner and kissed her grandmother's hand. "I love you, Gram. I'll see you later."

"Come back soon, honey. I've made a new friend I want you to meet. She works as a volunteer, and we're getting pretty chummy. I think you'd like her."

"Only if you promise no matchmaking."

"Who, me?" Izzy feigned hurt feelings as Regan blew her a kiss and left.

On the short drive home, Regan thought about the brunette from the club and about her own reactions to the scene she'd witnessed. How had she let herself get so involved in watching? It *had* been a long time since she had sex but *that* certainly wasn't her style. Still, she had to admit she'd been aroused by something that she'd never considered, the whole dominance/submissive thing. Even though she was the control freak, Martha had always directed their sex life—when they had it, how they had it, and if they had it. To be aroused by something different was natural, Regan decided, yet something else had happened. She had allowed her compassion for a complete stranger to get the best of her. She'd looked beyond the obvious lack of self-respect such a display implied and seen something deeper. But any woman who would allow herself to be fist-fucked in a public restroom was not someone worthy of her interest.

Regan pulled into the garage of her contemporary-style home and forced the image of the orgasmic brunette from her head and the sharp pangs of arousal from her loins.

❖

"You lose the lottery or something?" Jesse Finn asked as Syd plunked herself back down on a stool at the bar.

"Actually, I good as won it." Syd pulled a memo from the back pocket of her slacks and flattened it out in front of her best friend. "Take a look."

Jesse had been out running an errand when Syd marched triumphantly into the Cop Out an hour earlier. The owner, barista, and bartender, Jesse served coffee and tea all day to the workforce around city hall, in the middle of High Point's revitalized furniture district. After five, the back room opened into a small dance floor with intimate seating and the transition from café to club began. Everyone from judges to college students frequented the downtown hot spot. Jesse's previous law-enforcement experience allowed her to run her establishment with the right combination of discipline and decadence.

"Does this mean what I think it means?" Jesse tilted her head expectantly, a wide grin spread across her slightly weathered face.

"Yes, ma'am. Internal Affairs finally cleared me on that robbery shooting. Cleared by the shrink. I go back to work Monday. It's all good." Syd tried to sound cavalier, but Jesse had lived through the investigation with her as only a best friend could. She knew exactly what this meant.

"I'm so glad, honey. I know you're relieved." Jesse tousled Syd's hair. "Sounds like cause for celebration. What'll it be?"

"My usual, dirty goose." Syd neatly refolded the memo and slid it back in her pocket as Jesse mixed her favorite martini with Grey Goose vodka, a splash of vermouth, and three olives. "God, I'm glad this is over. This desk duty drives me nuts."

As she spoke, she let her trained gaze sweep the dance floor. The high of her sexual escapade in the restroom had been eliminated completely by the sneer of that disapproving bluenose, and she wanted to feel good again. She sipped the dirty martini Jesse slid across the bar and watched women tantalizing each other with their bodies. Searching eyes sought to connect hungry patrons with equally willing partners. Hands casually brushed strangers and, encountering no resistance, lingered and became more demanding. Body language and physical proximity provided clues to the level of intimacy between participants.

The visual stimuli summoned pangs of arousal between Syd's legs and loneliness deep in her chest. She thought of her latest attempt at a relationship, Tina. That had lasted almost a year. It might've gone longer if not for the investigation. Then again, Tina had grown impatient waiting for a commitment, and Syd's commitment lessened in direct proportion to her impatience. Why couldn't good sex just be good sex forever? Women always wanted more than she could give.

"Quite a show, isn't it?" Jesse followed Syd's gaze around the room.

"Yes, it certainly is." Syd loved Jesse's place. Since being on administrative leave, she'd frequented Cop Out in search of the excitement her job normally provided. She usually found plenty.

"It's a good thing you'll be back to getting your thrills on the job," Jesse said dryly. "You're going through my customers like a swarm of sand fleas at the beach."

"What am I supposed to do? A woman needs companionship, right?"

Jesse placed her hand over Syd's, forcing Syd to meet her gaze. "My friend, you just need to find the woman who can ride you long, hard, and consistently, in spite of your puny attempts to buck her off. And when you do, I'm going to tell her that you're a femme trapped in a butch job mimicking a stud."

Syd pulled her hand from Jesse's and poked a fake pout with her lips. "You'll do no such thing. Besides, if she's half the woman I want her to be, she'll find out for herself."

"That could pose a challenge." Jesse started drying shot glasses. "You put up a hell of a front. Most lesbians have been married and divorced several times by your age."

"My point exactly. Why suffer unnecessarily?"

"And on that subject, was it Lacy I saw ducking out of the restroom after you?"

Syd shrugged. "Could be."

Jesse gave her a skeptical look. "What goes on at the Cop Out stays at the Cop Out as far as I'm concerned. But, like I told you last time, you don't want to go there."

"What do you mean?"

Jesse's drying cloth froze in mid-swipe. "You're kidding, right?"

Syd shook her head, trying to dislodge the cobwebs of confusion that camouflaged her memory. "Okay, so we've hooked up a couple of times. What's the problem?"

"Look, Syd, I'm not your mother, your conscience, or your girlfriend, so I don't tell you how to live your life. But going after another cop's wife? After everything you've just been through, are you nuts?"

"Huh?"

Jesse wiped her way down the long mahogany bar. "Just be careful."

"Wait, you're saying Lacy's married to a cop?"

Jesse nodded in the affirmative.

"And you already told me?" Another nod. "Jeez, I better get my shit together and fast."

A couple at the other end of the bar waved to Jesse. "Gotta go. See you later. Or not."

Syd returned her attention to the small dance floor, bemused. Her mind spun through question after question to which there were no answers. A desire to run clashed with a need to find out what was happening to her. Granted, she'd been distracted with the investigation and more sexually active the last few months, but she'd never completely forgotten a woman's face or their interaction, let alone the kind of important detail Jesse just mentioned. Maybe she was more distracted than she'd thought. Either way, she had to make some changes.

She wondered about the chasm between her reluctance to give her heart and the freedom with which she gave herself physically. Sex was easy, an expression of emotional turmoil combined with bodily hunger that she had no words to explain. But the giving of her heart was another matter. She'd never known deep intimacy or the passionate need to translate and communicate it into lovemaking. She'd been unable to trust anyone with both the light and shadow sides of her life. Did anyone else experience this kind of disconnect? Pushing the troubling thoughts from her mind, she returned to the sensual scenes before her.

Her body grew warm watching the women interact. Her hand slid down the length of her outer thigh and back up to rest at her crotch. She licked her dry lips as a young blonde ran her tongue over a potential lover's earlobe. When the blonde pressed her pelvis against the other woman's thigh, Syd squeezed her legs together.

She tried to remember when her feelings had become so intense and raw. Where sex was concerned, she'd always been ravenous. But since the shooting it was as if something inside her was trying to claw its way out, something beyond the need for physical connection. She'd lost herself in more sex, with more women, to salve the body and distract the heart.

But Jesse's warning coupled with the blond voyeur's disapproving sneer had thrown her off her usual game. Another hookup tonight was highly unlikely. She downed her martini with a gulp, waved to Jesse, and headed home to do the one thing that frightened her most, lately— be alone.

CHAPTER TWO

Regan stepped into the small elevator on Monday morning with only a cursory glance and obligatory greeting to the other occupant, a female police officer with cinnamon-brown hair feathered around her face and a hat pulled low on her forehead. When the doors slid together, the other woman's heady perfume permeated the cavity and sparked an involuntary response in Regan. The fragrance oozed and twitched through her system, tugging in her gut like something familiar.

Annoyed by the unsolicited response to a stranger, she surveyed her companion's reflection in the shiny doors of the lift. The black uniform was molded to her form, taut and revealing. Even the bulletproof vest, so obvious under her shirt, couldn't disguise the swell of ample breasts. The woman rolled her shoulders as if the cumbersome garment chafed in places she couldn't touch in public. She tugged at the weighty equipment belt around her shapely hips and leaned against the elevator wall.

Regan had seen women in uniform too many times to find the look a novelty and, typically, she wasn't attracted to the butch types who wore them, but something about this officer's carriage and presence seemed incongruous. It was almost as if her body was incompatible with the garb although, physically, everything fit quite well. Regan wanted to see the woman's face, to get a reading from her eyes about the person underneath the clothing barrier, but the shiny billed hat and dip of her head made eye contact impossible. Probably just as well. Her reactions had been off since the unseemly encounter with the couple in the bar three nights ago.

"Like what you see?" the officer asked without shifting position.

A surprised breath escaped before Regan could stop it. She realized she'd been openly staring since the lift doors shut. Of course the officer had been discreetly observing Regan's reflection as well. How stupid, she thought. Now what? She turned toward her, feigning unawareness. "I beg your pardon?"

The officer's head moved only slightly as she surveyed Regan's body with an up-and-down inspection. "I asked if you like what you see."

Her voice was soft and disturbingly provocative, without the slightest hint of arrogance or challenge. It was the kind of voice that would normally turn Regan's head. But these weren't normal times.

"I'm sorry if you thought I was staring. I was thinking about work, that's all." Regan wondered if her attempt at recovery sounded as lame as she thought.

The reflection hadn't done the officer justice. Her body was indeed shapely and highlighted by the tight fit of her uniform, but what didn't translate was the aura of total femininity that radiated from her. It screamed vulnerability and clashed mightily with the harsh accoutrements of her profession. The bill of her hat shadowed her face to just above her lips—lips deep rose and lush like they'd been kissed all night and were still ripe for a lover. Regan watched them move to speak.

"I do," said the officer.

"You do what?" Regan fidgeted with her briefcase and sent up two prayers simultaneously—that she could see this woman's face and that the lift doors would open and she'd be swallowed by the workday before embarrassment completely consumed her.

The officer stepped closer and whispered, "Like what I see."

Regan's heart thumped wildly against the walls of her chest. She felt rattled. Heat flushed her cheeks and she knew her reaction was evident on her face. She moved closer to the doors and, mercifully, they opened with a swish. As she exited the elevator she heard a soft chuckle behind her and some comment about her ass. If she didn't know better, she'd swear Izzy had put the Irish moxie on every woman in her path lately just to get a rise out of her. First the immodest couple in the bar, now this officer who thought it was okay to flirt with someone she didn't know in a public workplace.

But having a police officer come on to her so blatantly was a different twist, and it felt unsettling. Regan usually made the first move if she liked a woman. She was assertive and adept at handling any situation, verbally and physically. It wasn't like her to be surprised and, she had to admit, excited, by a total stranger.

Her thoughts returned to the woman in the club restroom. Like the officer, she was a brunette, but her hair had been drenched in perspiration and swept back from her face. They both had firm, curvy bodies, the kind that said they were all woman and took care of themselves. Their attitudes were also similar, bold and unafraid. And like the pub crawler, the officer gave off the vibes of a woman on the prowl, always ready for her next conquest and never really having to work for it. Women like that considered fidelity a nuisance and would probably lobby to have the word removed from the English language.

Heat gathered between Regan's legs as she reached her desk and plopped into the swivel chair. She could not understand why her reaction to both women had been so visceral. Whatever the reason, she needed to enjoy the fantasy for what it was, the momentary diversion of a sex-starved divorcee. She was disciplined, she could redirect her energy to her work. But the tingling in her crotch as it strained against the seam of her slacks let her know that would be easier said than done.

❖

Syd chuckled and propped her foot against the elevator door as it started to close. She couldn't resist the urge to watch Miss Friday Night Snob strut off in righteous indignation after being caught looking again. "Nice ass," she said as the doors slid shut, blocking her view of the gorgeous pinstripe-covered bottom.

She'd recognized the blond voyeur from the bar as soon as she'd entered the elevator, and had tugged her hat down to shield her eyes. The last thing she needed was a city employee reminding her of her private indiscretion in a public facility. She wasn't sure if the woman recognized her or not, but Syd couldn't forget the icicles those blue eyes had scraped across her postorgasmic skin. There had been something in their depths that called to Syd in a haunting, almost pleading way.

But that look had been fleeting, quickly replaced by disbelief and eventually distaste. Upon closer inspection today, Syd decided the tall, androgynous prude might not be so genteel after all. Anyone who would openly scope out another woman in a public elevator had to have some sexual virtues. And her voice. The moment she spoke, Syd was captivated. Her tone was sanguine and inviting, the kind of voice you wanted urging you on during sex.

Something else about this woman attracted Syd. Perhaps it was her not-too-femme appearance, or her air of assertiveness, or just the sense that she was ripe for a foray into her untapped sexual treasure chest. Blondie gave off all those vibes and more, the more being cause for hesitation. This woman's restraint was the result of pain, deep and unresolved. Syd recognized the look. The same one haunted her any time she'd gazed into a mirror the past eight months. The stranger couldn't hide that kind of hurt, not with her confident demeanor, swaggering walk, or unconcerned looks. It was still there visible through the windows of her soul.

This was the kind of woman that intrigued Syd. She liked the challenge of cracking open that hard exterior shell of protection and safety and finding the creamy filling of love, nurture, and trust. So far she'd been disappointed. The women she'd dated either had layer upon layer of shell, or no filling at all, no real substance, just a need to be attached at the hip for identity purposes. Syd had no use for another appendage beyond the occasional lover's strap-on. She wanted an equal, a real partner, a challenge. Someone who didn't bore her within a week of their meeting. But she'd had that wish for years and it wasn't likely to be granted today. Today was about getting back to work, and that in itself was a cause for celebration.

When she stepped off the elevator on the police-department level, her entire squad descended on her like a "hot now" sign at the donut shop. They kidded and jostled her all the way to the lineup room, where a big cake occupied the center of the sergeant's table.

"Let's eat this thing before it melts," Sergeant Miller grumbled, but his big smile said he was just as happy to have her back as the rest of the squad. They were like a family, with one new addition, Gil Brady, who stood off to the side.

Syd motioned for him to join the group as she dug hunks of ice-cream cake into plastic saucers and handed them out. Gil was a shy, thirtyish country boy who had recently returned from a stretch in Iraq and was newly married. Syd couldn't imagine the reentry problems he was having. Just coming back from that hellhole was enough, but with a new wife in tow, a wife who was also a war veteran, it couldn't be easy. He'd been assigned to the squad just before the shooting so she hadn't gotten to know him at all yet. He seemed nice enough. Time would tell.

After the party and assignments, they all hit the street. As she walked to the patrol car and stowed her gear, Syd was amazed at how unchanged everything seemed: same procedures, same criminals on the wanted list, same job, and same zone partners. These guys really cared about her, and this job meant something in the whole scheme of things. But a nagging sensation in her gut told her that something had definitely shifted. No matter how vital the job, it should never require her to take a life.

Feeling physically in her element but emotionally disconnected, she started the cruiser and maneuvered into the light morning traffic. As she drove along the block, she wondered if she could ever reconcile killing, "justified" or not, with the person she imagined herself to be. But self-evaluation would have to wait as the radio crackled to life with her first call of the day.

❖

Regan had barely settled at her desk and calmed her traitorous libido when the phone rang and she was summoned to her boss's office.

Terry Blair was a physically fit baby boomer. His sharp blue eyes beamed with penetrating intelligence from beneath a crinkled forehead and a shock of white hair. They'd been working together for a year, and Regan had been honest with him about her reasons for leaving a high-paying, high-profile job for an assistant city attorney's position. He'd been sympathetic and fair, enthusiastically accepting her into his cadre of lawyers. And as he'd become more comfortable with her abilities, he'd assigned progressively more difficult cases to her.

She took one of the two sleek leather club chairs in front of his oak desk and waited for him to finish the notes he was scribbling. When he closed the file he rounded the desk to sit beside her in the matching chair.

"How's it going?" he asked, rubbing his palms together in a gesture Regan had come to recognize as a nervous tic.

"Good. So now that the pleasantries are out of the way, what's the bad news?"

The surprised look on Terry's face was priceless. "Bad news?"

"I may be the newest kid on the block but I wasn't born yesterday. You've got something on your mind and I'm not going to like it, am I?"

"Probably not, but hear me out before you go postal on me. Okay?"

"If I were going postal, you wouldn't be at the top of my list," Regan replied dryly. "What are we looking at?"

"I've really been impressed with the caliber of your work. I want to give you another case, a more difficult case." He hesitated.

Regan knew his reluctance to deliver unpleasant news was a result of his kind heart and appreciated him for it, but sometimes it was just annoying.

"It's a civil suit against the city, the police department, and an officer involved in a line-of-duty shooting. I received the papers this morning."

"And you want *me* to handle this?" Terry knew what had happened in the Fowler case she'd screwed up in Nashville. She was amazed he had enough confidence in her to entrust something similar to her so soon.

"You're the best attorney I've got, Regan, and you've had the most recent experience."

"Which, if you recall, was a bad one?" The last thing she needed right now was another complicated case full of uncertainty. Building a track record of losing those could tank her career.

"We all lose cases," Terry said. "It's part of the job. But we move on and you've done that."

"If you could call quitting my job and relocating almost five hundred miles away moving on," Regan said with a slight edge.

"I can't justify leaving you in the spill-and-fill division forever."

Regan smiled at Terry's reference to the landfill and employment cases she'd been handling since her arrival. "I don't think I'm ready, for obvious reasons."

"You're being too hard on yourself," Terry responded softly. "And we both know you're more than ready for a challenge. You're so bored I'm amazed you can stay awake."

"Point taken, but can I at least think about it?"

"Sure, you've got five minutes. We're on a short turnaround for review and recommendations to the manager."

The discomfort in Regan's chest increased. Not only was she being asked to handle a case exactly like the one she'd lost in Nashville, but she would also have the added pressure of the political microscope scrutinizing her once again. On the other hand, if she refused she'd be letting Terry and herself down.

"What about my other cases?" She stalled for time while she considered her options.

"You mean that single employment case you've been milking for days?"

Regan laughed despite herself. "Okay, so I'm procrastinating."

Terry shrugged. His expression grew more serious. "I'll be honest with you, Regan. This is going to be a messy, high-profile case, and the outcome will affect the city's budget in a big way."

"All the more reason to give it to someone else."

He shook his head. "No, I think you need to do this."

She had to admit, he was probably right. She was going through her assignments with less and less enthusiasm. But that didn't mean she was ready to take full responsibility for a case that could burn the city. There could also be ramifications for the police department, with a review of their policies and procedures, not to mention the bad press. And last, but certainly not least, the officer involved would have to live through the events at the center of the lawsuit over and over again until it was settled. Regan had heard horror stories from the parents and friends of her last client. The thought of going *there* again made her nauseous.

She took a deep breath to steady her nerves. "All right. I'll do it. I appreciate your confidence, and I'll try not to let you down." Collecting her scattered thoughts, she asked, "What's our turnaround time?"

"Two weeks from today."

"Two weeks? You're kidding, right?"

"I'm afraid not. Here's the file." He handed her a six-inch-thick accordion folder. "Try to skim the highlights as soon as possible. We'll be meeting with the officer at two o'clock tomorrow. After that we'll develop a strategy."

"Will do." Regan tried to sound enthusiastic as she scooped the folder under her arm and exited Terry's office.

Even before opening the file, she could feel its contents dredging up thoughts and emotions she didn't want to face. As she walked back to her desk, the weighty documents she carried might as well have been a ball and chain around her neck.

CHAPTER THREE

Preparing for her second day back at work, Syd pulled on her tailored uniform pants and was once again amazed at her rush of energy. She'd been wearing this outfit for work every day for twelve years, but the transformation never ceased to excite her as she slid into character. It was like a Jekyll and Hyde mutation. Maybe the fabric came with testosterone woven in. Out of uniform she was just an ordinary person who wanted the same things every other femme wanted, to meet the right woman and live a normal, happy life. But once that uniform molded itself to her body, her breasts cupped by the snug flack vest, her hips weighted by the powerful tools of her trade, and her crotch constantly massaged by the rough wool-cotton blend pants, she morphed into an adrenaline-powered, sex-seeking junkie. It had been like that her entire police career.

Women had always been drawn to her, and finding willing partners was never an issue, but since the shooting, her appetite had grown out of control. Her therapist had implied that the only way Syd would allow herself to feel anything right now was through physical intimacy. Therapists didn't know everything, and Syd certainly hadn't been completely forthcoming about the extent of her escapades since the shooting. After all, the shrink's job was to evaluate her and get her back to work, and Syd was helping the process along. Besides she was probably just bored and trying to fill time until she was back on the street.

And that day had finally come. As she smoothed the creases of her freshly pressed uniform, she released a grateful breath and looked around her third-floor loft. Light flooded in from all sides and gave the space an openness and freedom that defined her. Soon everything would return to normal. Work was almost like old times already and soon she'd have women lining up at her door again. The thought simultaneously pleased and saddened her. Was that really what she wanted or had it simply become her default way of life? She discounted the latter as premature performance anxiety, but her mind flashed to the blonde from the elevator and a tinge of uncertainty crept back in. She shook the vision from her mind, locked the loft door, and maneuvered through the noisy furniture-market crowd on her short walk to work.

By midmorning she'd already answered three alarm calls, taken two burglary reports, and was assisting Gil Brady with a personal-injury vehicle accident. They compared notes while sipping coffee at Mitzi's, a diner on the outskirts of town that catered mostly to police, EMT, and fire patrons, which suited the public servants just fine. An uninterrupted meal or cup of coffee wasn't the normal fare for folks in uniform.

As Gil traced out the accident diagram from a template, Syd noted his studious attention to detail. His tanned complexion was sprinkled with white crow's feet at the corners of his eyes and worry lines across his forehead from frequent frowning. As he worked, he occasionally rubbed his bony hand over the stubble cropping up on his shaved head. He divided his attention between the paperwork in front of him, the front door, and the other patrons in the diner. Bluish gray eyes took in every movement and returned to his task only in short spurts. Syd wondered how many people this seemingly mild-mannered young man had killed during his tour in Iraq and if those deaths tormented him as much as her shooting did.

"What're you staring at me for?" Gil asked in his slow Southern twang without looking up from his drawing.

"How did you know I was staring?"

"I can feel it. Am I doing something wrong?" His expression showed an eagerness to please.

"No, you're doing a great job. I was just wondering—"

"About the war." The look in his eyes changed from open and receptive to pained and distant.

"I'm sorry. It's obvious you don't want to talk about it." Syd didn't want to cause any discomfort but obviously had.

Gil pushed the diagram toward her and slid his pen into the tiny cutout on the flap of his left shirt pocket. "It's okay. I'd rather folks ask than just stare at me and wonder, or act like it never happened. You've killed somebody. You know what it's like."

Syd flinched at the word. It was the first time she'd heard the K-word stated so bluntly out loud. During the investigation her taking of a life was referred to as neutralizing the suspect, bringing him down, stopping the advance, terminating the threat, anything but killing. "Yeah," was all she could say.

"Funny how they dress up the truth with administrative jargon and flowery bullshit, huh? In wartime we depersonalize the victims even more. We call them targets, bogies, incoming, bad guys, and a bunch of other names I won't repeat."

"How many people did you—"

"Kill?"

Syd nodded without making eye contact.

"I don't really know. When you're using rockets and tanks, it's hard to keep a head count. There were only a couple in one-on-one situations." Gil's drawl slowed even more. "And before you ask, yeah, I think about them daily. I see their faces every night and wonder about their families. You know what I mean."

Syd nodded. Her eyes stung with unshed tears. "Yeah, it feels like somebody else fired those shots. It makes me wonder sometimes what kind of person I really am."

Gil reached across the table as if he was going to touch her hand but withdrew. "You're a fine person. If you weren't, it wouldn't bother you. I know guys who never give killing a second thought. It's like any other job. But those are guys with no conscience. You don't strike me as that type."

"Thanks," Syd replied, "you don't either." She felt a sense of validation that she hadn't experienced since the shooting. Finally someone understood the intangible nuances she could never explain to her therapist.

Gil's cheeks flushed slightly and he nodded at the accident diagram. "That look okay?"

"Yeah. Good job." Syd gathered their paperwork together, preparing to leave, but Gil didn't move. "You ready?"

"I was wondering if I could ask you a question." His gaze shifted uncomfortably around the room but settled on Syd.

"After what we've just talked about, you can ask me anything."

"It's about my wife."

Syd's heart dropped. She had hoped to return Gil's favor. "I'm not sure I'm the best person to give advice on stuff like that, Gil. My track record's not very good."

"But you're a woman. That's what I need, a woman's perspective."

She wondered how far her confidences with her new squad mate should go and then decided if they were to be true friends, she had to put it out there. "But I'm not the best person to ask about men and women because—"

"I know you're gay, if that's what you're hedging about, and it doesn't matter. You're still a woman."

Syd leaned back in her seat. The air between them seemed more casual, like just two friends talking. "I'll do my best."

"I think Priscilla is cheating on me." The statement hung in the air like a foul odor.

"Oh." Syd waited for the rest of the story.

"We got married in Iraq just before we came home. It's only been nine months. How can you get tired of somebody in nine months?"

Syd was definitely not the right person to answer that question. She'd been known to get tired of a woman in less than nine minutes. "How long have you known your wife?"

"A little over a year. We served as MPs together. I fell for her right away. She was the kind of woman I always dreamed of. Tall, gorgeous, great body. She goes after what she wants, and she wanted me. At least for a while."

The description made Syd smile. That was exactly the kind of woman she dreamed of too. Her mind drifted to Miss Friday Night Snob. Syd wondered if she was the assertive type who went after what she wanted. Did she even know what that was? She returned to Gil's dilemma. A year wasn't long to know someone, and getting married after such a short period seemed unwise, but stranger things happened in the pressurized military bubble of wartime Iraq.

"What makes you think she's cheating?"

Gil hung his head. "She doesn't want to make love much any more."

Bad sign, Syd thought, really bad sign. She knew the symptoms and causes of waning sexual interest all too well. But she couldn't bring herself to hurt him. "Maybe she's just going through an adjustment period, too. It hasn't been that long since you got back. I can't imagine what that was like for either of you. Add to that the guilt of leaving your friends back there and the pressures of conforming to 'normal' society again. It must be really stressful."

"She *has* been upset about something lately but she won't talk about it. She can't find a job and doesn't want to go into civilian law enforcement. She'd be great at it."

Syd noticed the softness in Gil's voice as he talked about his wife. He obviously loved her and wanted their marriage to work. "Why don't you just give her some time? Be patient, don't push for sex. Let her come to you when she's ready."

"That's so hard to do." Gil pushed his coffee cup aside and stood to leave. "She's so damn hot. Even you'd like her."

Syd took the good-hearted ribbing as his way of getting back into work mode. As she placed the accident report in her clipboard, communications relayed a message for her to call the city attorney's office. She waved good-bye to Gil and dialed the number on her cell phone, wondering what person with friends in high places she'd pissed off now. The receptionist who answered was unable to provide much information. She merely said that Syd should attend a meeting at two o'clock in the city attorney's conference room on the second floor.

As she hung up, Syd mentally reviewed the cases she'd made recently and decided this had to be a wrap-up of the shooting investigation. She went through the rest of the morning excited that soon the entire incident would be behind her.

❖

Regan retrieved her next Diet Coke from the mini-refrigerator beside the desk in her small office. She popped the tab and took the first fizzing sip. Her eyes were burning and tired, and it was only noon. She'd started reading the new civil-case file Terry gave her yesterday, reviewing witness statements and mapping out a timeline of the actual shooting. The cleaning crew had finally run her out of the building after midnight.

When she got home sleep proved impossible. The facts of the new case had mingled with the old one from Nashville, keeping her tossing and turning. Her last client was so traumatized by the act of killing another human being that he'd found it impossible to cope. He had horrible nightmares, flashbacks, bouts of drinking, and blackouts from booze and drugs in the final days before he took his own life to escape the pain. Regan had failed the young officer, the City of Nashville, and her employer. She'd allowed her personal turmoil to take priority over her job. She'd had the case for only a week when Martha announced that she wanted out of their relationship.

At first Regan didn't take her seriously. Martha often vied for her attention when a big trial occupied most of her time. But this time she was serious.

"I'm not in love with you anymore," she'd informed Regan with the precision of a practiced response. "I'm not happy and haven't been for a long time. And don't try to talk me out of it with your legalese.It won't work." Then the final blow. "I've found someone else and I want out."

She moved out the next day, and Regan felt like she'd walked headlong into a brick wall. Her mind went completely blank, all function overtaken by the emotional swell inside. She couldn't argue. She was in such a state of shock that she didn't even cry for several days. But when she did, the crying didn't stop for weeks. By then it was too late. Martha had moved in with her new girlfriend and Regan was left to thrash about in their half-furnished home, wondering what had happened to her once-happy life.

Obsessed with finding out who had sabotaged their relationship and trying to fix it, Regan worked on the case by day and her former lover by night. She followed Martha home from her office and discovered that the culprit was not some babe who had suddenly invaded her life, but a woman Martha knew very well, the athletics director at the university and her boss of eighteen years. They'd traveled together to all their out-of-town games and had sworn time and again nothing was going on between them but work.

Armed with this new information, Regan tried to persuade Martha to return. She offered to forgive her and start over. Martha requested half the appraised value of their home as soon as possible. Regan's substantial negotiating skills were of no use on her own behalf. Was it any wonder she hadn't been able to fully apply herself at work? She'd tried to give the case and the young officer her best effort, but it hadn't been enough. She couldn't concentrate on the small details that were usually the trademark of her litigating skills. No one blamed her for the loss of the case, but she knew the truth.

Even now, she found it hard to separate her professional impressions of the new case from her emotional responses to the past. She felt an attachment to the High Point officer she would be representing, yet she had never even met her. The past produced magnified feelings that made no sense in their present context, and she was growing progressively less enthusiastic about handling the case. Portions of the new file were scattered across every horizontal space on her desk and on the floor surrounding her chair. She was reviewing the case summary for the final time before meeting with the officer this afternoon and making a to-do list of the information she would need.

The shooting incident itself seemed clear-cut. An armed robber had exited a jewelry store and opened fire when confronted by Officer Cabot. The officer had returned fire and killed the suspect. Witness statements supported her account of events. Even though the suspect was only eighteen years old, his actions limited the officer's options. The family had probably brought the lawsuit out of sheer grief, which was understandable, but not actionable by the court.

In criminal proceedings a good attorney first attacked the evidence, looking for loopholes and problems with the State's case. If that didn't work, the focus shifted to the victim to find "justification" for why he was victimized, how he contributed to his misfortune. If all else failed, the final mode of defense was to question the police and their procedures. But in a civil process those strategies didn't necessarily apply.

Regan needed to find the weakness of this case before opposing counsel did and neutralize it. In criminal prosecutions the burden of proof was high, beyond a reasonable doubt; civil cases merely required a preponderance of evidence. And in her years of civil work, Regan had learned that anything could sway a jury in favor of mourning relatives. While she completely sympathized with the family, from all she had read, it seemed that Officer Cabot was just doing her job. Regan wasn't about to let another police officer become the victim of misguided grief.

And she wasn't about to lose another case like this one. Her pride and professional prowess were on the line. There was no personal upheaval to distract her this time, and she intended to keep it that way.

CHAPTER FOUR

Syd ducked into the third-floor restroom for one last look at her uniform. She wanted to make a good impression on the attorney who would deliver the final clearance from her eight-month ordeal. Straightening her uniform shirt where it tucked into her trousers, she was grateful for a relatively slow morning on patrol. She hadn't had to wait in sweltering businesses for owners to respond to false burglar alarms or spend long hours directing traffic. Her uniform felt relatively fresh.

As she slid her hand down the front of her trousers, her thoughts strayed to the woman in the elevator yesterday and she felt a tingle of excitement. Maybe they would run into each other again. Blondie had definitely piqued Syd's interest, but city hall was a big place and you could work here thirty years and never meet all the folks who filled the myriad public-service positions. Their paths had crossed twice already. How often could lightning strike in the same place?

Satisfied with her appearance, Syd checked her watch and headed for the city attorney's complex. She arrived fifteen minutes early and surveyed her surroundings. The circular reception area was the hub for a maze of offices shielded from the waiting area by heavy wooden doors. People popped in and out of their private workstations like jacks-in-the-box on a merry-go-round. The receptionist showed her into an empty conference room that housed a shiny, rectangular mahogany table with twelve leather-upholstered chairs. A bank of windows on the opposite wall made the grouping appear to float against the city's skyline. Floor-to-ceiling bookshelves lined the walls on either side of the table, filled with thick procedurals and statute books.

Syd pulled out the cushy chair at the head of the table and was enjoying the view when a distinguished-looking white-haired gentleman entered the room followed by a woman. Syd recognized her immediately, Miss Friday Night Snob, the woman from the elevator. Her tailored black slacks clung to her body like idol worshipers to a rock star. A flint blue mock-necked sweater ignited the cobalt hue of her eyes and cupped palm-sized breasts that bounced perkily as she crossed the room. The only detractor to the attractive package was an oversized black blazer that hung from her shoulders like a decade-old housecoat and yelled Don't Notice Me. But it was already too late.

Stunned, Syd rose. She couldn't suppress a slight smile or the involuntary flutter of her heart. The gentleman spoke first, introducing himself as City Attorney Terry Blair. He motioned to the tall woman across from him. "And this is Assistant City Attorney Regan Desanto. She's recently joined our staff from Nashville."

Syd shook his hand and turned her attention to Regan. As their hands closed around each other, Syd noted the strength of Regan's grasp and detected a quickening of her own fluttering heartbeat.

She maintained her grip until she felt a slight tug and knew she'd forced the attorney to purposely withdraw. The cool blue eyes that had gazed so unabashedly upon her body after orgasm now evaluated her with obvious confidence. Was it possible she hadn't recognized Syd from the restroom? Or even the elevator? Syd's ego felt a bit bruised. For her, Regan Desanto was instantly memorable.

"Officer Cabot, I'm pleased to meet you."

The voice was just as cheery, sincere, and sexy as Syd remembered from the elevator. She wanted to urge her to say more just so she could listen to its easy cadence and soothing quality. And that stare. The intensity and all-encompassing nature of it made Syd feel she was the sole recipient of her attention.

"My name's Sydney...Syd," she said weakly.

The attorneys took their seats on either side of the table, with Syd at the head. Terry Blair rubbed his hands together and seemed to be evaluating her. Regan Desanto's gaze hadn't left her since she entered the room. Now her left eyebrow was arched and a questioning look was etched across her face.

Blair must've realized he didn't have either woman's attention because he cleared his throat and said, "Let's get started." Directing his next comment to Syd, he continued. "I'm a little surprised, Officer. In the history of our police department we've never had a female officer involved in the fatal shooting of a suspect." His face flushed bright pink. "I guess that sounds sexist, doesn't it? Believe me, I didn't intend it to be. It just makes this conversation more difficult."

Syd stared at him and a sick feeling gathered in the pit of her stomach. This was supposed to be a meeting to exonerate her once and for all from this nightmare, wasn't it? "I'm afraid I don't understand. I thought I was here to get a final all-clear on the shooting."

Terry Blair looked like a politician who'd been caught taking money from the widows and orphans fund. He shuffled the papers in front of him and avoided Syd's eyes. She would've felt sorry for him if she hadn't been struggling to contain her rising anger. She turned toward Regan Desanto and saw sadness and concern on her face. She could feel compassion emanating from the attorney and a lump formed in her throat.

"Will someone please tell me what's going on?"

Regan scooted her chair closer to the table, stretched her long slender fingers across the slick, flat surface toward Syd, and leaned forward as though to reach out to her. "What Terry is trying to say is that we're not here for that reason."

Syd swallowed hard. "Then what?"

"The family of the young man you shot has filed a civil suit against the city, the police department, and you personally." Regan paused. "I'm very sorry, Officer Cabot. These situations are never easy."

"These situations?" Syd pushed back from the table and jumped to her feet. "These *situations*? We're not talking about a situation here, Ms. Desanto. We're talking about my life." She grabbed the side of the table to steady her shaking hands. "Do you have any idea what I've been through in the last eight months?" She didn't wait for a response. The pitch of her voice rose and trembled with each word. "Of course you don't. All you're concerned about is saving the city's precious money."

Syd felt as though the sky had opened up and was showering liquid lightning down on her. Perspiration popped out on her forehead and dotted her skin underneath the heavy vest. The entire shooting incident was being revived and pummeled anew into every muscle, fiber, and nerve of her being. How was this possible?

"And *you*?" She turned her fury on Terry Blair. "Do you really think my being a woman makes this harder? Ask anybody who's ever killed someone. Killing doesn't discriminate by gender, age, class, or culture. It rips us all apart, the killed and the killer. The only difference is the wounds are visible on the ones who die. You have no idea what we've been through. And when you pretend to understand, you just come off as patronizing."

Regan stood and moved toward Syd. Gently grasping Syd's upper arms, she gazed directly into her eyes. "I'm so very sorry, Officer."

The grip on her arms sent a jolt of conflicting emotions through Syd. She wanted to scream and cry, but at the same time she wanted to rush into the strong embrace and be comforted by the compassion flowing from this stranger. Self-preservation took charge.

"Don't touch me." She deliberately backed away and swept her fingers through hair that clung to the sides of her hot, sticky face. "You have no idea what you're doing to me, either of you. I can't go through this anymore. It's not right. It's supposed to be over."

White heat flushed her skin, and tears threatened to reveal the depths of her despair. She felt completely out of control and exposed in front of the two people who were ripping her world apart.

Regan's face paled. Her eyes filled with confusion and she backed away from Syd so quickly that she bumped into the table and slumped backward into her chair. "You—you're—"

It appeared that she'd had some great epiphany and was at a loss to express the extent of her awakening, but Syd could only struggle to maintain some semblance of control.

"This is very unfortunate for all of us, Officer Cabot," Terry Blair said, "but we have to address the issue. We're being sued and we must respond. Would you like to take a short break before we continue?"

His voice was direct and all business. Its effect on Syd was immediate. She drew a deep, deliberate breath to disperse the pressure in her chest. Although she knew she was being illogical, she regarded these two people now as her adversaries. Few situations in the field left her feeling so violated and vulnerable. She batted her teary eyes until they felt dry and clear.

With every ounce of self-control she could summon, she dug her nails into her palms and returned to her seat.

"I don't need a break. Let's get this over with, please. Tell me what it means."

Terry Blair looked at Regan, obviously expecting her to assume charge of the meeting. She was staring at her unopened file folder, as she had been since returning to her seat. When the silence became too conspicuous, he prompted, "Ms. Desanto will be handling your case."

His comment seemed to drag Regan from her mental distraction. "Terry, I think we should discuss this further before locking into any particular course of action, or any specific case handler."

"We've had this discussion, Regan. I see no reason to go over the same ground."

Watching the exchange between the two attorneys, Syd tried to understand what was happening. They had lowered their voices to whispers but continued heatedly. The confidence she'd seen earlier in Regan Desanto's face and bearing had vanished. It had been replaced by uncertainty and something bordering on fear.

"Excuse me." When Syd could not get their attention, she repeated, "*Excuse me*," and this time they fell silent. "If you two can't make a simple decision about who's going to handle this case, I'm not sure I want either of you on my side. Nobody has more to lose here than I do, so what's going on?" She rested her gaze on Regan.

"Excuse us for a minute, Officer." Regan stood and signaled her colleague toward the door. "We'll be back in just a second."

As the conference room door closed behind them, Syd's emotions began to calm. She replayed the events of the last few minutes and formed another possible scenario. What if Regan had suddenly recognized her from the club and decided she wanted nothing to do with her? Should seeing someone naked in the throes of orgasm interfere with job responsibilities? If that was the case, then many couples would be rendered professionally inept.

On the other hand, Syd wasn't sure about having Regan Desanto defend her under these circumstances. It really shouldn't make any difference. It wasn't like *they* had sex. Regan had simply witnessed Syd in the act with someone else, and if her expression that night was any indication, Regan was disgusted by her and would try her best to pass this assignment off to another attorney. Disappointment crept over Syd. She shook it off and told herself that she wanted the very best representative the city had. If Regan Desanto was so prudish and judgmental about witnessing the sex act, how did she perceive the moral ambiguity of killing another human being in the line of duty?

The door opened and Regan entered, having shed the oppressive black blazer. Her body seemed to bristle with vitality, more at home in the form-hugging slacks and sweater. Her eyes never left the file in front of her as she and Terry Blair returned to their seats. Setting a Diet Coke on the table, she flicked through the pages.

"What all this means, Officer Cabot, is that now we start building a civil case to defend the cited parties." Her tone was matter-of-fact. "Since the incident itself has been deemed justified by Internal Affairs and the district attorney's office, we have to assume you will be the sole subject of scrutiny."

Her entire demeanor had changed. She'd obviously lost the coin toss but was now entirely intent on the task before her. Any hint of distraction had vanished. If Syd hadn't seen it herself, she wouldn't have guessed that less than five minutes ago this woman had been seriously rattled. Now the words flowed from her kissable lips with precision and authority. Syd marveled at the demonstration of control. Whatever she was selling, Syd wanted it. At this moment she couldn't imagine anyone more perfect to handle her case. But Regan's last statement worried her.

"What do you mean I'll be the sole subject of scrutiny? When haven't I been?"

Still engrossed in the documents before her, Regan replied, "I know it feels like that, but the plaintiff's attorney is going to pick you apart. He'll be looking into your past job performance. He may even be granted access to your Internal Affairs and personnel files."

"Is that allowed? Can't you do something to stop it?"

For the first time since reentering the room, Regan looked directly at Syd. "Do we need to be concerned about something in them?"

Their eyes locked, and Syd was momentarily distracted by the gaze, which felt much more personal than the question. Regan's eyes were a luminous shade of azure blue and sparkled with flecks of gray.

"No, of course not," Syd answered. "Would you want someone going through your entire personnel history and every nitpicking complaint in twelve years? I don't think anyone would welcome that kind of public review of their lives."

Regan returned to her notes and mumbled more sympathetically, "Of course not."

Her boss seemed to be satisfied that they were now on track. Assembling his documents, he said, "Well, I think we have some idea of what we're up against. We just wanted to let you know what was coming, Officer. Needless to say, we'll expect your full cooperation. Regan and I will be developing a strategy, and then she'll meet with you. Any questions?"

"I suppose not." Syd knew they were waiting for her to leave, but she hesitated. "Ms. Desanto?"

Regan looked up. "Yes?"

"Do you think you can win this?" Syd asked baldly.

She noticed the almost-undetectable falter in the fluid motion of Regan's hands as she gathered the paperwork. Her gaze shifted slightly upward and to the left. Syd knew her response would be professionally and politically correct, though not completely honest.

"The facts of the case are definitely in our favor. There's no reason to doubt our success. I know it's difficult, Sydney…Syd. But try not to worry so much—and have a little faith in your attorney."

Syd stared at her, appreciative of her attempts to allay her fears and offer encouragement but still uncertain she could, in fact, place full confidence in her. At this point, she had little choice, and she needed to do whatever she could to make sure Regan Desanto was on her side.

"I'm sure you'll be doing your best," she said as sincerely as she could. With a nod of deference, she rose and walked toward the exit.

As she reached for the door handle, Terry Blair added, "And by the way, you're back on administrative leave for the next two weeks. Your assignment will be to this office. It won't be necessary to report here every day. Just call in with Regan and be available."

Syd tightened her grip on the doorknob. Her shoulders tensed and drew forward as the weight of inactivity settled upon her again. Fighting an urge to throw up, she jerked the door open and replied through clenched teeth, "Yes, sir."

❖

Regan dropped back into her seat as soon as Terry left the conference room. Thankful to be alone, she reflected on the meeting that had just taken place and the unforeseen complications that could arise in such a short period of time.

Sydney Cabot had instantly seemed familiar in some intangible way. Maybe it was the uniform that made all officers appear the same. But that wasn't right. This woman appeared at odds with the costume of her trade, too feminine in body, too quiet in temperament. Perhaps the sultry voice reminded Regan of someone from the past. But that didn't fit either. She couldn't remember ever really noticing another woman's voice as an element of attraction. And Syd's intoxicatingly earthy fragrance struck a chord of familiarity too specific to dismiss, drifting through the room and settling on her like a caress. It was possible that those gem-colored eyes were simply too distracting for her to think properly. The most likely scenario was that she had been alone too long and the attributes of a gorgeous woman simply registered more acutely than normal.

A few minutes into the meeting Regan had discovered just how wrong she was. When the reason for their briefing became clear, Syd had transformed from the seemingly quiet femme into a raging specimen of unleashed passion. Perspiration glistened on her forehead and dampened the straight hair feathered around her face. As her agitation increased and her emotions seemed to peak, the tone of her voice crested into an almost agonizing plea. She swept wet strands back from her forehead and the green of her eyes deepened to shimmering moss. The emotion emanating from those eyes was what registered with Regan, that look of vulnerability, confusion, and deep loss. She'd seen it before and it touched her heart once again.

Suddenly everything and nothing made sense. *This* was the woman from the club on Friday night and the elevator yesterday. The room felt like it was spinning as Regan lost concentration and the thing she feared losing most—her control. This was the third time she'd seen Sydney Cabot, and on each occasion she'd come away from the encounter feeling unsettled and inexplicably aroused.

It was worse this time. She'd allowed herself to become emotionally attached to the officer in this case before ever meeting her. After reviewing the file, she'd made a commitment that Officer Cabot would be completely vindicated. She had vowed that her personal drama would not affect her work the way it had last time. She'd given her word to this woman, and once Regan made a commitment she kept it. But there had to be a universal opt-out clause that covered such quirky twists of fate. How could she possibly represent *her*?

She'd seen this officer naked at the most intimate of moments and been disgusted by her lack of dignity. At the same time she'd been so mesmerized by her vulnerability that she'd been unable to turn away. She certainly couldn't be expected to work with her now. The rapport and trust that needed to exist had been destroyed before it had a chance to develop. Syd deserved someone who was totally committed to her case. According to her file, she had suffered serious trauma that required therapy after the shooting. Anything less than a one hundred percent effort would be unconscionable. But how could Regan explain her withdrawal from the case to Terry? Their brief tête-à-tête in the hallway had proved less than satisfactory.

"You want to *what*?" he'd asked.

"I need you to reassign this case, Terry."

"We've already covered this ground, and you agreed."

"The situation has changed. Something has happened that makes my position as first chair unwise."

"You're just getting cold feet. You'll have to do better than that."

"I can't. It's personal." Regan made eye contact, hoping he would see the gravity of the situation in her expression.

"Did you sleep with her?"

"*No!*" The idea had sent shivers through Regan's system.

"Then we don't have a problem. And even if you did sleep with her, it's not like a normal attorney-client situation. Your primary defendant is the City of High Point, then the police department, and Sydney Cabot last. You're on the case, so get back in there and act like it."

As she'd settled back at the conference table, Regan had admonished herself for even bringing the withdrawal up in the first place. It made her look unprofessional to her boss. That's what losing control did to her. It attacked her confidence and made her question tried-and-true methods of coping. Not again. She would remain on task and disregard any interactions with Syd, past or future, that didn't directly pertain to the civil suit.

But every time she looked at that woman she saw her naked and vulnerable, with another woman's fist inside her. The last thought ignited a burning ache in her chest that she'd never felt before. A deep need tugged at Regan and threatened to pull her in. How could she possibly remain unbiased and logical, when Syd elicited a savior complex that could easily cloud her judgment? The most disturbing aspect of today's meeting was the realization that Sydney Cabot didn't exactly fit into the box Regan had put her in after their anonymous encounters. The woman she'd seen today was obviously sensitive and deeply affected by the shooting. She tried to mask her vulnerability with the cloak and attitude of her profession, but remained partially exposed. Regan couldn't understand why Syd engaged in sexually inappropriate behavior like hooking up in a ladies' room or overtly flirting in an elevator. Maybe her acting out was part of an elaborate coping device to disguise deeper feelings. If nothing else, the woman was a walking, frustrating contradiction.

Regan couldn't believe her bad luck. Finally, she had an opportunity to redeem herself, at least in her own eyes, with this case. She couldn't allow herself to be steered off course. She had to win, and once fully centered on her mission, she felt confident that she'd be able to handle her annoying distraction with the officer.

CHAPTER FIVE

Syd stalked out of the municipal building mumbling under her breath, "…and by the way, you're back on administrative leave. Call in with Regan and be available."

That was just freaking great. The woman hated her guts at first sight, and now Syd had to report to her daily. To make matters worse, Regan Desanto was in charge of representing her in the most important case of her life. The meeting hadn't gone at all like she'd imagined. What else could go wrong?

"Hey, Syd, wait up." Gil's deep Southern voice echoed from across the street.

If she just kept walking maybe he'd go away. She wasn't in the mood to listen to stories about his day. It was bad enough that she'd been sidelined again, but hearing about somebody else's hot calls would be rubbing her face in it.

"Syd," he caught up to her at the corner as she turned toward home, "didn't you hear me?" He was the epitome of a soldier: tall, athletic, and good-looking even with a shaved head. In his blue jeans, T-shirt, and deep tan, he seemed too young to be a police officer. Meeting her eyes, he backed away. "What happened to you?"

"Nothing." Syd wanted to rip something apart with her bare hands. All the frustration of the past eight months surged through her anew like a vile, flesh-eating disease.

"You've got that I-want-to-hurt-somebody look."

"I'm back on desk duty." Syd wrapped her arms around her waist and rocked back and forth on her heels.

"Why? I thought you'd already been cleared."

"Civil suit."

"Holy shit, I'm sorry, Syd. This calls for a drink. Want to meet me at the Cop Out?"

"Gil, I'm not sure—"

"Don't even think about trying to blow me off. Go home and get changed since you're off the clock. I'll go ahead and grab us a table. If you're not there in twenty minutes, I'll be forced to initiate an extraction."

She really didn't want to spend time alone stewing over how Regan Desanto was going to make her life hell for the next two weeks. What she needed was to find an attractive, available, out-of-town visitor, bury herself between her legs, and forget this day ever happened. But Gil was trying to help. She could vent with him for a few minutes and check out the possible candidates while enjoying a much-needed drink.

"All right, I'll see you there shortly. Order me a dirty goose."

Syd made it home in record time and changed into a pair of black jeans and a crisply ironed cotton blouse in teal that highlighted her eyes and usually made women claim they were drowning in her stare. When she walked into the club, Gil was waiting and Jesse was just bringing their drinks to the table.

Syd scooped the martini up and downed a sip before taking a seat. "Thanks, girl, I needed that." She introduced Gil, adding, "Jesse is the proprietor of this fine establishment and my best friend."

The two shook hands and Jesse said, "I'll talk to you later, Syd. The furniture market has got us hopping."

As she walked away, Gil entwined his fingers around the frosty Miller bottle. His manner was relaxed, but Syd was uncomfortable. She stabbed at the olives in her glass with a red plastic toothpick. She wanted to be angry with somebody, to shout and proclaim the injustice of it all. But Gil's patience touched her with its unassuming sincerity. This mess wasn't his fault and lashing out at him wouldn't be fair.

"What?" she finally muttered.

"I'm just waiting for you to settle down. If you want to talk, I'll listen. If you don't, it's fine by me. I'm just happy to be in a safe place and have somebody to share a drink with."

She punctured one of the jalapeno-filled olives in her drink, popped it into her mouth, and sucked out the liquor. "I thought it was over. I'm not sure I can take another round of this."

"I really hate that. I know how it feels to be on that skewer again."

"It was like being in a tear-gas chamber when they told me. Everything got foggy, my eyes burned, and I couldn't catch a breath. And then to have this condescending woman tell me the plaintiff's attorney could be rifling through my Internal Affairs files. That was the kicker." Syd's tone had risen steadily and was starting to draw attention from nearby tables. "*And* I'm back riding a desk and have to report to *her* every day."

"What woman? I thought the city attorney was a guy."

"It is but he's handed my case off to an assistant. An uptight prude."

Gil stretched his lanky legs out in front of him and took another long pull from his beer. "Yeah, she got to you."

"Don't be ridiculous. I'm talking about being sued here and your mind is in your pants. Typical."

But the truth was Regan Desanto had irritated and intrigued her, and she didn't like either feeling. One minute this woman was a brick wall of unreadable calm and control and the next she was blushing because she'd gotten caught cruising Syd.

"I'm just saying the civil case is a pretty routine thing," Gil said. "After all, you've been cleared by everybody but the pope. Give the woman a chance. She might actually be good at her job, like you. And if you don't trust her, check her out. You're a cop."

She felt like Gil had just handed her the winning lottery ticket. That's exactly what she'd do. She had friends in the Nashville Police Department. They'd know the scoop and wouldn't be shy about sharing it. "You're a genius. I could just kiss you."

Gil held up his hands in mock surprise. "Oh, no. I'm a married man, remember?" The laughter in his blue-gray eyes vanished almost immediately. "At least I took the vows."

The pained expression that invaded Gil's face was sobering. "How are things going at home?"

"Your advice helped. I haven't been pressuring her and we're talking more. But we're still not sleeping together. She said she's having trouble adjusting to married life and coming back home from Iraq."

Syd watched the gray in Gil's eyes turn dark as his facial features changed from relaxed and happy to tense and uncertain. There was probably big trouble ahead in their marriage but she couldn't bring herself to say so. It would break this gentle soul's heart. He was such a Southern gentleman he couldn't even talk about *sex*. He referred to it as sleeping together.

She made eye contact with a tall, dark-haired butch ordering a drink at the bar, licked her lips seductively, and filed her as a possible hookup later. The woman didn't look familiar, which was a good thing. Maybe she was a furniture marketer out for a walk on the wild side. Well, Syd would be glad to help her with that little experiment and afterward wish her a safe trip home. Yeah, all her useful advice about relationships could fill a thimble.

"How did the two of you get along while you were in Iraq?"

"It's different when you're in country. You live each day like it's your last. When you get a chance to relax, have a drink, or make love, you take it. And whenever you do, it's great. Knowing you literally might not live to do it again puts you right on the edge." Gil stopped and took the final sip of his beer. "Sorry, I sound like a recruiting commercial. Guess I better get going. Priscilla is due home in a few minutes and I want to cook dinner for her."

Syd smiled at him. "You're a good husband and a good friend. Thanks for listening."

"Don't sweat it. Check out your lawyer lady, keep your head in the game, and it'll be fine." He strode toward the exit, then called one last cliché over his shoulder. "And keep it in your pants."

Syd waved him off and scanned the club for the butch she'd eyed earlier. One quick trip to the restroom and she'd be ready to play.

❖

Regan was driving home after another ten-hour day when the flashing red-and-blue neon sign caught her attention. Cop Out glowed in alternating colors and caused a slight quickening of her pulse when she remembered her first visit. She slowed and surveyed the parking lot, which was overflowing, no doubt a hot spot with the market crowd. An irritated driver honked his horn from behind, and she realized she had stopped in the street. Waving and mouthing her apology in the rearview mirror, she turned into the parking lot and cut the engine.

"Mr. Impatience, I hope you're happy." As she said the words aloud, Regan laughed at their absurdity. She could hardly blame some nameless driver for her impulsive detour. But *what* was she doing here? She blushed and reached for the open Diet Coke in the Acura's console cup holder. Her last visit should've cured her of this place forever.

She turned the ignition key and the car roared to life. Just as quickly, she shut off the motor again. This time it's business, she told herself. Regan needed to get a better sense of what Sydney Cabot was really like. She wasn't sure how Syd had coped after the shooting, other than having sex in public bathrooms—if that wasn't the norm for her. But if the case in Nashville was any indication, her reactions probably ran the gamut. If she was as reckless and unpredictable as Regan thought, she might be prone to drinking and acting out when stressed, and today would've been a perfect trigger to tip her over the edge. If this place was one of her usual haunts, Regan should take a quick look in the door and make sure she wasn't providing extra ammunition for a character assassination. It would be a nightmare for the city and for Syd. She wouldn't let that happen. It was her job to see that it didn't.

Regan took the final sip of her lukewarm Diet Coke, as if it could miraculously infuse her with the courage she wasn't feeling at the moment, and headed toward the club. She told herself, not for the first time, that her desire to check up on Syd was driven by the case and had nothing to do with the attraction she felt in her presence.

She shook off the little warning voice in the back of her head and entered the club. As she approached the bar, a dark-haired woman with a welcoming smile and Northern accent greeted her.

"Welcome back. Diet Coke, not much ice, right?"

Regan looked behind her to see if anyone had followed her in.

"Sorry, too many years on the job. I didn't have a chance to introduce myself when you were in on Friday. I'm Jesse."

Regan wasn't sure how she felt about being recognized by the bartender, but she nodded and tried to sound cordial. "Regan. Nice to meet you. Put my Coke on hold, will you? I'll be back in a second."

She weaved through the sea of bodies that mingled in the small space. Their heat closed in on her like a wave of tropical air. She felt vulnerable and slightly aroused as she made her way through the wall of strangers to the restroom.

When she opened the door, she came face-to-face with Sydney Cabot and stopped abruptly. Tight jeans and a teal blouse clung to Syd's body and highlighted the curves of her tempting frame and the sparkle of her green eyes. Her skin shimmered with a light sheen of perspiration and her cheeks glowed with color. The scene from Friday night flashed through Regan's mind.

"Counselor, back for a repeat performance?" Syd's tone was seductively mocking. "You strike me as more of the hands-on type."

How could she do this again? Didn't she understand the possible ramifications of her actions or didn't she care? "We have to talk about this." Regan took hold of Syd's arm and guided her from the restroom, past the inquisitive-looking bartender, and out the front door.

"See, I knew you'd need a more active role," Syd taunted. "Lead on."

Regan pulled Syd into an alley between the club and a closed bakery. The smells of beer and roasted peanuts were replaced by a combination of fresh-ground coffee and baker's yeast. "*What* are you thinking? Or do I really want to know?"

Light from the street lamp on the opposite corner bathed Syd in a muted yellow haze. The color settled around her like a halo and illuminated her delicate features. In that light, Regan thought she appeared innocent yet rakishly alluring. Syd returned her stare and seemed to be considering how to respond. The gleam in her eyes said the answer would not be what Regan needed.

"I'm thinking if you wanted to go out with me all you had to do was ask. While I really like that Bogart thing you've got going on, it's not necessary. Verbal assertiveness works just as well for me."

Regan was increasingly aware that she still held Syd's elbow, which brought their bodies too close for her to stay on point. She let go and stepped away. "You actually think I came back here for you?"

"Well, I have to admit, it could be Jesse's drinks. She's superb. But I'd bet on me."

"Are you really that self-absorbed or is it just an elaborate ruse?" This woman's audacity was surpassed only by her arrogance, or so she wanted everyone to think. But Regan had acquired the skill of reading body language and subtle shifts of expression at an early age. Her observation powers had helped her survive and keep peace in a home dominated by violence and upheaval. It was this ability to discern truth from fiction through the fine-spun nonverbal communications of others that drew her to the legal profession. The alternative had been psychology, and she couldn't handle the emotions that other people's suffering generated inside her. One thing was certain, Sydney Cabot's act didn't ring true. But this wasn't the time to try to figure her out.

"Speaking of ruses, you seem to be the expert," Syd taunted softly. "Are you seriously trying to suggest you came into the club, found me in the restroom, and dragged me into a darkened alley to talk about work?"

Regan evaluated each word as Syd spoke. She had to admit it would sound pretty unbelievable to anyone who might be watching and didn't know better. But she knew better. "This is a professional issue. Nothing more."

Syd inched closer. "You need to lighten up a bit."

You just need to lighten up, Regan. This time it was Martha's voice she heard, urging her home from work early, convincing her to try something new or pleading for a little more spontaneity. The memory was sharp and jagged, tearing through her like a serrated knife.

"You don't have to be so cautious," Syd urged. "I like you, and I know you like me."

"You're not hearing me, Officer Cabot. This *is* about work." But Regan couldn't deny the series of shivers Syd's words evoked.

"What? You're kidding, right?" Syd looked as if the comment had distinctly distasteful qualities.

"I am not. I stopped by because I was afraid you'd do something irresponsible. We can't afford to have things like this come out at trial. You need to be much more discreet. In fact, it would be best to curtail this altogether until the case is resolved."

Syd looked at her as if she'd suddenly sprouted three heads. "And what exactly is *this* that we're talking about?"

Regan waved her arms toward the club. "You know, *this* this. You, in the restroom with women, having—sex." She felt like an inept mother trying to scold a child and failing miserably.

The look on Syd's face shifted from flirty to mildly amused. "You don't have to be jealous. There's enough of me to go around."

"This is serious, Syd. You have *got* to avoid these sexual encounters in public, at least until the trial is over. Then you can do whatever you want. But I'm not about to risk my reputation and career on someone who's on a self-destruct mission. Do you understand?"

In the blink of an eye, the glimmer of flirty amusement on Syd's face vanished. It was replaced by something dark and painful. Syd stood her ground, remaining within arm's length but seeming emotionally miles away.

"I understand perfectly, Counselor." Her voice was as sharp and steady as bladed steel. "Somehow you're under the mistaken impression that handling my civil case gives you the right to handle my life. It doesn't."

"I'm just saying that public sex isn't the best choice right now."

"And I'm telling you that I wasn't having sex in the restroom tonight. Not that it's any of your business. I was here with one of my squad mates. We were just talking."

"Right." Regan's tone made it clear she didn't believe Syd's explanation.

"What's your problem anyway? Are you so uptight that the sight of two women enjoying each other offends you? Or was it just too exciting for you to handle? Can't give up that control?"

Regan's insides tensed as Syd's words revived desires long suppressed. It was like Syd was reading her mind and knew her most closely guarded fear. She struggled to prevent the shock of her thoughts from being played out across her face.

"That's it, isn't it? You liked it and you're too afraid to do anything about it. Hell, you probably can't even admit it to yourself." Syd leaned into Regan's body space and lowered her voice to a whisper. "It's okay to admit it." She licked the edge of Regan's ear. "Really."

Regan recoiled from the moist contact and the stirring of arousal it dredged to the surface. "Sex in a public restroom is not my idea of excitement. Besides, we're not talking about me. We're talking about your case. A case that, need I remind you, could have a serious impact on your life. Doesn't that matter to you at all?"

Syd backed deliberately away from Regan and fixed her with a look that clutched at her heart. Her matter-of-fact tone had lost its flirty playfulness. "You have no idea what matters to me or what I've been through the past eight months. When you do, maybe then you'll understand just how far a person will go to feel whole again." She turned and walked from the alley, leaving Regan staring open-mouthed.

She's got you there, Desanto. Regan knew the pain of uprooting herself from cherished friends, of losing a lover, of being betrayed on the deepest personal level, and of having her lifelong dreams annihilated.

But she had no idea how it felt to make a split-second decision that would end another life and then have to live with that horror every day. She truly could not imagine what toll that kind of responsibility took or what extreme measures one might embrace to alleviate a psyche so haunted.

Was that the demon Sydney Cabot tried so desperately to conceal? Was that the reason for her false bravado and blatant womanizing? And she was absolutely right. Regan could never truly understand what Syd was going through, on the most fundamental level. A swell of sadness gripped her as she realized that this time her overdeveloped sensitivity and empathy could not help. And for some reason beyond mere compassion, she wanted to fix it and make everything better for Syd.

❖

Syd scuffed her Cole Haan drivers against the pavement as she dodged loud and intoxicated pedestrians, traffic barricades, and off-duty officers on her way home. The furniture market had been in full bloom for two days and the downtown square resembled Mardi Gras. Furniture might be big business during the day, but liquor and women ruled at night.

What a delicious combination, she thought, liquor and women. That had been all she wanted tonight: a couple of drinks, an innocent liaison with an out-of-town marketer, and a huge dose of decompression. Instead she'd come away with nothing but an unpleasant tongue-lashing from Regan Desanto. She replayed the encounter again as she took the long way home.

It was surreal when Regan opened the restroom door and almost collided with her. The blue eyes staring back at her flashed surprise only for a moment before shifting into heat and anger. Syd realized she should probably have objected when Regan dragged her from the club, but something inside her screamed, *Oh yes, finally.* Just the thought that someone cared enough to save her from herself was amazingly exciting.

That thought quickly vanished as she realized that Regan had no idea she wanted to be saved or from what. Syd's mood shifted from excitement to confusion. Of course she didn't need to be saved, she loved her life. But the woman tugging on her arm stirred up something different inside her. She could hardly wait to hear the prim, proper attorney explain this behavior.

It didn't take long. Once outside in the alley, Regan simultaneously called her a fraud and a slut in one long rant that sounded like a courtroom summation. Her mood and tone were so intense that Syd was slightly amused, even though her comments were hitting too close to home. Regan didn't know her well enough to see through her smoke screen of sexual bravado, false confidence, and misdirected humor, and yet she'd nailed her behavior as "an elaborate ruse."

Regan's assessment sent Syd into her first default mode, flirting as a diversion. If she allowed herself to examine the ramifications of Regan's astute observations, she would've clung to the woman there in the alley surrounded by the swirling scents of coffee and pastries. Instead, she went for her weakness, that obvious need to be in control. And it worked. She challenged Regan to lighten up and let go. Her shot hit the mark as Regan's cool blue eyes became clouded and distant. Syd felt momentarily ashamed for having triggered such an unhappy memory.

But Regan wasn't distracted for long. She finally got to the point of her seemingly coincidental visit to the Cop Out. She was checking up on Syd, certain that she was so disturbed by their earlier meeting that she would fling herself into the arms of the first available woman she met. Bingo. Syd hated to admit it, but she was right again. If the dark-haired butch had followed her into the restroom and come on to her, she would've gladly obliged. But she wasn't about to admit that to Regan Desanto.

Instead, she accused Regan of being attracted to her and maybe even a bit jealous. Heat rose in Regan's eyes when she mentioned their first encounter at the Cop Out. Regan shifted her stance uncomfortably, moving slightly away from Syd. She repeatedly licked her kissable lips in an involuntary motion indicative of sexual arousal and invitation.

And when Syd inched toward her, whispered that she should admit her attraction, and rimmed the edge of Regan's ear with her tongue, the response had been immediate. Too immediate and too strong. It had been Syd's experience that reactions that intense were usually employed to hide equally fierce feelings. The thought sent a shiver of uncontrollable delight through Syd's body. She could easily imagine this emotionally contained woman letting herself go and allowing Syd to please and pleasure her.

But Regan's release came in another form—a brilliantly orated sermon about Syd's irresponsible behavior and its possible effect on her civil case, her job, and the City of High Point. Again, she nailed Syd with her insight and made her consider things in a broader context. How could this woman arouse her sexual interest and emotional curiosity, and challenge her professional commitment all at the same time? The latter rocked Syd. No one had ever questioned her job performance or dedication. And to have the woman who was supposed to be defending her do so spun Syd into her second default behavior—anger.

She completely withdrew from Regan, all flirting and playfulness carefully tucked behind her impenetrable screen of self-protection. Ice water pulsed through her veins as she stepped intentionally away from her attorney. How dare she assume to know what mattered to her, to have any concept of what killing another human being had done to her, or to understand the lengths she'd gone to in order to cope with and forget that night for even brief moments. She was wrong. Regan Desanto had no idea what made her tick, and that intellectual and compassionate void might cost Syd her livelihood.

Chapter Six

Two days had passed since Regan's ill-advised stop at the Cop Out, but the heated exchange with Syd kept replaying in her mind at the most inopportune times. This particular version occurred during the morning staff meeting: Syd standing toe-to-toe with her, whispering that she should accept the attraction between them. A warm, moist tongue sliding seductively around the rim of her ear.

A slow burn started low in Regan's belly and crept lower.

"Regan?" Terry Blair and the rest of the legal staff were staring at her, awaiting the answer to some question she'd obviously not heard.

"Yes?" Regan knew her face telegraphed her lack of attention and embarrassment at being caught. She made a mental note to have her hormone levels checked at her next physical. There had to be some organic reason for her uncustomary states of arousal and lapses into sexual fantasy.

"I asked for an update on the Cabot case."

"There's not much to tell at this point. I've been going through the file more thoroughly, and I've requested her Internal Affairs and personnel records."

"Is she calling in as we requested?"

Regan thought of the clipped phone exchanges the last couple of days. "Yes, she is. And we're meeting this afternoon to go over a few things."

Terry hesitated before asking his next question. "Any problems I need to know about?"

She knew his question referred to her professional lapse in trying to get off the case. "No, no problems at all." She ignored the nagging voice in the back of her mind.

The remainder of the morning disappeared in a quagmire of phone calls back and forth between her and the police chief, as she tried to explain that full Internal Affairs and personnel files did not mean a redacted version. She wanted the secret files kept on each officer that even they weren't shown. She needed all the good, bad, and questionable pieces of Sydney Cabot's file intact. It was almost two o'clock when the receptionist buzzed and informed her that Syd was waiting in the conference room.

Great, another day with no time for lunch. Facing Officer Cabot fully fortified had proven challenging; this time she'd have to depend on mental mettle to sustain her.

When Regan entered the conference room, Syd was standing at the wall of glass windows overlooking downtown. Crisp linen slacks in a warm chocolate color hugged the perfectly rounded orbs of her butt, and a white sleeveless shell shone in stark relief against the pants and her tanned arms. Chiseled muscles along the back of her upper arms flexed and released as she clenched her fists in front of her. Her straight chestnut hair kissed the top of her shoulders, and the layered strands blew lightly with the circulating air in the room.

Regan felt an urge to simply stand and watch the shapely officer silhouetted against the backdrop of the city. She hadn't wanted to just look at another woman since the early days with Martha. Why this particular woman? At that moment Syd sensed her presence and turned.

"Good afternoon." Her tone held a cool, guarded edge mirrored in her evasive gaze.

Regan elected a briskly professional response. "Syd, thanks for coming in."

"I didn't exactly have a choice. I *am* assigned to you for the next two weeks." Syd chose the chair farthest from her.

Very encouraging, Regan thought. Syd's voice sounded hollow, with a sense of resignation. The timbre of it filled her with compassion. "Is it really necessary for you to sit way over there?"

She realized, with more than a moderate amount of surprise, that the words carried a double meaning. One was a professional concern for their ability to communicate easily and effectively about this case. The second was an uncomfortable desire to be physically closer to Syd. Something about this enigmatic woman yelled *sex* while simultaneously eliciting compassion and asking for help.

"Probably as necessary as the rest of this."

Regan understood that Syd didn't want to be in this situation. Reliving every detail of the shooting, exposing her unorthodox coping mechanisms, and waiting for a barrage of professional and personal judgments wouldn't appeal to anyone. Steeling herself against further invasion into her life by giving as few details as possible was likely her method of self-defense.

"I'm really sorry about all this," Regan said. "I can't imagine how it makes you feel."

"No, you can't. Could we just get this over with, please? I'm meeting someone for drinks later and I don't want to be late."

Syd's tone had changed from resignation to defensiveness, and the sharp contrast stimulated Regan's Irish temper, reminding her just who she was dealing with. "Fine, let's get started. Wouldn't want you to be late for a date, now would we?" She could care less about Syd's personal life. Her job was to defend the City of High Point, in spite of Sydney Cabot.

"Don't you think we need to talk about something else first?"

"What did you have in mind, Officer Cabot?"

"The first time we saw each other."

After a lengthy pause, Regan felt her face flush with heat. "If you're referring to that scene at the Cop Out, I don't believe it needs to be discussed. It was—unfortunate."

"Unfortunate? That's what you call a look that could send most women in search of a confessional?"

Regan's skin prickled as the visual of that night returned. Syd's screams of pleasure reverberated in her head. "I was merely surprised by two grown women behaving so irresponsibly. I hadn't seen that type of behavior since college."

"That look was way beyond surprise. But the point is, how do you feel about it now?"

Regan folded her arms across her chest, hoping Syd wouldn't see the traitorous nipples dimpling beneath her sweater. "I don't feel anything," she lied. "It was an unfortunate first impression. Neither of us knew we'd be working together. And now that we are, it's history and we move on."

"There's that word again. *Unfortunate.* I'll tell you what's unfortunate—you not staying longer that night so we could get acquainted. I think you wanted to, but you were too afraid."

"Then you don't know me very well. And as to who's afraid of what, why don't we get back to the business at hand, namely your civil suit. Are you ready to talk about that or do you want to continue this evasive banter in the hopes of intimidating me or getting your case reassigned?"

"I just thought we should clear the air. If we have to work together, I have a right to know that you'll do everything you can to represent me without prejudice."

"You have my word that I will represent you to the best of my ability, regardless of the circumstances of our first un...comfortable encounter. Now, can we please get to work?"

"Sure, so, why am I here?"

"I've asked the police chief to release your files to me for review and—"

"You've *what?*"

"If you'll let me finish, I'll be glad to explain."

The anger Regan had seen in Syd's eyes at their first meeting returned and burned even brighter. What was in these files that Syd didn't want her to see? Was she one of those officers who got her kicks pushing the use-of-force policy? Regan didn't think that was the problem. Besides, she'd already had a firsthand look at how Syd got her kicks.

The stately African-American woman's back, rippling with sexual tension and power, flashed through Regan's mind. She stifled a gasp at the memory of Syd's thighs wrapped around that body. The vision of her humping and begging for more shot through her like a dose of pure adrenaline. She squeezed her legs together and wondered what evil deed in her past justified the physical torment visited upon her each time this woman was near.

She looked up into Syd's waiting gaze and quickly glanced away. Even an unobservant woman would be able to see the desire that raged inside her, and Syd was trained to search for nuance. Regan wanted desperately to understand why her body had chosen this time and this woman to betray her meticulous control. Maybe years of a sexless relationship had finally taken its toll. Maybe the upheaval of living in a new place with a new job and no social outlets had rendered her vulnerable to even the most subtle hints of sexual interest.

"Counselor?"

Syd's stare was a combination of innocence and temptation. At times her openness was intoxicating and at others she tested the bonds that tethered Regan to her tenuous patience. She wondered how many other women had wrestled similarly before Syd bedded them, wanting her and not wanting her, craving her and fighting to reject her. Whatever the reason for this push-pull of emotions, she had to stop the unproductive turn her mind and body had taken and get back to work.

"Yes, as I was saying, I've asked the chief for your files. I'll be looking at your past uses of force, complaints, evaluations, supervisory remarks, and overall job performance. The purpose is to make a preemptive strike if necessary. The more I know about you and your history, the better I can defend you against anything the plaintiff's attorney may dredge up. If there's anything you think could be viewed as unfavorable, please let me know now."

"I can't think of anything."

Regan regarded her with skepticism. "I have a feeling you wouldn't tell me if there was. I can't impress upon you enough how important it is for you not to keep anything from me."

"I am unaware of anything in my file that would be cause for concern. But, then, I'm not an ambulance-chasing attorney hell-bent on destroying a hardworking cop's life."

The pain in Syd's voice was covered by a thin coat of anger, but Regan had mastered the art of discerning the two emotions as a child. "That's not the intended result but sometimes it certainly can be." She took a sip from her Diet Coke and rolled the can between her palms. "I know this is difficult, but I need you to tell me about the night of the shooting, if you can."

"That's why I'm here, isn't it? Why didn't you tell me before I came in?"

"I honestly didn't think you'd show up if you knew."

"You're absolutely right. It's a waste of time." Syd rose from her seat and paced back and forth in front of the windows. "It's all in the report. I've given my statement so many times I've lost count."

"Yes, it's all here, but I'd like to hear it from you." Regan felt Syd bristle from across the room and braced herself for the response.

"What's with you people, anyway?" Syd whirled on her as if prepared to strike. "Do you get some perverse pleasure out of putting me through this over and over? Why can't you just read the damn file?"

"I wouldn't ask if it wasn't important. I need to verify the repeated consistency of your version of the incident, and, more importantly, I need to get a sense of you as a witness."

Anger and pain alternated in equal parts across Syd's tortured face. "You mean I have to tell it again?"

"We hope that won't be necessary, but it's a possibility."

Syd shook her head. "Is there no end to this?"

Regan knew the last question was rhetorical. She waited for Syd to calm enough to tell her story once again. This was a critical part of her case and could not be rushed.

"It was August twentieth and hot as hell."

Syd's voice was almost inaudible. Regan leaned closer but didn't speak.

"Some of the shops at Oak Hollow Mall were having a sale. It was closing time. I got the call of a robbery in progress at Bradford Jewelers. They gave a description of the suspect. I rolled to the scene blacked out."

Regan looked up from taking notes. "I'm sorry, blacked out?"

"I didn't run lights or siren. It's the recommended response if you're close to an incident and don't want to alert the suspect of your arrival. So, I parked out of sight of the entrance and approached on foot."

Syd stopped and drew several deep breaths. "That night, it was hot and humid. I could hear the traffic on the surrounding streets and the calm of the mall parking lot. The area stunk of rotting garbage from the overfilled Dumpsters and stale beer from a nearby bar. Everything was sharply focused but in freeze-frame snapshots.

"I was flattened against the wall making my way to the entrance when the door burst open and the suspect ran out. He had a gun in one hand. I announced myself and told him to stop. He turned toward me, brought the gun up, and aimed it at me. There was no cover anywhere around me."

Regan watched Syd swivel, looking for cover, as if reliving the event in real time. She had no frame of reference for the feelings that must have overtaken her.

"I hit the ground, yelling for him to drop the weapon. He kept aiming at me. I rolled out of his sight line and fired twice. Everything else was just aftermath."

Syd stopped as if further explanation was unnecessary. Silence seeped into the stacks of books around them and swelled like a liquid invasion. Regan stared at her, amazed at the range of emotions that had played out on her face during the recitation. Now her shoulders sagged and she looked almost lost, her expression downcast and her brilliantly green eyes shadowed. Something in that look twisted Regan's insides into a knot of confusion and hunger. Suddenly she was back in that alley denying accusations of jealousy, with Syd's gaze burning her skin, seeing through her façade to the truth she didn't want to admit.

"Syd," she said quietly, "I'm sorry about the other night. I had no right to seek you out at the club. That was terribly unprofessional. Invading your privacy is not part of my job description and neither is trying to control your personal activities, sexual or otherwise."

"You did that so easily, apologizing, I mean. It sounded as effortless as saying good morning when entering a room." She seemed to be considering her next statement. "It's not so easy for me, but I'm sorry for lashing out at you. It's not your fault my life is in the crapper."

"Still, I overreacted, made an assumption that was unwarranted." Regan reached over and took Syd's hands in hers. "I wish you didn't have to go through this whole thing again."

Regan felt heat rising between them and stood, intending to move away and return to work. She hesitated before asking her next question, knowing it had less to do with the case and more to do with her curiosity about Sydney Cabot. "Do you remember what you were feeling during the incident?"

"Feeling?" Regan's hands were still on hers. She released their grasp, took a deep breath, and cupped Regan's face in her palms. "*This* is how I feel now, and now is what matters." She brushed her fingers over Regan's bottom lip and tugged the moist, soft skin between her thumb and forefinger. "God, you're beautiful."

Regan felt as though her lips were on fire. The rush that accompanied Syd's touch blazed deep inside. She was lost in green eyes that sparked heat but produced moisture in her most private places. Her hands moved upward to taut biceps that quivered with suppressed desire. Her body ignored all mental attempts at control, and she allowed herself to be pulled closer to Syd's luscious mouth.

"Kiss me," Syd whispered.

"Yes." Regan thought the voice sounded like hers but the body response was definitely foreign. She felt the warmth of Syd's breath on her face and inhaled her earthy fragrance. She waited to be consumed by the passion that was Syd, the passion she'd seen so freely shared and had so unabashedly craved since that night at the club.

The memory registered like a cold shower. She didn't know this woman. *This* was what Sydney Cabot did. She seduced women to escape from her pain. *I won't be one of them.* It took every ounce of energy Regan could summon to pull back. Her body screamed for connection, to be joined with the only thing she had lusted desperately for in her entire life. The thought itself was sobering.

"I can't do this, Syd." She walked toward the door, talking as she went. "Please check in tomorrow."

In disbelief, Syd watched Regan move away from her. Their lips had been so close that she could almost taste the mixture of peppermint and cola on her breath. In the next instant she was gone. What had happened?

As she replayed the last few minutes in her mind, it became clear. *She* had happened, her typical response to anything that came close to feelings—divert and run. They'd shared a few honest moments, let their respective guards down, and then *bam*—she regressed into a hormone-driven, emotion-dodging, pitiful excuse for a human being. Uncomfortable feelings had started to surface and she burrowed further into her protective shell, letting her body and libido take charge. It was probably just as well; she was in no condition to offer anything beyond the pleasures of the flesh. And it seemed Regan had troubles of her own, aside from defending her in this case. Tragedy averted.

She left the conference room and walked toward the Cop Out.

Regan Desanto was the first woman to resist her advances in a very long time. But it wasn't her ego that was shaken. It was a nagging feeling that something inside her had shifted and could never be righted. One thing was for sure, she needed to find out more about this woman who had charged into her life, disrupted a perfect orgasm, and taken on the defense of her professional life. She could not summarily relinquish such monumental responsibilities to the unknown, or the unworthy. Syd wanted to know the woman she was counting on.

CHAPTER SEVEN

Regan exited the conference room without acknowledging the stack of phone messages the secretary waved in her direction. She darted into the ladies' room and locked the door. Her skin burned where Syd had touched her, and the ache between her legs would not stop. She turned on the faucet and repeatedly splashed handfuls of cold water on her face.

What in God's name was wrong with her? She'd almost kissed Syd during an interview about an ongoing case. It was obvious she hadn't been thinking, at least not with any part of the body capable of intelligent cerebral function. Syd's recounting of the shooting had been intense, and she'd gotten caught up in the progression of feelings. She translated Syd's words and reactions about that night into emotions and internalized them. Her empathy for Syd was profound and she'd allowed the feeling to overwhelm her. Instinctively, she'd reached out to offer comfort. And that's when her reality clashed with Syd's.

Regan told herself she meant only to show compassion. Syd had interpreted her physical touch as sexually motivated, because that's how Syd related. Regan had never met a woman who wore her sexuality so blatantly, like a badge of honor. Where Syd was concerned, most encounters with women seemed to be filtered through a sexually enhanced prism. But in this case, Syd had read the signals all wrong. Hadn't she?

Splashing another round of cold water on her face, Regan replayed the scene in her mind. Had she somehow encouraged Syd to come on to her? The flush in her body remained as she tried to convince herself that Syd's advances were unprovoked and unwelcome. She was not the kind of woman Regan would be interested in. Syd was gorgeous enough, that part appealed to her, but she was obviously irresponsible, irrepressible, and incapable of loyalty to one woman.

And, Regan acknowledged, Syd had avoided mentioning her feelings about the shooting. Her body language and expressions relayed an emotional component, but she never articulated what she felt. In fact, she'd deflected the question by overt physicality and inappropriate touching.

A conversation about the young officer in Nashville came to mind. Friends of his had told Regan of the changes the officer suffered after the shooting incident, about too much alcohol and drugs, withdrawal from friends and family, and sexual promiscuity. A wave of sadness and loss washed over her. Perhaps the same thing had happened to Syd. Maybe she was trying to compensate for the emotional numbness with physical contact. Or maybe sexual excitement substituted for the feelings she no longer experienced. Either way, Regan's initial impression of Syd remained unchanged. She needed to keep the officer on a short professional leash for the sake of the case and a very long personal leash for her own sanity. In the meantime, more information about Sydney Cabot, her past, and her work would be an easy distraction.

❖

"Line me up a flock of dirty geese, Jesse," Syd called as she perched on her favorite stool at the end of the bar.

"Looks like desk duty isn't any easier the second time around."

"Oh, it's great if you like waiting at home for the phone to ring. It's worse than the first time. At least I was at the station and could see the guys and talk to people. I'm stuck in nowheresville now. And this, this *woman* is driving me nuts."

Syd suddenly had Jesse's total attention. She slid the first Grey Goose martini in front of Syd and propped herself across the counter on her elbows. "There's a woman involved? Do tell. I want details." Her thick New York accent brimmed with teasing.

"It's nothing like *that*. She's the assistant city attorney who's handling my case. And, God, is she a pain in the ass."

Jesse grinned devilishly at her and waited.

"Get that stupid look off your face," Syd said. "I told you, it's not like that."

"But you have to admit, she's the first woman to get a rise out of you in years, without getting in your pants."

"She's snooping around in my life like it's really her business, asking questions about the shooting, my past—"

"But that's not really the problem, is it? You've answered those questions at least a dozen times now."

"Yes, and I just don't like going over everything again." Syd took a sip of her martini and looked around the bar, wishing more people were there so she'd have a legitimate distraction. Guzzling martinis and avoiding eye contact would only last so long with Jesse.

"Syd, look at me."

As if on cue, the front door opened and Lacy sauntered in, scanning the room as she walked. She caught sight of Syd at the counter, nodded in recognition, and took a table near the back of the room.

"Look at *me*," Jesse repeated. "She's not the answer to your problem, darling. None of them are."

Syd shifted uncomfortably and did what Jesse asked. "What?"

"You know what I mean. You're running from your life. It's time to figure out what you really want. Bedding women like a mating rabbit isn't going to give you the answer."

"You sound like that departmental shrink they sent me to."

"Yeah, and you didn't listen to her either. Don't try to bullshit a bullshitter. I was a cop once, too. I know how we operate. Have you been honest with anyone about how this has affected you?"

Syd couldn't lie to her best friend so she said nothing.

"I didn't think so." Jesse reached across the counter and squeezed Syd's hand briefly. "I gotta go see what your latest paramour wants to drink. This isn't a lecture, Syd. I just want you to be happy. And if this attorney has you at least thinking about your feelings, I say that's a good thing."

Regan Desanto had Syd doing more than just thinking about feelings. The soft tone of her voice, her compassion, and the tenderness of her touch had brought Syd to the edge of her closely guarded emotions. Her assumptions about Regan's controlled demeanor suddenly seemed hypocritical and cruel. She had no right to criticize anyone for something she so blatantly practiced herself. But they had different motivations. Regan's control was about bridling life and all its possibilities. Her own inhibitions were about self-survival and sanity—

not at all the same thing. She fully explored all her possibilities, didn't she? Her mind and gaze wandered to Lacy. Was Jesse right? Were these women just an attempt to salve a wound too deep to heal by itself?

She recalled the feel of Regan's fingers wrapped around her hands, the emotional warmth, and the singularly directed focus of Regan's attention. Her body responded again to the current that had swept through her at the time. It was sexual, no doubt, but it was also foreign and frightening. She'd wanted more, and for the first time in years, she wasn't sure if her desires were purely physical.

One thing was certain, she wanted to know more about Regan and her Nashville police contacts could make that happen. She downed the rest of her martini, waved to Jesse, and exited the club. As she reached the sidewalk, a deep throaty voice sounded from behind.

"Leaving so soon?" Lacy came alongside and finessed an arm around her waist. She edged Syd back against the building. "I was hoping for a replay of Friday night. Any chance?"

Hot breath swished past her full lips when she spoke and tickled Syd's ear like the feather touch of a lover. Syd tilted her head to accommodate the kiss she knew was seconds away. As if summoned by the spirit of a cruel April fool's joke, a gray Acura cruised by the front of the club occupied by one very gorgeous assistant city attorney.

Syd jerked away from Lacy. "Sorry, I can't. I've got something to take care of."

❖

Regan cursed when she saw Syd pinned against the building by her tall companion from the restroom. Hadn't she learned that driving by this place was a bad idea? But it was the fastest and shortest distance between the office and home, and she shouldn't have to alter her routine because of Syd's indiscretions. The woman was incorrigible. Obviously Regan's mini-sermon about appropriate behavior had had little impact. Syd had simply moved her rendezvous from the semi-privacy of a bar restroom to the full view of a public street.

She slowed her car and watched the strong woman's hands slide up Syd's thighs and pause at her waist. She leaned closer to Syd's ear as though whispering some enticing endearment designed to lure her into her bed or the nearest bathroom stall. Regan tightened her grip on the steering wheel as the heat of her temper crawled up the back of her neck. How could Syd allow herself to be mauled in public like a common streetwalker?

The memory of Syd's hands on her face and lips returned anew and with it a fresh flare of Irish ire. Less than an hour before, she and Syd had been on the verge of kissing. Evidently the out-of-control cop couldn't even make it home without a sexual outlet. Regan wondered why it bothered her at all. Syd's personal life was not her concern. Her only interest was how this woman's behavior might affect the suit against the city. She glanced back at the intimate scene one more time before turning the corner toward home.

Regan jerked her car to a halt and grabbed her briefcase. Fighting the temptation to go back to the club, she stalked to her front door, shouldered it open, and stepped inside. Grimly, she looked around her small home. A transient seemed to live here among the sparse furnishings and stacks of business files piled on top of her dining-room table. She'd only bought the place to reinvest some money, and it had never felt like a real home.

To her, home was where the heart and soul received nourishment, and she hadn't had such a place since Martha left. This house was merely a stopping-off station for rest and food between long stretches of work. If possible, she'd live at work and never face the emptiness of another dwelling again. But tonight the solitude seemed more dense and unbearable.

She dropped her briefcase on the dining table on her way to the bedroom. How had she allowed the interview to get so out of hand? She was usually excellent at controlling situations, especially ones that involved her feelings. But something about Syd took her on a different path, a dangerously sinuous path mined with deeply gouged potholes and cleverly disguised quagmires. The threat of emotional disaster felt imminent with each step she took. Everything about Syd spelled trouble, yet Regan thought about her constantly.

She peeled off the business attire redolent with the scent of Syd's earthy perfume. The fragrance still intoxicated her and was entirely too distracting for an evening of productive work. As she changed into a pair of worn sweats, her thoughts returned to Syd and again she chastised herself for the near kiss in the conference room. Her body definitely wanted that kiss. Hell, her body wanted more than a kiss, and the memory of that physical hunger still throbbed like a deep bruise on her flesh.

Shaking off the image of Syd in the arms of another woman, she grabbed a Diet Coke from the fridge and pulled Syd's personnel file from her briefcase. The High Point Police Department hadn't provided the full complement of information she'd requested. They were doling it out piecemeal as if they were reviewing the contents before surrendering them to her. She'd made it clear she wanted the files unedited. Surely they understood the necessity of being fully prepared, of methodically reviewing every detail so as not to be ambushed in court. This type of case demanded frequent and religious reevaluation and preparation. But her numerous requests hadn't speeded up the delivery.

The level of bureaucratic procrastination in a government agency had been one of Regan's most difficult adjustments after working in the private sector. If the city was trying to hide something about their officer, she'd find it, but an hour later Regan closed the file with an exasperated sigh. She hadn't uncovered anything damaging in the personnel records, but she had a little more insight into Sydney Cabot. Syd was an only girl in a family of four children. Her working-class parents and three brothers still lived in Atlanta. Until about two years ago Syd had moved often during her twelve-year tenure with the department. The list of home addresses filled most of a typewritten page. What was not mentioned was the reason for the frequent moves. The latest address was one Regan recognized as a loft in the downtown business district within walking distance to city hall and the police station.

What Regan found most useful was the psychological profile the department had done on Syd as a new hire. It told the story of a young woman raised in a strict household with a domineering mother. Syd had a rebellious streak and tested her independence in college before eventually entering law enforcement, a profession as restrictive as her upbringing. Syd was labeled as an introvert with a suspicious nature, a perfectionist quick to make decisions, impulsive at times, reliable, and totally loyal when she believed in something. Her potential as a police officer was projected to be an eight out of a possible score of ten, well above average.

But like everything else associated with Syd, these tidbits of information could prove to be advantageous or detrimental to their case, depending on how they were manifested on the job. Regan hoped that Syd's Internal Affairs file would help her establish a pattern of professional behavior that would benefit their case. Mentally reviewing her encounters with Syd, she prayed nothing in those files would paint an unflattering picture of the officer, on or off the job.

❖

Syd left Lacy standing on the sidewalk and returned to her loft with one goal in mind, to find out more about the woman who was haunting her life. Taking the stairway steps two at a time, she reached the landing of her apartment, opened the door, and rifled through the basket of business cards on the entryway table. She pulled the Nashville PD embossed card from the stack and dialed the private number scribbled on the back.

Keith Rickard answered, and after a few minutes of idle chitchat, Syd got to the point of her call. "I need some information on an attorney from over your way. She moved here not long ago and took a job with the city. I was wondering if you could check her out for me."

"Sure thing. What's her name?"

"Regan Desanto."

"I don't need to do any research on that one. She was a hotshot lawyer with Tuggle, Diggins, Mershaw, Thompson, and Elrod here in Nashville for years. They're the top civil-litigation group in the state."

"Really?" Syd's pulse kicked up and she tucked the phone closer to her ear. "So what happened?"

"She was on the verge of becoming a partner and was handling one last pro-bono case for the city. A wrongful-death suit. A thug shot and killed by an officer in the line of duty and his family sues, you know how it goes."

Syd's throat tightened. "Yeah, tell me about it."

"The case seemed pretty open-and-shut, but she lost it. Cost the city big bucks and the officer quit the force."

She lost the case. That was just great. "Anything else?"

"I guess she couldn't take losing. She left town. There were articles in the papers for weeks, talk about whether the officer's family would sue her firm. All I can say is, I hope she's not defending you."

"Thanks, Keith, I appreciate your help."

"But there's more."

"I think I've heard enough."

Syd hung up the phone with a sick feeling. The information made sense and it made her nauseous. That explained why a high-priced attorney had left a prestigious law firm and taken a mediocre city-service job in a town five hundred miles away. Regan had lost her edge and blown one of the most expensive cases in the firm's history. And instead of staying to face her failures, she'd run away and started over. Great, Syd's attorney was a coward.

For some reason the image of Regan Desanto running away from anything didn't fit Syd's impression of the woman. She seemed to have too much confidence and pride in her work. On the other hand, it fit perfectly. Regan did seem like the kind of person to be sympathetic to the misfortunes of others, especially if she caused them. And having cost the firm money would weigh heavily on her mind. She would have insisted on taking responsibility for her actions. So why did she leave? And didn't Terry Blair know about her history? Surely he wouldn't have given her this case if he did.

The lights of the city sparkled and danced beyond her window, reminding her of the challenge and satisfaction her work provided. It seemed unimaginable that her future as a police officer might be in jeopardy. Suddenly Regan's objections to handling her case during their first meeting made perfect sense. She had tried to persuade her boss to reassign it to someone else, but he'd refused. Maybe she hadn't told him all the details about the case in Nashville. Syd would gladly provide them. She needed the best representation the city could offer, and if that wasn't Regan, she had no qualms about having her removed. She felt vindicated in exposing her past.

But as she envisioned having Regan taken off the case, conflicting feelings ignited inside Syd. She'd seen another side of Regan and had sensed the spark of deep caring that burned just below the surface. And what about the tiny flicker of feelings Syd had experienced when Regan tried to console her about the shooting? Would she ever allow anyone to explore those dark places inside her if she shut Regan out now?

Her mind told her to call the city attorney first thing in the morning and expose Regan's past. But her heart held out for a better option.

CHAPTER EIGHT

Regan's drive to work the next morning was filled with images of the previous night's sidewalk show of Syd. Her phone was already emitting its annoying multitoned ring as she entered the office and deposited her briefcase on the desk. She answered with her usual professional identifiers and soon realized this wouldn't be just another day at the office.

"Desanto, this is Dean Bell, attorney for the family of Lee Nartey. I understand that you're representing the city in our wrongful-death suit."

Regan dropped into her swivel chair and rolled her eyes toward the ceiling. She'd never met Bell but had heard he was a shark in the courtroom who took only cases that had the potential to sustain his exorbitant price tag and bolster his flashy career. "Yes, that's correct. How may I help you this morning, Counselor?"

"Actually, I'm calling to help you." His high-pitched voice sounded condescending and presumptuous.

"I'm always open to cooperation between peers, Mr. Bell. What did you have in mind?"

"I've just gotten my hands on Sydney Cabot's therapy notes and a copy of the so-called secret file from Internal Affairs. After reviewing it, I thought we should talk before this case hits the press. And trust me, it will."

The not-too-subtly veiled threat in the man's voice shot up Regan's spine like the twinge of a bad back. How did he get a copy of those documents before she did? A subpoena for therapy notes wasn't easily or quickly obtained without a compelling reason. And how *dare* he threaten a public airing of such private information, regardless of the content.

Based on her own recent encounters with Syd, Regan shuddered to think what Bell had uncovered. Whatever it was, he obviously thought it would make juicy grist for the mill of public outrage and win points for his case. "What is it that you find so interesting and worthy of public revelation?"

"You're kidding, right?" His smug-sounding voice was laced with superiority and distaste. "This woman is like a feral cat that should be spayed. But then she's not really in danger of reproducing, is she?"

The comment soured in Regan's system, and she bit her tongue to keep from firing back the response this man really deserved. "I'm not sure I follow."

"Come on, Desanto, haven't you read this stuff? It seems that Officer Cabot has an insatiable hunger for the fairer sex. And she's not real picky about when or where she meets them or how she dumps them. Sounds like she failed the class on discretion in the academy."

Regan's heart tripped a beat as she reached for a jolt of cold caffeine. She couldn't imagine Syd revealing intimate details of her personal life to a therapist, especially not in the context of a fitness-for-duty session. The department's mandatory FFD examination centered on the precipitating event and getting the officer back to work. Syd was savvy enough to understand the process and to disclose only the pertinent facts, if that.

"And what exactly do her personal proclivities have to do with this case, Mr. Bell?"

"It's pretty obvious she's too preoccupied with scoring snatch to keep her eyes or her mind on the job. She'd probably just had a little rendezvous in that alley at the mall when she shot my client's son to death."

Regan couldn't believe the vulgar tone and blatantly prejudicial comments spewing from Bell's mouth. She'd never met this man, and yet he thought it acceptable to talk to her in such a fashion. Then another possibility occurred. What if he was taping their conversation to goad her into an unfavorable or compromising remark about Syd or the case? Even though such a remark wouldn't be admissible in a legal proceeding, it could tarnish her reputation and credibility if he leaked it to her client or the press.

She checked her temper and replied in her most professional and impassive tone, "I'm sure the facts presented in court will show exactly what happened that night, Counselor. Why don't we wait and try the case in that venue?"

Silence at the other end of the phone line confirmed Regan's suspicions. After a lengthy pause, Bell replied, "Well, uh, if you're sure you want to do that. Officer Cabot's background won't make her a very sympathetic witness. I just thought you might appreciate an opportunity to settle this and save the city a lot of money."

"Thank you for your concern and your generous offer, but we'll take our chances."

As she hung up the phone, Regan had a sinking feeling in her gut. Obviously Bell thought he had something very damaging in those documents. She needed a copy. *Now*. It wouldn't help to have Syd portrayed in the media as a wanton lesbian on a rampage to devour the city's female population. And Syd certainly wouldn't handle public exposure of her personal life with any degree of calm. It was her job to see that neither Syd nor the City suffered at the hands of an opportunistic attorney.

The remainder of Regan's day vanished in an array of phone calls and personal visits to secure the Internal Affairs file and Syd's therapy notes. After receiving assurance from the chief of police that the information would be on her desk first thing in the morning, Regan fished her cell phone from her briefcase and headed toward the elevator. As she waited for the door to open, she punched in the number she'd memorized the day she received it. This was not a conversation she wanted to have but knew in her gut she had to. Her call was answered almost immediately. She chose a guarded tone when she really wanted to blurt the news and be done with it.

"We need to talk…no, not there, somewhere more private."

❖

Syd teetered on the four-inch-wide rock parapet that encircled her penthouse and enjoyed the surge of energy that accompanied this gravity-defying feat. The idea of cheating death while skimming the perimeter of her third-floor residence had helped sell her on the place. Granted, she probably wouldn't die from such a fall, but the odds of a soft landing weren't great. Still, it brought the adrenaline highs of the job home and within her control.

She wobbled precariously above unsuspecting pedestrians, doubting if any of them felt half as alive as she did at this moment. She doubted if most people found it necessary to go to such extremes to feel an emotional connection with their own bodies. Why was it so hard for her?

She remembered growing up in the warm Southern hospitality of Atlanta. While her parents hadn't been overly affectionate, Syd had always known she was loved and had felt connected to them and her brothers. They seldom discussed their emotions, but family activities that centered on teamwork and challenge had bonded them together. She felt supported and encouraged to experiment, within the parameters set by her mother. But when Syd went to college, she branched out and tested her own boundaries. Lovers became the new "activities" of her life and she engaged her feelings based on the circumstances. It seemed pointless to give her heart to someone she knew wasn't the right one. Until now *she* had always drawn the emotional line.

But since the shooting, Syd's ability to connect on a personal level had seemingly been surgically removed. When that bullet left the barrel of her Glock, it took a piece of her soul and she'd been unable to reconnect with it. Tina had been her lover for a few months when it happened, and until that day Syd had allowed herself to think they had a chance at a long-term relationship. Or maybe she was just still in lust. When Syd was placed on administrative leave, Tina started making demands about moving in, taking care of her, and seeing a counselor to keep their relationship on track. The pressure was too great and Syd bolted.

She tiptoed to the end of the parapet, jumped in the air, pivoted, and started back in the opposite direction. If she was honest, she'd have to admit that no one had really aroused her interest until Regan. But that was before she'd found out about her past in Nashville.

There was something compelling about the woman who pushed all her buttons, but Syd couldn't forget that her career rested firmly in the hands of an attorney who'd lost a case just like hers. Last night she'd been determined to report her findings to Terry Blair and demand that Regan be taken off her case. But she didn't actually want to believe the worst about Regan and she didn't want her replaced. She simply wanted to understand what happened.

Her thoughts returned to their near kiss in the conference room: the silky softness of Regan's face between her hands and her hot breath mingling with her own. A sharp stab of desire rattled Syd and she momentarily lost her footing on the wall, tilting sideways over the street.

"I assume this note on the door was for me." Regan entered the loft waving a piece of paper in her hand. When she saw Syd dangling over the wall, she stopped mid-step and clutched the note to her chest. "Dear God, will you come down from there?"

Syd regained her balance and jumped from the wall, landing directly in front of her open-mouthed attorney. "I wouldn't leave my door unlocked for just anyone. What's the matter, Counselor, afraid of heights?"

Regan glanced at Syd's mouth as she spoke, then backed away from her. "It's not the heights that bother me as much as the reckless disregard for life. I certainly hope this isn't a tendency that carries over to your job."

The comment was like a solid jab in the gut. "I assure you that if I seem reckless, it's only with my own life." She motioned to a pair of Poang chairs on the balcony and settled into one. "Would you care for a glass of wine or a Coke?"

"No thanks. This is a professional visit."

"Your call sounded urgent. What's happened that would require a home visit on Friday evening?"

Regan squirmed uncomfortably in the chair and looked out over the city. Her blue eyes sparkled with light from the street below, but her face appeared drawn and serious. Syd waited patiently for her to get to the point of her visit. After Regan had her say, she intended to find out about Nashville. She could not rest until she knew what had caused such a highly competent woman to lose that case and leave town.

Regan's gaze shifted around the balcony, back to the city skyline, and finally came to rest on Syd. "I got a call from Dean Bell today. He's representing the plaintiff in our suit."

Regan was finally coming to the point. In their brief association

Syd had already learned that she believed in delivering bad news eye to eye. This gesture alone told her volumes about Regan's character and made her seriously doubt what she'd heard from Nashville. Syd met her stare with equal candor and waited.

"Bell has copies of the Internal Affairs secret file and your therapy notes."

Panic oozed through Syd like an arson fire from its source. She'd spent her entire career facing physical danger, but this threat seemed more vague and insidious. The defensive weapons of her job couldn't help her now. She felt unprepared and afraid. "How?"

"Discovery and a well-crafted subpoena. He's threatening to leak the contents to the press, obviously to damage your reputation and sway public sentiment."

Syd recalled the few sessions she'd had with the department's shrink and felt relatively sure she'd adhered to the unwritten rule of "deny everything and demand proof." But the so-called secret IA cache was another issue. She had no idea what juicy tidbits, personal or professional, were relegated to those smut files. The information was never shared with officers, even on request. The IA files reputedly consisted of calls and letters that never rose to the level of a complaint or were simply not actionable under departmental rules and regulations. It was also rumored that the brass often reviewed them when considering officers for promotion. Anything of an unsavory nature could affect an officer's chances for advancement and he'd never know it.

"What's in the IA file that could possibly be so bad?" Syd asked.

"I was hoping you could tell me."

Syd shook her head in dismay. "You haven't seen it? Their attorney has it and *you* don't? How is that possible?"

Regan's lips were drawn into a thin line. "The department has been giving me the runaround. But the chief promised I'd have them in the morning. I just couldn't risk you hearing about this in the media if Bell makes good on his threat. I'm so sorry, Syd. I'm doing the best I can."

Helplessness blanketed Syd. "Is that what you told Ken Fowler?"

Syd immediately regretted her angry outburst. Her words registered like a slap across Regan's face and made her blue eyes darken and her face pale. There was obviously more to this story, and her callous delivery had injured Regan. Her usual composure crumbled. Wanting to mitigate the damage, she said, "I didn't mean to blurt it out like that. I just needed to know who was representing me, so I checked you out."

Regan's posture was stilted as she rose and paced the balcony. She answered in a low, deliberate tone. "And you still don't know who I am. If you believe one lost case defines me or my career, you're more naïve than I thought."

Syd tried to regain some of her initial righteous indignation, but the pain in Regan's eyes tugged at her heart and demanded further explanation. "I'm really sorry for upsetting you. There's obviously a lot I don't know. Can you tell me what happened?"

She considered the hypocrisy of her question. How could she ask Regan to share something that caused her such pain when *she* was unwilling to reveal her feelings about the shooting? Such disclosures required more trust than she'd given.

Regan paused at the parapet, surveying Syd as if evaluating whether to answer her question. Her internal struggle was emphasized by several deep inhalations and exhalations. When she finally spoke, her voice was barely audible over the street noises below.

"I've never told anyone the entire story. I trust you'll be discreet." Without waiting for a response, she said. "I received the Fowler case a week before my partner of fifteen years left me for her boss. Turns out she'd been sleeping with her the entire time we were together. I guess it took that long to choose between us."

Regan delivered the information with the composure of a court brief, but Syd struggled to dislodge the knot of emotion that gathered in her throat as Regan spoke. She had no idea what a fifteen-year relationship felt like, but the range of feelings that contorted Regan's face was almost tangible. She wanted to comfort her but wasn't sure she knew how without being misunderstood. It had been so long since she'd reached out for any reason other than sex that she didn't trust herself. Clenching the chair arms, she listened as Regan spoke.

"I spent the days on my feet in court and the nights on my knees begging Martha to come home. I just couldn't hold my world and someone else's together at the same time. In the end, my job and my relationship both came apart."

Overcoming her internal resistance, Syd joined Regan at the parapet. She awkwardly slid her arm around her waist and stood beside her. "I'm so sorry. I had no idea."

"I'm not making excuses for losing the case."

"I know. You're not the type."

"There's more."

"You don't have to go on. This is obviously hard for you. I appreciate you sharing it with me. And I *will* be discreet."

"You need to know the rest. The young officer, Ken Fowler, left the department after I lost the case. Three months later he committed suicide. So, you see, I do know what it's like to kill another human being."

Syd's body stiffened. She felt as if she'd explode from the stew of feelings bouncing around inside her. She was angry at herself for not getting the whole story from her contact in Nashville. She was scared that the same thing could happen to her if they lost. She was worried about Regan's ability to handle the case. Yet a small part of her was relieved that Regan had some idea of the guilt she felt about killing someone, though the circumstances were vastly different. But mostly, Syd was deeply sad that she'd caused Regan to relive this devastating part of her life.

The pain in Regan's eyes turned liquid and rolled down her cheeks; her body trembled and she swayed forward. Syd instinctively wrapped both arms around her and held her close. She felt an immediate connection where their skin touched and a tactile craving where fabric separated flesh. The joining was more intimate than any she'd ever experienced, less physical but decidedly more arousing. Her default sexual response seemed anemic compared to the feelings of empathy and nurturing that had overtaken her.

"I can't imagine how painful it must've been to lose a partner in the middle of all that."

The muscles along Regan's back tightened and she pulled back from Syd. "No, you can't. You're a serial polyamorist who's probably never had a relationship last longer than your orgasm."

Regan's words stung, but rather than her usual impulsive reaction, Syd considered the comment and decided it was close to accurate. "My track record isn't very good, but I know pain when I see it. I'm amazed that you haven't given up on love altogether."

"What makes you think I haven't?"

"You feel things too deeply, Regan. And you're not bitter. That means your heart is still open."

"And what about you? You never answered my question about how you felt during the shooting. Do you remember?"

Syd gazed at her as if she'd asked the most idiotic question in the world. The muscles of her abdomen knotted. Regan had been honest with her. Why the hesitation? She stifled the emotions bubbling unbidden to the surface. "I felt absolutely nothing. I'm certain of it."

She could barely speak through the shroud that seemed to surround her, as if she were in a coffin. Then tears rushed from a small part of her that still seemed alive and stung her eyes. She squeezed them tight to keep them from betraying her.

"Can you just wave your magic lawyer stick and make it all disappear?"

"I really wish I could." She took Syd's hands in hers and gently stroked the backs with her thumbs.

Syd watched Regan's thumbs slide across her hands and allowed the sensation to soothe the tension in her chest and calm the urge to run. She'd been physically closer to numerous women in her life but never felt as intimately touched. For someone who wanted to be in control of her surroundings, Regan didn't seem concerned about allowing herself to nurture and comfort. If she was worried about exposing herself, she did not allow her reservations to change her behavior. The innate courage in that choice touched Syd on a level she couldn't quite explain.

"I'm all right," she said.

"No, Syd, you're not. And don't give me that tough-cop crap. I'm not buying it."

"What makes you think it's an act?"

"It doesn't go with everything else I see in you."

"And what exactly do you see?"

Regan smiled. "A sensitive woman trying to survive in an insensitive profession. A human being torn between her personal values and the ones that the job imposes on her. An officer traumatized by a decision to live or die, to kill or be killed. A woman struggling to cope with anguish so profound that any attempt to feel is like ripping open an old wound."

"Stop. Please stop."

"I'm sorry. I just hate to see you suffering so much."

Syd gently squeezed Regan's hands and released them. "I can't do this. Please don't ask me to do this."

"Do what?"

Syd vacillated between her need for self-protection and the raw emotion in Regan's eyes. If nothing else, that look demanded honesty. "Feel."

"The only thing worse is not feeling."

Regan brought their bodies together again in a warm embrace that elicited another round of uncontrollable emotion in Syd. Her muscles tensed in their usual defensive response, then released as if fatigued from months of exhaustive overuse. Regan's firm body against hers felt like a haven of refuge. Syd tried to disengage but was transfixed by a sensation more compelling than any she'd ever experienced. She rested her head on Regan's chest and was comforted by the rapid pulse of her heart. Tears escaped and soaked the soft cotton fabric of Regan's shirt.

Sliding her hands up Syd's back and over her shoulders, Regan cupped her face, brushing away her tears. Her long fingers combed through Syd's hair and palmed the back of her head. Syd gazed into azure blue eyes that sparked with heat as Regan licked her trembling lips and lowered her mouth to Syd's. When their lips touched, the warmth of Regan's mouth made Syd light-headed.

Regan tentatively traced Syd's lips with the tip of her tongue, moistening and requesting entry. Syd opened to her and met Regan's tongue with equal reverence. The moment their mouths fused together, all hesitancy vanished. Regan's tongue plunged deeper as if reaching for Syd's soul. Her mouth pressed forcefully against Syd's like a protective covering to seal even the air out.

"Mmm." Syd was unsure if the sound came from her or Regan as their kiss deepened. She tried to remember the last time a first kiss, or any kiss for that matter, felt this perfect. Her entire body was on fire. They were only kissing but she felt like she was being stroked and stimulated all over. She leaned into Regan and rubbed against her muscled thigh, physically begging for flesh and blood to replace her imaginings. Syd couldn't suppress the need building inside her for long. It was like a craving for something she'd never had but knew instinctively she must experience.

She drew Regan's arm from around her waist and guided her hand to the heat between her legs. "Touch me."

Regan broke their kiss to catch her breath and looked down into Syd's face. "I want you so much."

"Then take me. Please."

Closing her hand over Syd's crotch, Regan squeezed. "You're so wet."

The physical evidence of Syd's arousal seemed to release a vampire in Regan. She kissed and sucked Syd's uncovered flesh wherever she could make contact: her face, neck, ears, arms, and hands. Regan's mouth was hot and hungry against Syd, whose tingling skin and normally cool face and neck were afire with patches of red heat. Regan rubbed and clawed the denim fabric between Syd's legs with one hand while simultaneously tugging at the hem of her T-shirt with the other, to dislodge it from her jeans.

Syd reached down, ripped the shirt from her waistband and over her head in one swift motion. Her unencumbered breasts rose and fell with each labored breath as she waited for Regan to touch her exposed skin. Regan looked at her with lust-hooded eyes, her breathing heavy. Then all movement stopped. Her gaze swept up and down Syd's body as if taking stock while she made a conscious decision. Syd had seen that look of hesitation too many times to ignore it. Rational thought was trying to interrupt and discount the body's needs.

She gripped Regan's right hand, holding it in place between her legs, and reached for her left. She cupped their joined hands over her left breast. "You want this as much as I do."

Regan gently massaged Syd's breast and it puckered to life in her hands. She jerked the tender flesh between her legs one final time and backed away. "You have no idea."

Syd followed the retreat. "We don't have to stop."

"Yes, we do. This is wrong and I apologize. You were vulnerable and I took advantage."

"But you don't understand, I—"

"I understand enough to know that this is not right, even if you weren't my client." She paused, and her tone was sorrowful more than accusatory when she spoke again. "I'm not willing to be another notch on your sexual belt. Good night, Syd."

Regan turned and walked out of the apartment, leaving Syd with a hunger she knew no one else could fill and an ache that prevented giving chase.

CHAPTER NINE

Gil Brady caged a fresh beer between his fingers and avoided Syd's questioning gaze. He'd asked her to meet him at the Cop Out for a drink on the way home from his Saturday shift. He hadn't talked much about his wife in a few days, and Syd hoped that was good news for their marriage. His sullen demeanor said otherwise.

"Well, we've covered every call you went on today," she said after they'd spent half an hour. "Are you ready to tell me why we're really here?"

Syd knew she sounded short but she'd been irritable since last night. Images of Regan Desanto kissing and touching her body resurfaced when she least expected them, constricting her breathing with jolts of emotion too intense to categorize. Her entire day had been an exercise in self-control as waves of desire overtook her when she should've been thinking of other things.

She decided she must have been more tired than she realized. She'd not only allowed Regan to take charge of their interaction, but she'd enjoyed relinquishing control. Normally her submission in sex play was a conscious choice and was still about *her* control. While partners appeared to be in charge, the final decisions were always hers. But with Regan, she'd simply let go and felt completely safe. Even more telling was her inability to verbally respond when Regan disengaged, practically insulted her, and left. Her usual reply would've been some quip about what Regan was missing, but Syd felt like she was the one losing out.

She wondered what was happening to her. Her life was getting more bizarre by the day. Last night she'd kissed her attorney, loved it, and wanted more. Today she couldn't stop thinking about her. It was infuriating. Still, her distraction level was no excuse for being unkind to Gil. "I'm sorry for being snappish. Something's bothering you…want to talk about it?"

Gil looked around the club again before finally asking, "What's so special about this place?"

"What do you mean?"

"My wife loves it. It looks like any other bar to me."

"I'm not sure I can answer that one. Jesse runs a tight ship and doesn't put up with any nonsense. That makes all kinds of folks comfortable coming here."

"All kinds of folks, huh?" His slow, deep voice sounded flat and sarcastic.

Syd detected an unasked question. "What do you want to know, Gil?"

"I wish my wife could read me as well as you do." He took a long pull from his beer. "Do you meet other women here, you know—like that?"

Syd felt the blood rush to her face. She and Gil were developing a friendship, but they'd never discussed her personal life. It seemed he was more comfortable avoiding that specific topic.

"I have, but mostly I come to support Jesse. If you're asking if gay men and women hang out here, the answer is yes, but so do straight people. It's not strictly a gay-and-lesbian club."

"I think Priscilla meets women here." The look on Syd's face must have been one of obvious shock because Gil added, "It's just a feeling I get. I don't think she's sleeping with another guy. She says she loves me and wants our marriage to work."

"Then why would she want to meet women?"

"That's what I need your help with. I was thinking you—"

"No."

"You haven't even heard me out."

"The answer is still no. I'm happy to offer advice, but I'm not going to be bait for some experiment to lure your wife."

He grimaced. "It's not like that. I just want you to help me stake out the place and see if she shows up. Is that too much to ask?"

Syd had a shaky gut feeling that told her to haul ass in the opposite direction. But Gil was becoming her friend and he was confused and worried. "Why don't you just ask her outright? Sneaking around spying on her is not the way to build trust in your marriage."

"I need to know the truth. Please, Syd. There's nobody else I can ask."

The desperation in Gil's voice tugged at Syd's heart. Her head said this was a bad idea but her heart was just beginning to understand that strong feelings for another person could create internal turmoil that had to be resolved. She wanted to help. "And what happens if she *is* sleeping with women?"

"I just want to know if she still loves me. Nothing else matters."

Syd couldn't believe she was letting her emotions rule her judgment, but Gil needed a friend and she was it. "When do we start?"

"How about right now? I left my car at the station so she won't see it. We can use the parking garage across the street for high-ground surveillance."

Syd finished her martini and walked to the bar to pay Jesse.

"Do you know what you're doing, Syd?" Jesse nodded toward Gil. "He's—"

"Don't be crazy. We're just friends."

"But do you know who that is?"

"Of course I do. I introduced the two of you. He works on my squad."

Gil walked up behind Syd. "You ready?"

"Sure." Syd gave Jesse a reassuring smile, touched by her obvious unease. It felt good to have someone who looked out for her. "See you later, Jess."

She and Gil exited the club and climbed to the fourth floor of the parking structure. An hour later, staring out into the night, she wondered what she was doing. She was perched on the fourth floor of a parking deck with a squad mate spying on his maybe-cheating, maybe-lesbian wife. This was crazy.

"Hey, Syd, get over here. There she is. How did she get in without us seeing her?"

Syd rushed to Gil's side and peered below. "She probably went in the back door."

Two women exited the Cop Out holding hands and leaning into each other. A tall, mocha-skinned African-American in tight leather pants and T-shirt pinned a short blonde with pale skin against the wall and kissed her roughly. The tall woman plunged her hand under the blonde's skirt, eliciting a loud moan of pleasure that resounded off the building-lined street. Muscles rippled along the stronger woman's back as her hand worked feverishly between the blonde's legs.

A shiver shot up Syd's spine, and the hairs on her neck prickled to attention. Her mouth felt dry and sticky as she recognized the woman humping the blonde as her sometimes-paramour Lacy.

When she found her voice she asked, "That blonde is your wife?"

Without turning to face her, Gil said, "No, the other one." His voice held no hint of anger, only sadness.

"*That's* Priscilla?"

"Yep. We can go now. I've seen enough."

Stunned, Syd allowed Gil to lead the way down the stairs. She didn't trust that her mouth wasn't still hanging open. "Lacy" was actually Priscilla, Gil's wife. She had trouble believing it. Jesse's anxious face flashed through her mind. She knew. *This* was what she'd been trying to warn her about. Lacy was obviously a regular, so she must have been in the bar with Gil occasionally. Syd couldn't remember ever seeing them together, but the last eight months had evaporated into a haze. She had to wonder what else that she'd forgotten or suppressed would come back and bite her firmly on the butt.

"I'm really sorry, buddy." And he had no idea just how sorry she was. She wanted to tell him the truth, but her mother used to say, "If it ain't a gift, don't give it." Syd wondered if she was just being a coward. Maybe she would let him know, but not right now. Not after what they'd just seen.

Gil stopped at the bottom of the stairs and turned to her. "Please don't spread this around."

"I won't. Trust me. What are you going to do?"

Most men would've charged their wife's lover like a raging bull and done serious bodily damage. Maybe it was just Gil's nature to take things in stride. His self-discipline had probably made him an excellent soldier. It was certainly an asset for a cop.

"I'm not sure," he said. "I need some time to think. All I really want to know is if she still loves me. I think I could forgive everything else."

They circled around the back of the parking deck, Gil's shoulders slouched as he moved like a man carrying too much pain. Syd didn't linger, afraid she might somehow reveal her role in Priscilla's double life. As she walked home she felt as though everything around her was changing form. Another piece of her life had suddenly been twisted into a new shape. She was disoriented, no longer at home in her world. Yet she wasn't sure if she wanted things to go back to the way they were before the shooting. Could she just step back into her life as if none of this had happened? Syd didn't think so.

Things kept changing around her, but there was more. She was changing too.

❖

Crushed Diet Coke cans filled the wastebasket near Regan's desk, and scattered papers covered the floor of her den. She'd received the files she requested from the chief and had been reading ever since. Saturday had blurred into Sunday with little sleep as she tried to forget kissing her client. But the memory was branded into her mind just as Syd's touch was tattooed on her skin. A foreign longing permeated her entire being. Her skin prickled with sudden shudders of sensory recall. Muscles in her legs and arms tensed and simultaneously weakened with a yearning so intense it seemed to attack the very framework of her body. Nerve endings quivered with an appetite for something obscure to her sexual palate but vital to her emotional survival. She felt like a live electrical wire severed from its source and floundering dangerously.

What about this particular woman affected her so powerfully? Syd would look great fighting crime in her uniform or making dinner wearing only an apron. She was certainly attractive, with a body that curved, dipped, and swelled in exactly the right places. One of Regan's fetishes was full, soft breasts that she could nurse, tease, and suck. Syd's fit the bill perfectly. Burying her face in cleavage and being surrounded by the yielding mounds could almost bring Regan to orgasm. She also enjoyed rounded hips that she could hold and sink her fingers into while making love.

Her body thrilled as she remembered the masterful feeling of holding Syd's breasts in her hands and manipulating them into pinpoints of arousal. She'd wanted to take Sydney Cabot right where she stood, on her loft balcony, for anyone who cared to watch. Her restraint had been so weakened by their interaction that she'd blatantly disregarded the voice of reason that screamed in her head, grabbing and clawing her flesh like a cannibal hungry for her next meal. And when her lips touched Syd's she was lost. Truly, deeply, irrevocably lost. She knew she could never go there again, or she wouldn't be able to leave. It had taken all her willpower to walk away that night.

Regan quivered, and the file she was holding fell from her hands. Looking at the papers on the floor, she realized she'd been staring at the same pages for almost an hour, but only now did she grasp their significance. Syd had only one reported use of force in her twelve-year tenure with the police department—the fatal shooting of Lee Nartey.

That was unheard of in police work. Most officers used their mace or ASP batons numerous times, in addition to physical restraint. To have no reported instances was unusual. However, reports of on-duty injuries seemed to be in abundance in Syd's history. These documents, one after the other, told the story of an officer more interested in verbal than physical resolution to dangerous situations. Syd tried to talk suspects down, which often worked. Other times her repeated attempts at communication annoyed an already-hostile suspect and he took out his frustration on her. Copies of medical-services forms detailed Syd's many visits to the city nurse or hospital for injuries ranging from a bloody nose to stab wounds.

Regan shivered at the thought of a weapon piercing Syd's soft skin and causing her pain. Her temper flared and she wondered why Syd hadn't defended herself better. Taking a sip of lukewarm Diet Coke, she smiled at her protective attitude. If Dean Bell thought this file would help his case, he was mistaken. These documents squarely supported Syd and the training she received from the city.

Regan sighed in relief and reached for the yellow padded envelope marked Confidential. This was possibly the last obstacle between Syd and a complete dismissal of the case, and it was the file Regan feared most. She ripped the protective tape from the envelope and emptied the contents onto the floor. Several lined index cards fanned out around her. Each contained a woman's name, address, and telephone number, along with a brief summary of an unsatisfactory personal encounter with Syd. As Regan read the reports, her spirits sank. "Unsatisfactory" seemed to be a relative term. The women's issues centered mainly on dissatisfaction with the longevity of their interaction with Syd, not with her performance during it. Six women in the past twelve years had an encounter or a relationship that ended badly enough for them to complain to her boss.

If six had come forward, how many more had not? The memory of kissing Syd suddenly felt cheap and inconsequential. She was just another dissatisfied customer and the thought sickened her. Forcing the unpleasant idea from her head, Regan willed herself to examine the cards more closely. Most of the complaints had occurred during the past eight months, since the shooting. This fact seemed to support her theory that Syd had tried to assuage her professional guilt through personal pleasures. But, with one exception, none of the incidents had been pursued beyond the collection of preliminary data. Taped to the back of one of the index cards was a microcassette tape marked "Gina Lorrey complaint; received by phone."

Regan turned the tape over and over in her hands. It seemed to scorch a fiery path up her arm and into her heart. Her body already knew what was on the tape without hearing it. Her mind wasn't sure it wanted confirmation. The warring feelings sparred back and forth like a feedback loop caught in continuous repeat mode. She didn't want to hear another woman's voice maligning Syd's reputation or her private life, and she wasn't sure she could endure any other woman describing the physical pleasures that Syd was capable of providing. But she needed to know what was on the tape because Dean Bell had obviously listened to it. If she had any hope of defending Syd, she had to know what the opposing counsel intended to use against her.

Filled with trepidation, Regan found her cassette player and started the tape. A deep male voice spoke first, providing the routine details of a conversation taped in August, the month of the shooting. The officer who took the complaint was Detective Ramon Boudy with the Internal Affairs Division.

The female complainant provided the information requested in a tone designed to arouse speculation and fantasy. Her soft, breathy voice oozed sexuality. Regan pictured a diminutive blonde batting her baby blue eyes, cooling herself with a hand-painted paper fan, and sipping a mint julep. After a feeble protest about getting anyone in trouble and a few over-exaggerated attempts at modesty, Gina Lorrey began her tale.

"It was August twenty-first. I remember specifically because it was my birthday and I was supposed to meet some friends at the Cop Out club, to celebrate. I parked in the back lot and was walking to the door when this cop came up to me. She was in uniform but I didn't see a cop car anywhere. Of course my first reaction was, 'What have I done?'

"She seemed to be in a daze or something. I asked if she was okay. I mean it looked like she was going to cry. Being the kindhearted person that I am, I reached out to comfort her. Well, that was the wrong thing to do. She grabbed the front of my jeans. Don't misunderstand. I'm no prude when it comes to sex, with men or women. It was just a surprise, that's all. Then she kissed me, and it was pretty clear what she wanted. I've never been kissed like that before. It was like she sucked the energy out of my entire body."

Regan crushed the Diet Coke she held in her hand and the sticky liquid spewed everywhere. She'd experienced that kiss, and listening to another woman try to explain its effects was like exposing raw flesh to acid. She didn't want to hear anymore but knew she had to. Wiping the spilled soda with the hem of her T-shirt, she concentrated on the breathy voice.

"She never spoke a word. She just backed me into a dark corner and onto the hood of a car. It was still hot. It felt like my ass was burning. She ripped my blouse open like a mad woman. Then she yanked my jeans down around my ankles."

Grabbing the pillow from her desk chair, Regan put it under her head and lay down on the floor. Tingles of excitement rippled through her as she remembered the texture of Syd's skin beneath hers and the pleading look in her eyes. Regan slid her hand down the length of her torso and cupped the quivering flesh that begged for attention. She'd never been the kind to enjoy girlie magazines or even dirty talk, but ever since she'd seen Syd having sex in the restroom, fantasies had played incessantly in her head like porn movies. Something about Syd called to the primeval urges of her body and soul.

"When I was completely naked, lying there on the hood of the car, she stopped." Gina Lorrey's tone hardened. "I'm not sure what happened but she just stared for the longest time. It was getting a little awkward, if you know what I mean. So I asked if she was okay. She started apologizing and told me to get dressed. But I was already too far gone."

After a long hesitation the voice changed. Regan had the impression that Gina Lorrey had decided to play a game with the detective at the other end of the phone.

"I grabbed her by the gun belt. She put up a bit of resistance, but I unzipped her pants and stuck my hand right in there. God, she was wet like you couldn't believe."

Regan plunged her hand into the band of her sweats and into the liquid warmth between her legs. She imagined Syd's hand there smoothing and stroking the engorged shaft of aching flesh. She pulled and kneaded the tender folds of skin. It had been entirely too long, and touching Syd on Friday night had rekindled her appetite for physical satisfaction.

"Well, she was having none of that," Gina continued. "She wanted to be in charge. She took her nightstick out and flicked the tip across my breasts. Do you have any idea how that feels?"

The detective made an impassive sound, like he'd heard it all before.

Gina's voice took on a taunting lilt as she said, "It's like the hardest dick in the world begging to be fucked. I felt like I could've taken the whole thing if she'd given it to me. She twirled it around between her thumb and palm like you cops do and started rubbing me with the handle."

The idea of making love with Syd in her uniform had played itself out more than once in Regan's imagination, but being seduced by the tools of her trade was a new spin. The delicate skin around her nipples dimpled in anticipation. She massaged her left breast in time to the intensified stroking between her legs. *She* was the woman on top of that car in the dark parking lot behind Cop Out. Syd was teasing and tantalizing *her* with her nightstick, bringing her closer and closer to orgasm.

"That handle has these ridges on it, you know. And when she dragged it between my legs, I thought I was going to come right then. She knew I was in a bad way. I started humping that stick. The harder I tried to get a piece of it inside me, the more determined she was to keep it away. I was on the edge."

Regan was starting to lose control. Like the woman on the tape, she'd long since abandoned any sense of modesty or decorum.

She writhed on the hardwood floor, her clothes oppressive with their confinement. All she wanted was the precious release that only Syd could provide.

"I was desperate, I'm not ashamed to say it. A girl can only stand so much torment. I begged her to fuck me with that long, hard stick. Then she finally said something. I still remember it. 'Every woman deserves to come with something hot and throbbing inside her.'"

Regan sighed. The voice droned on, blurring with the sounds of her own rapid breathing.

"Oh, God, I've never been fucked so good. It was like she knew exactly how much I needed and how hard. I'd get right to the edge and she'd back off. When she told me I could come, I didn't ask questions. I blew."

Regan's climax ripped through her and weakened her extremities. Her muscles contracted, relaxed, and then trembled before she slid into complete euphoria. She inhaled deeply and allowed Syd's imaginary hands to once again run the length of her body and persuade her to rest. How long she had waited to feel this kind of liberation.

The tape droned on. "By the time I composed myself, she was gone."

Regan looked around her empty home, alone, postorgasmic, and craving more. The tape was silent and she reached to turn it off. Just before she hit the stop button, Detective Boudy spoke.

"Um…well, I guess I'm confused, Ms. Lorrey. What exactly is your complaint?"

"I'd think it was obvious."

It certainly was to Regan. Syd had loved and left, as usual, and this woman was angry.

"Isn't it against the law to use those, those weapons on a person without arresting them, or something?"

"Does this cop have a name?" Boudy asked blandly.

"She never told me, but I saw her in that club again a few weeks later so I asked. It was Sydney Cabot. She acted like nothing had happened, and she wouldn't see me again. That sounds criminal to me."

There was a sound on the tape that resembled a muffled laugh before the detective spoke again. "We'll look into your complaint, Ms. Lorrey, and give it the attention it deserves."

Now Regan understood why this particular grievance had ended up in the secret file. There was nothing to investigate. A horny woman looking for a fuck was routine in the police world and was hardly grounds for discipline, unless, of course, the cop failed to uphold the brotherhood's reputation for exceptional performance. And from what Regan had heard, Syd represented the team quite well.

A feeling crept over her, an odd mix of anger, nausea, and insecurity. She struggled to identify the emotion. Jealousy?

"Ridiculous," she mumbled. "I've never been jealous in my life."

But the image of Syd pleasuring another woman on the hood of a car summoned the alien feeling with full force. Regan's hands shook as she turned the recorder off and shuffled through the index cards one more time. If this was the ammunition Dean Bell planned to use to discredit Syd, it was her job to render the tactic ineffective. She grabbed the phone and stared down at the contact information on the first card. Steeling herself, she dialed.

CHAPTER TEN

Dean Bell's puffy red face looked as if it was ready to explode when he hurried into Regan's office on Monday morning. His costly Italian suit strained at the seams and buttonholes meant for a leaner specimen as he wedged himself into a chair across from her desk. "How long have you been practicing law, Ms. Desanto?"

Regan stifled an equally demeaning comment, pleased that her latest move had unsettled her opponent. She took a Diet Coke from her mini-fridge and asked, "Would you care for a Coke or a cup of coffee?"

"No, I would not care for a Coke or a cup of coffee." Bell studied Regan with the disdain he probably reserved for the very poor or the very ignorant. "What is the meaning of this motion for a bench trial? This just isn't done in wrongful-death cases. We *always* have a jury trial."

"Actually, one of the first things I learned in law school is that we don't *always* do anything. The law is very fluid, with lots of room to negotiate. As attorneys, we see to that, since we write the statutes in the first place."

Bell squirmed uncomfortably in his ill-fitting suit, and the red of his cheeks deepened. "I didn't come here for a damn lecture on the law, Ms. Desanto. I want to know what you hope to gain by this stall tactic. No judge will agree to hear this case without a jury. It's too potentially volatile, and he wouldn't want his ass on the line when it hits the media. Judges defer that pleasure to twelve less politically aspiring citizens."

Regan liked the fact that she'd caught Bell off guard. He was obviously unsettled and already playing the political card. This usually meant that opposing counsel was not as confident in his case. She chose to believe it also meant he considered her a worthy opponent. Good thing too, because she aimed to win this case, whatever it took.

"You might be surprised," she said. "I'm sure there's a judge with enough integrity to take on public opinion in the name of justice. But I was actually trying to save us both a bit of embarrassment and to settle this quickly and amicably."

"You just don't want a jury to see the seedy side of your officer and how she gunned down my client's teenaged son without provocation."

"Is this the same teenager with a criminal record dating back to age twelve and covering charges from shoplifting to assault and two counts of robbery? That teenager?" Regan hated to speak ill of the dead, but it was obvious that Bell intended to vilify Syd and downplay the youngster's criminal past. If a judge or jury was going to reach an informed verdict, they'd have to know all the facts.

Bell straightened in the chair and flashed his perfectly capped teeth at Regan. "You must be pretty desperate if you're already trying to malign the character of the victim."

"Isn't that exactly what you're trying to do to Sydney Cabot? Her personal life has no relevance to this incident, yet you're planning to parade it out in the open."

Bell stood and leaned over Regan's desk, his coffee breath heavily laced with last night's garlic. "That's where you're wrong. Her personal life is exactly the reason she overreacted and shot that young man. She's been on a downward spiral of sex and booze for months. Read her files. There's one complaint in particular that you might find stimulating."

Regan wanted to reach across her desk and strangle Dean Bell until his bulging eyes popped out of his fleshy face. Remembering Gina Lorrey's explicit complaint, she was nauseous to think Bell might have been titillated by it. Listening to Syd satisfy another woman was bad enough, but to imagine this pompous blowhole getting off on the recap was too much.

"Judge Marie Chamberlinck has agreed to hear both sides of the motion this morning. I assume that's why you're here." Regan rounded her desk, moving as far away from Bell as possible. "I suggest we not keep her honor waiting."

"It's a waste of time," Bell mumbled as he collected his briefcase and followed her.

They crossed the concrete-and-stone courtyard that separated the municipal building from the courthouse in silence. The door to Judge Chamberlinck's office was open and she motioned them in.

"Thank you for seeing us this morning, Your Honor." Regan had researched the judge as soon as she'd been awarded the hearing. She was a respected member of the bench, with a reputation for fairness and no nonsense.

"Mr. Bell, I assume you're here to oppose Ms. Desanto's motion for a bench trial in this matter." Judge Chamberlinck directed them to a conference table in the corner of her modestly decorated office. Her totally white hair and crystal blue eyes projected an image of keen intelligence.

"Yes, Your Honor. This case cries out for justice," Bell declared. "Not that an impartial judge couldn't render such justice, but I believe the facts deserve the due diligence of a jury."

Regan half listened as he prattled on with his benign excuses for a jury trial. She looked around the deep cherrywood walls of the judge's office. There were no grandly matted and framed diplomas as homage to her college or law school. The only photos were of two thoroughbred horses in varying stages of competition ridden by an exquisite-looking redhead.

"In other words, you think a jury would award more money in a wrongful-death suit," Judge Chamberlinck translated, nailing Bell's intentions perfectly.

It was all about the money for this guy, and Regan was gratified that the judge wasn't going to pretend otherwise.

Bell recovered nicely. "Not at all, Judge. I simply believe the facts of this case will take time and a lot of consideration. The officer involved has a complicated history that needs to be taken under advisement."

"I've read Ms. Desanto's motion regarding her client's so-called history. I've also seen the background of the victim. If we get into character assassination, I'd have to side with Officer Cabot. At least her indiscretions were consensual."

Regan liked Judge Chamberlinck more with each passing minute. She had a good feeling about this case and this judge and decided to press her luck. "Judge, I'd like to go ahead with a bench trial as soon as possible. I see no need to cause the family or the officer further anguish by prolonging these proceedings. My witnesses are on standby. I'm ready to move forward."

The judge smiled at Regan and turned her attention to Bell. "Is the plaintiff ready, sir?"

"Yes, Your Honor, but we still object to a bench trial."

"Are your witnesses available?"

"Yes, ma'am."

Judge Chamberlinck rose from the table. "Then the motion for a bench trial is granted. The issue for trial is whether or not this shooting was in fact wrongful by statute, not the questionable histories of the parties involved. I caution both of you to stick to the facts of the case. Do not wander off into personal quagmires that have no relevance. It's I who will hear your case tomorrow morning."

"Thank you, Judge." Regan glanced at Bell as she left the room. He was looking back and forth from her to the judge like a bobblehead. His mouth opened and closed but nothing came out. She smiled. "See you tomorrow, Counselor."

❖

On her way back to the office, Regan stopped by Terry's office to tell him the news and talk over her strategy. He seemed pleased and optimistic about the outcome, picking up the phone to update the city manager as she left.

She dropped the list of witnesses on her assistant's desk, asked her to notify them of the hearing, and gave special instructions for their arrival at the court building. Her next task was to call Syd with the news. As she stood by her desk and dialed the number her heart rate quickened. The granting of her motion was cause for optimism but not reason enough for such an excited physical response. Had she become so enamored with Syd that just the thought of talking with her raised her pulse? She momentarily searched for a profound answer, then settled for the obvious one: *Duh.*

When Syd answered, Regan realized she was in even more trouble than she imagined. Her mind stalled in pause mode while her body replayed their kiss once again. The texture of Syd's lips, the radiant heat, the weight of her breasts as she palmed them, and her craving to devour Syd overcame Regan and she collapsed into her chair.

"Hello. Is anybody there?" Syd's voice penetrated her daze.

Regan took a deep breath. "Syd, we need to talk. Our case is being called tomorrow. Come by my office as soon as you can."

She was not looking forward to telling Syd that she'd subpoenaed some of her past lovers as witnesses. It was a given that Syd would consider her action intrusive and a borderline betrayal. After all, Regan was supposed to represent her, not air all her dirty little secrets. Regan sighed at the thought of comparing herself to a parade of exes. She was certain she had nothing to offer a woman of Syd's diverse and expansive tastes.

"How's two o'clock?" Syd asked.

"Fine. See you then." Regan hung up realizing that she'd responded in one long frustrated breath.

Could she be in the same room with Syd and not think about kissing her? Her very presence sparked feelings and bodily responses Regan couldn't control. Her desire to make love to Syd verged on obsession. Regan wanted the surrender that only comes with trust and true intimacy. The thought brought her up short. She'd only kissed Syd once, and already she was fantasizing about making love with her. What was next, the moving van? It was probably best not to think about the kiss again and definitely best not to discuss it with Syd. Their parting that night had been awkward. The hearing was only a day away and they both needed to focus on it.

As Regan reviewed her notes for court, mindlessly picked at a salad for lunch, and waited for time to pass, she wondered what would happen between her and Syd when the case was over. They would probably never see each other again. The case was really the only thing keeping them in contact. Beyond that, they had nothing in common. Their lives were simply too different. Syd was a reckless cop who bedded women as a second career and had no plans to change. Regan considered herself a settled, no-frills person who simply wanted a satisfying job and eventually a compatible but definitely hot lover. An affair didn't have to last forever, not much did anymore.

The thing that had suffered most in her relationship with Martha was her libido. Martha's appetites had been sated elsewhere, leaving Regan to fend for herself. Maybe she could be happy with semi-permanence and consistently hot sex, such as Syd could provide. The thought dispatched a tingle of excitement down Regan's spine that ended between her legs with a flush of heat and a shudder of desire. She slid her hand toward the chronic ache that had become a constant companion the past week.

She had Sydney Cabot to thank and to curse for her renewed passion, damn her.

❖

Syd stumbled into the Cop Out soon after the phone call from Regan. Her eyes felt like they were filled with sawdust. Sleep had been impossible since seeing Lacy morph into Gil's wife, Priscilla. Syd maintained clear boundaries about sex partners, and cops' wives were always at the top of the do-not-touch list. She'd unknowingly betrayed Gil and then lied by withholding the truth. She knew she needed to clear her mind for her afternoon appointment and tomorrow's hearing, but she was filled with regret and shame. If Gil found out, their growing friendship would end.

"What's up with you?" Jesse slid a tall latte in front of Syd at the bar. "Anybody you want to talk about? I could use a little vicarious pleasure."

Syd took a sip of the coffee and prayed the heat and caffeine would magically awaken her from this nightmare of a situation. "No, but I found out about Lacy. Or should I say Priscilla? I guess that was what you were trying to tell me."

"I told you months ago that she was a cop's wife. I just didn't know which one till they came in together one day. Was he pissed when he found out?"

"I didn't tell him." Syd rolled the coffee mug in her hands and waited for Jesse's inevitable admonishment, which Syd was sure she deserved, and much more. She'd apparently been too traumatized by the shooting, too lust-crazed by Lacy, or too drunk most nights to hear Jesse's earlier warning. Either way, she'd landed neck-deep in an untenable position. She couldn't see how she could reach an uncomplicated, friendly resolution.

"You didn't tell him?" Jesse looked appalled.

"I know. I know. We staked her out Saturday night and saw her pawing some blonde on the street. He was pretty devastated. I couldn't tell him after that. He loves her so much."

Jesse stepped back from the bar and wiped her hands on the front of her apron. "Jesus, Syd. You helped him spy on his wife? And when he caught her playing grab-ass with another woman, you said nothing?"

Syd couldn't meet her disapproving stare. "Yeah, I was a total coward. I just couldn't dump one more thing on him. But I'm going to make it right."

"And how do you plan to do that? It's not exactly an easy fix. You didn't take his parking place, you know. You took his fucking place, and men don't forget that quickly."

"I haven't figured that part out yet, but I've got to do something."

"Get your shit together, will you, before you go up in a puff of smoke." Jesse shook her head and walked to the opposite end of the bar to take an order.

Syd knew Jesse only had her best interests at heart. When she needed an honest answer about anything or a swift kick in the pants, Jesse was always the right choice. When she needed nurturing and comfort, Jesse steered her toward other friends. This time she'd gotten exactly what she needed, a cold, hard look at her behavior and where it had landed her.

As she sipped her latte and wondered about her next move, the front door opened and her problem strolled in. Gil's wife scanned the room and chose a booth near the back door. When she passed Syd, she just smiled and kept walking. To anyone watching, the gesture would have seemed like innocent acknowledgement from a stranger, but Syd knew it was a signal.

She considered her options and decided it was time to confront her demons. What better place to start? She ordered two more lattes and, ignoring a warning look from Jesse, crossed the room to Priscilla's booth.

"Mind if I join you?" she asked.

"I'd love it." The low, sexy voice summoned memories of promises whispered and pleasures delivered.

Syd's skin tingled. She shook off the sensation and reminded herself why she was here. She had to correct this errant course she'd embarked on before she took others down with her. The truth was always a good choice. "Gil and I saw you with the blonde in front of the club Saturday night, Priscilla."

Priscilla's skin seemed to blanch a lighter shade of mocha. Her cocoa brown eyes glistened with moisture. "Oh, shit." She lifted a trembling hand to cover an exclamation that had already escaped. Her confident military posture slipped into the defeated and frightened carriage of a trapped animal. She searched Syd's face for the answer to an unasked question that seemed to claw its way up her throat and die before she had the courage to utter it out loud.

Syd gave the answer. "I didn't tell him about us."

Priscilla released a heavy sigh and slumped back against the bench.

"I couldn't. He was too upset." Syd waited for her words to sink in and for the other woman to regain her composure. "I had no idea you were married—to a cop—and a friend of mine. Why didn't you tell me?"

Syd considered her accusatory tone. What gave her the right to sound so self-righteous and scorned? All she'd wanted was sex and Priscilla had provided it, no questions asked. Hell, Syd didn't care enough to get her real name, to ask about her life, or follow up with an actual date. She'd been perfectly content to fuck her in the restroom and leave.

"I'm sorry, Priscilla. I have no right to accuse you of anything. I'd just like to understand and try to make this right, if we can."

Priscilla's cheeks were wet from tears she seemed unwilling or unable to control. Syd handed her a napkin, amazed at how easily she expressed her feelings. She wondered why she hadn't noticed this woman's sensitivity before.

"What do you want to know?" Priscilla asked shakily.

"Do you love Gil? Are you a lesbian? Do you want out of your marriage?" Syd stopped firing questions to allow her an opportunity to answer. "Sorry."

Jesse approached the booth cautiously and placed two lattes on the table between them. She looked from one to the other. "Are you two all right here?"

Syd patted her hand. "Yeah, we're fine. Thanks, Jess."

Priscilla waited until Jesse was out of hearing range before she answered. "I love my husband very much. I'm not a lesbian. And I don't want out of my marriage."

"Then what's going on? You're in here almost every night picking up women and having sex in the restroom. That's not the behavior of a happy woman. What are you running from?"

"I could ask you the same question, my serial paramour."

"It's not the same thing at all." As the words rolled off her tongue, the bad taste they left startled her. Priscilla's eyebrows arched toward her hairline in an equal expression of disbelief. "Well, it's not. I'm not married to a wonderful man who loves me."

"But you *are* running."

Priscilla's statement gnawed at her. She hadn't been herself since the shooting. And she'd been distracting herself with women to avoid dealing with the difference, but she didn't consider that "running." She'd simply needed to divert her thoughts for a while and enjoy something like the rush she'd come to expect from her job. But Syd had to admit that Priscilla could be right. Maybe she *was* running from the reality of her situation, from her feelings, from dealing with the uncertainty and dissatisfaction of her life. She swallowed a choking sensation in her throat.

"You're probably right." Syd hardly recognized her own voice as it squeaked from her. "I killed a man who was robbing a store. I guess I haven't been dealing with it. Sex was my avoidance mechanism and my adrenaline substitute for the job. It's easier to engage physically and tell yourself you're alive than to hurt emotionally and know it."

Priscilla reached across the tabletop and took Syd's hands in hers. "Oh, baby, I know exactly what you mean. In Iraq everything I did was planned and executed by someone else. After I got back home, I had to be in charge of my life. When I saw you in here the first time, I knew you were a kindred spirit. Something in you called to me. I knew I had what you needed and vice versa. And I was right. It worked for both of us, didn't it?"

Embarrassed as she was by her behavior, Syd couldn't pretend she'd been reluctant or blame alcohol for the decisions she'd made. "Yes, it did. But it can never happen again. We both need to get our lives back on track."

Priscilla nodded. "I know. For me, having sex with women here is about taking control and the adrenaline high of the conquest. For you, I guess it's about giving up control and denying that heavy responsibility you carry every day. We both have to learn to handle things without our crutch."

Syd thought about the primal way they'd connected. Their bodies appeared to know exactly what their souls needed and joined to provide that comfort. The sad part was neither of them thought beyond those intense moments. They'd made choices that could harm others they cared about.

"I love Gil. I really do," Priscilla said. "I guess I have sex with women because in some twisted way I believed it wouldn't hurt him as much if he found out."

Syd recalled the look on Gil's face that night when he saw Priscilla with the blonde. "It hurts just as badly. Betrayal is betrayal. The good thing is that he loves you. He just wants to know if you still love him."

"Are you planning to tell him about us?"

The possibility of causing Gil more pain was totally unacceptable to Syd. On the other hand, she had contributed to his marriage troubles and it was time to pay for her actions. "We've become friends and it feels dishonest not to tell him."

"Even if it would destroy our marriage and your friendship? He likes you, Syd. And I know he respects you as an officer and a person."

Guilt swept over Syd like a cold chill. Maybe this was why she ran from anything emotional. The decisions and their ramifications were always much more difficult and potentially devastating when feelings were involved.

"It might be better coming from you. He needs to know what you've been doing and why. Be honest and let him know that you still love him." Syd hoped her decision and advice were the right ones. "I'll leave it to you to decide what you want to say about us."

"Gil is a wonderful man and I know he loves me. He'll be able to distinguish between intent and misguided behavior. I have to believe that."

Priscilla finished her coffee and rose to leave. "Take care of yourself, Syd. And who knows, maybe someday the three of us can be friends without you feeling like you're trapped in the middle."

"Thanks. I hope so."

She watched Priscilla walk away, her gait the determined stride of a soldier on a mission. She seemed so confident, Syd wondered if she was being completely realistic expecting Gil to understand. Her faith in him was astounding. Syd wondered how it must feel to know you are so loved. She'd never imagined that anyone could love her unconditionally, in spite of her irresponsible behavior and need for excitement. She sought her thrills on the job and in the bedroom. She'd always assumed she would have to hide those needs from a partner, if she had one, and Syd didn't want to live a dishonest life. Now she'd inadvertently hurt someone she cared about by being selfish and reckless. Maybe she needed to reevaluate. Maybe it *was* time to manage her life without her crutches.

She'd been following her errant impulses like a man with a permanent hard-on. But change always proved challenging. It was so easy to fall back on tried-and-true methods of survival. A not-so-old saying came to mind: *If you do what you've always done, you'll get what you've always gotten.* Syd thought about continuing on her way, making the same choices and dodging bullets like she had with Gil and Priscilla. Did she want to spend her life moving from one high to the next, hoping she could avoid mistakes that would blow up in her face? What was the point?

The kiss she and Regan shared came to mind. It was hot in a way that shocked and surprised Syd. She'd guessed at the passion Regan tried to hide behind constant control and professionalism, but never imagined it could be so intense. Regan had taken charge of her body and orchestrated responses that were immediate and profound. Sex was sex, but something different about their brief interlude had excited and frightened her.

It was more than physical, much more. They'd connected on an emotional level that Syd hadn't experienced before. Regan had bared her soul, something that required tremendous trust. Syd seldom received such a precious gift and avoided giving it. Regan's willingness to be vulnerable and open, even after such a betrayal by her lover, had allowed Syd to connect with feelings that she had denied and suppressed for too long.

Perhaps it was possible to have a life that was both physically and emotionally satisfying. Perhaps it would be just as thrilling as her brief, casual encounters. Maybe she wouldn't need substitutes if she built something real. Just maybe.

CHAPTER ELEVEN

Syd stood outside Regan's office wondering how she would feel seeing her for the first time since their kiss. No woman had ever gotten her so excited, been equally turned on, and then walked away. That required a great deal of control. She didn't understand how to contain that level of desire. She'd never tried to do it before, never felt it necessary. Knowing that Regan had such physical fortitude made Syd want to dissolve that restraint into a puddle of quivering need.

But the urge to overcome this particular woman's resistance was not just about meeting a sexual challenge or evening the score after a blow to her ego. Her desire transcended physical attraction. It seemed almost emotionally magnanimous. If she helped free Regan from the repression of her physical desires, Regan would be grateful and much happier.

And then what? That's where Syd's rescue fantasy ended. She stared at Regan's office door, her hand poised to knock until she heard what sounded like swearing from inside.

"Go ahead and knock. She's expecting you," the assistant urged from her workstation a few feet away.

She did as she was told and Regan invited her in. "You wanted me to come by?"

Regan jumped from her desk chair as if it were spring-loaded and swiped awkwardly at the front of her trousers.

"I'm sorry. Did I interrupt something? Your assistant said I should knock."

"No, no. Just a phone call." A flush crept up Regan's neck and colored her cheeks. Blushing seemed so out of context for this self-assured, take-charge woman that Syd was intrigued. "I need to go over a few things with you before trial. Please, have a seat." Regan motioned to a couple of worn leather chairs beside the windows. As they sat, facing the city skyline, the afternoon sun bathed Regan's profile in streaks of light that shimmered with floating particles. Caught up in the halo effect, Syd forgot to say something meaningless to open the conversation and cover any awkwardness from their last encounter. More than anything, she wanted to hold Regan and bask in her warmth. She wished they could just stay right here until the sun surrendered the city to the possibilities of night.

After an extended silence Regan asked, "Is something wrong? You look a million miles away."

Surprised by her own lapse into sentimentality, Syd replied, "I was just wondering why I'm here. What do we need to discuss?" She prayed that it wasn't the kiss. Having that incredible moment reduced to a series of rationalizations and apologies would be dishonest and insulting. Perfection should remain simply that. Regan had walked away from her immediately after it; wasn't that comment enough?

"I don't want you to be surprised in court tomorrow morning." Regan paused, seeming to weigh her words carefully before stating, "I made a motion for a bench trial, which, as you know, means no jury. It will be better for us in the event that Dean Bell tries to bring up your personal life during the hearing. I don't think the judge will allow it, but he might be able to worm something in."

"Okay, that's good news, right?"

"Absolutely."

"Then why do you look so worried?"

"I'm usually better at hiding my feelings." Regan seemed to be talking to herself more than Syd. "I better bone up before trial." She stared out the window for a few seconds and the frown left her face. Once again she was the serene professional Syd had observed the day of their first interview. "When we go into the courthouse, you might come across some people you haven't been around in a while and wouldn't necessarily expect to see now."

A sense of dread told Syd she didn't need to ask her next question, but she wanted to hear Regan's response. "What people?"

"Women you've had sex with over the past year." Regan couldn't look her in the eye. Perhaps she had some idea how offensive this whole thing felt. "I realize it's a little unorthodox. After all, these women filed complaints against you. But when I explained your situation, some of them agreed to testify on your behalf. However, there are others who are not so eager to assist, as you can appreciate."

"But doesn't their very presence give credence to Bell's argument that I'm a wayward, woman-devouring lesbian? Why couldn't you just get depositions?"

"There wasn't time to depose everyone. And the judge made it clear that character assassination won't be allowed. We may not even need the girls, since we're stipulating to the facts of the case. I'm hoping our arguments will be enough to secure a decision."

Syd was skeptical. "I don't get it. I used them for sex and dumped them without another thought. Why would any of them agree to come to court?"

Regan cupped Syd's hand. "Every one of these women had sex with you because she wanted to. And some of them wanted to help. Do you know why?"

Syd shook her head. She didn't want to remember her callous behavior, and she certainly didn't want Regan to witness it. The thought of having her ex-lovers lined up like Herefords at a slaughterhouse made her ashamed. They shouldn't have to be dragged into her problem.

"They all agreed to be here even without a subpoena," Regan said, "because you were kind, attentive, and respectful. That speaks well of you."

Syd started to respond when Regan's office door burst open and Dean Bell swaggered in. Regan gave Syd's hand one final, reassuring squeeze and withdrew, but not without Bell noticing.

"Excuse me, ladies. I seem to be interrupting."

"Don't be ridiculous," Regan responded in a bored drawl. She stood and Syd followed suit. "Have you come to concede?"

"You wish. I thought I'd come meet your officer and try to talk some sense. You've still got time to settle."

"Not likely. Dean Bell, this is Officer Sydney Cabot. Syd, Mr. Bell is counsel for the plaintiff."

Syd shook the proffered hand and cringed at the clammy feel

of his skin against hers. The man's expensive brown suit made him look like a mole, in spite of his attempts at fashion with a beige shirt and multistriped tie. His bulging eyes swept her up and down and she wanted to hurl.

Regan must have sensed her discomfort because she placed a hand on her shoulder and steered her clear of Bell's grasp. "I won't detain you, Officer Cabot. Thank you for coming in." As she guided Syd toward the door, she said softly, "Get a good night's sleep. We're going to win this."

❖

"I'm a little surprised you chose to wear your uniform," Regan said as they made the short trip across the courtyard to the judicial building. It felt like the dead-man's walk to Syd.

"Why wouldn't I? I'm being sued for an act committed during the performance of my duty. Wearing anything else would be disrespectful to the uniform and, quite frankly, would seem as if I'm trying to distance myself from the job, which I'm not."

Syd heard a snort from the squatty man a few feet to one side. Regan had positioned herself between Syd and Dean Bell, but he kept modifying his pace and jockeying back and forth to stare unabashedly at her.

"Did you say something?" Syd challenged him.

Before he could reply, Regan said, "You look very competent."

Syd ignored another salacious glance from Dean Bell. Right now she had more important things to worry about than some pervert eye-groping her. Her stomach seized into a bundle of knots as they entered the courtroom. She'd been in every courtroom in this building, and the federal equivalent, hundreds of times in her career, but never as the defendant. This judge's bench seemed more imposing, the defendant's table more ominous, and the bailiffs she normally spoke to and joked with seemed more detached. It was as if some cruel master had reached into her life and jerked it inside out, making her the subject of a menacing legal system.

The room felt cold and unwelcoming with its institutional gray walls. Only a few people were scattered in the rows of wooden pews. Syd recognized members of the city attorney's staff, an assistant district attorney, a couple of Internal Affairs supervisors, and members of Lee Nartey's family. They stared at her like she was a leper.

The bailiff called the court to order as a kind-looking white-haired woman strode to the bench in the black regalia of her position. Syd recognized the judge and immediately felt more relaxed. Judge Chamberlinck had a reputation for fairness, integrity, and swift justice, and that's exactly what Syd wanted. The sooner she was out of this situation and could move on with her life, the better.

Judge Chamberlinck motioned for everyone to be seated, then looked at Regan and Bell with what Syd interpreted as a cautionary glare and began. "Counsel is reminded of my earlier warning regarding protocol in this proceeding. I assume you are both willing to stipulate to the events of the case and move directly to arguing aggravating and mitigating factors. Is that correct?"

Regan and Bell answered in the affirmative.

"Mr. Bell, you may begin."

Bell stood, pulled at his tie, and walked to the small podium in front of the judge. "Your Honor, on the night in question Mr. Lee Nartey, the deceased, was going home from the mall on foot, minding his own business, when he was accosted in a darkened corner of the parking lot. According to his dying declaration, all he saw was someone pointing a gun at him. By North Carolina law we are permitted to defend ourselves against the use of deadly force. Mr. Nartey tried to do so with a weapon that he had purchased for his personal protection. There was no evidence on Mr. Nartey at the time of his shooting to indicate that he had committed a crime, and no reason for the officer to confront him. His death was caused solely by the unwarranted actions of Officer Cabot. These facts are uncontested."

Syd wanted to yell her objection to the blatant distortion of events. Regan had been taking notes furiously while Bell spoke, but she must have sensed Syd's growing anxiety. Glancing at her, she mouthed, "It's okay." That simple reassurance, along with Regan's confident smile, settled Syd's jangled nerves.

"And as for the officer involved, and element two of the claim," Bell spouted, "the plaintiff contends that Officer Cabot was negligent and should be held strictly liable for the death of Lee Nartey. On this evening, she had just returned to work from a three-day weekend of—"

Regan jumped up so quickly that she startled Syd. But before she could speak Judge Chamberlinck waved her off. "Mr. Bell, I hope you're not headed where I think you're headed with this. I've made myself clear about straying into this questionable area."

"Yes, Judge, but I will be addressing the issue of impairment and culpability, not the matter we discussed earlier."

She gave him a stern look and said, "See that you stay on point."

"As I was saying, Your Honor, Officer Cabot had been off for three days and we have witnesses who've given sworn statements that she was drinking for a large part of that time in a club called the Cop Out. She was even seen there just before going on duty the night in question."

Syd rolled closer to Regan and gripped her arm. "Are you going to let him get away with this crap? Do something. He's making it look like I'm an alcoholic incapable of doing my job."

Regan covered the tightened grip on her arm and stared into Syd's eyes. "You have to trust me," she whispered. "I know it's hard to hear your life trashed like this, but we'll get our turn soon. Neither I nor Judge Chamberlinck will let this get out of hand." Her eyes remained on their joined hands for a few seconds before meeting Syd's. "Trust me?"

Something in her expression made Syd feel less apprehensive. "I think I can do that."

Bell continued his diatribe. "It is our contention that Officer Cabot was impaired the night of this incident and therefore negligent in the death of Lee Nartey. The surviving members of Mr. Nartey's family have been denied the pleasure of this young man's presence in their lives, not to mention the potential income from what could have been a very lucrative career in the retail business. He was only eighteen years old so his earnings could have been substantial. Then there is the matter of medical and funeral compensation for this grieving family, combined with the mental anguish of seeing his young life so brutally and unnecessarily ended. We are also asking for punitive damages against Officer Cabot, as this death was intentionally and maliciously aggravated by alcohol while on duty."

Bell retrieved a handkerchief from his back pocket and swiped at perspiration that had collected on his forehead. He shoved his summation back into the folder and returned to his seat.

Judge Chamberlinck simply looked at him. After several seconds of silence she asked, "And what, pray tell, Mr. Bell, do you see as reasonable compensation?"

Dean Bell sprang to his feet again like an unsteady jack-in-the-box. His chubby cheeks flushed with embarrassment as he realized that he'd failed to cap off his brilliant summary with a monetary price tag, a major legal faux pas. "The plaintiff respectfully requests monetary compensation in the amount of four million dollars, Your Honor."

Syd could've sworn the judge rolled her eyes before diverting her gaze to some papers on the bench in front of her. Without raising her head, she said, "Ms. Desanto."

Regan moved to the podium with the air of confidence Syd had glimpsed before. She was so elegant and self-assured that for a moment Syd forgot where they were and wanted simply to be alone in her arms, kissing her again. She scolded herself for the thought. Her professional future rested in this woman's hands. Now was not the time to fantasize about those same capable hands cradling her body.

"Your Honor," Regan began, "I'll be brief. On the evening in question, Officer Cabot received a robbery call at Bradford Jewelers in Oak Hollow Mall. Witnesses working at the store identified Lee Nartey as the robber because he had worked there one day. He exited the mall after the robbery, dumping the items he'd taken into a trash receptacle on the way out because he was being pursued by mall security. These items were later recovered with his fingerprints on them. The gun he drew on Officer Cabot was purchased from an undercover officer working a sting operation for illegal weapons. Warrants were pending at the conclusion of the operation. Officer Cabot identified herself as a police officer and ordered Mr. Nartey to drop his weapon. He refused. It wasn't until he raised the gun toward her, and Officer Cabot feared for her life, that she fired on him.

"Training records from the High Point Police Department document Cabot's excellent firearms qualifications. Their standards exceed mandated state requirements and Cabot has never had any difficulty meeting those standards. Her use-of-force file is exemplary for a twelve-year officer. This is the only instance during her career. She prefers peaceful resolution to conflict. She followed the use-of-force continuum that night as events escalated."

Syd sat a little straighter in her seat. Not only did the facts ring true this time, but the conviction with which Regan relayed them made Syd feel vindicated. She hadn't really believed in her own innocence in a long time. Too much avoidance, denial, women, and booze had clouded her thinking and prevented her from reconsidering her actions with detachment. Hearing Regan so vehemently argue on her behalf made her heart swell with pride and relief.

"As to any impairment on Officer Cabot's part, there was no indication that any existed. The fact that she had had a three-day weekend and whether or not she consumed some alcohol during that time is irrelevant. On the day of this incident, Officer Cabot stopped by the Cop Out on her way to work, as she did almost every day. It is her habit to drop by for a cup of coffee with the owner before reporting to duty. I have sworn testimony to this fact."

Syd stared openly at Regan, amazed that she had conducted such a thorough investigation into her background and habits. It concerned her that Regan knew so much about her without Syd having provided that information. How much more did she know that could prove detrimental later in their relationship.

What relationship? Right now the only thing that should concern her was that Regan had done her homework and it seemed to be helping her case.

"Now the issue of compensation, Your Honor. I have the utmost sympathy for the loss of any human life. My condolences go out to the Nartey family. However, I must contest monetary compensation when there is no earnings history on which to base a projection of future income. A financial review indicates that this family spent money on Mr. Nartey that might have better served the household and the minor children. The City of High Point does not object to covering the medical and funeral costs of the family, with the stipulation that neither the city nor Officer Cabot assume any liability." Regan gathered her notes. "Thank you for your attention, Your Honor."

Judge Chamberlinck thanked both sides and said, "I'll need a while to review my notes, the reports, and your statements. You'll be notified of my decision before close of business today."

The bailiff adjourned court and everyone except the Nartey family moved toward the exits. Syd waited while Regan filled her briefcase and shook hands with Bell. As they headed down the aisle, Lee Nartey's mother stepped in front of her. "Mrs. Nartey, I'm so sorry about your son. Please—"

"You killed my boy for no reason. Why, I'd like to—" The woman drew back her hand and was bringing it forward to slap Syd's face when Regan grabbed her wrist.

"No. This is not the way to deal with your grief."

Syd had seen the blow coming and hadn't tried to avoid it, perhaps out of disbelief. Or perhaps she thought she deserved it in some way. She was surprised that Regan had defended her at all. It was her job to represent her in court, not to protect her person or her honor.

"Why did you do that?" Syd had to ask as Regan steered her out another exit.

No one other than her fellow officers had ever taken up for her. Other women usually assumed she was the strong one because she was a cop, and she'd played along. It was easier to live up to a stereotype than to expose her vulnerability by asking for what she really wanted. Having Regan defend her was a huge turn-on, emotionally and physically.

Regan smiled at her as if reading her mind. "I'm not about to stand by and let anyone hit you, especially when you don't appear inclined to defend yourself." She edged closer to Syd as they walked back to her office. "It's not your fault that young man died. He made a series of bad decisions that left you no other choice. And when the judge gives her ruling, you'll be completely vindicated."

When they arrived at Regan's office, Syd closed the door behind them. "Thank you so much for everything you've done. I know I haven't made it easy for you."

"You're welcome. It's my job."

"Having said that, I hate to ask, but I need one more favor."

Regan eyed her. "Name it."

Syd bowed her head and studied a staple stuck in the carpet. "I'd like to see the women you brought in as witnesses before they leave. Could I speak with them in the conference room for a few minutes?"

Regan looked as if she wanted to object, her blue eyes turning from sparkling azure to deep sapphire. "Of course. I'll make it happen. Give me ten minutes." She started toward the door, hesitated like she thought Syd might reconsider, then she was gone.

Confronting the women she'd used was not something Syd relished, particularly on the day of her trial and especially not en masse, but they had come forward to help her, according to Regan. That deserved at least a personal thank-you.

A light tap on Regan's office door was followed by her assistant peeking around the corner. "Ms. Desanto said they're ready in the conference room."

"Thanks." As Syd walked down the hallway, for the second time today she felt like she was marching toward a firing squad. She'd barely had the courage to face these women one-on-one after bedding them. Now she was going to face them all at once. Pausing outside the conference-room door, she wondered if she'd lost her mind.

❖

Regan tried not to make eye contact with any of the women seated around the conference table. She'd formed a mental image of what each would look like from her phone conversations with them: gorgeous, sexy, and oozing with desire. Having her images confirmed in the flesh and finding herself lacking in all three areas was not her idea of a fun way to pass the time. Instead she looked at Syd.

She was still wearing her dress uniform, and Regan could barely contain herself. The trousers and shirt still fit Syd well, but she had obviously lost weight. There was just enough slack in her outfit that a carefully placed hand could easily fit inside the pants or shirt front. That thought sent a trickle of excitement scurrying down Regan's tense body. But what was even more compelling about Syd's appearance was a subtle softening between person and profession.

Regan's earlier recollections of Syd featured a harsh contrast between the woman and the job, an almost tangible struggle for balance. Now Syd's personal presence seemed to overshadow the rigid formality of her uniform. Regan could look beyond the outer veneer to a poignantly vulnerable creature. More than anything, she longed to reassure Syd that her world could be safe again. Winning this case would go far toward proving that point, and Syd would be able to return to her normal life. Soon they would know the judge's decision.

The moment Syd closed the door behind her a young shapely redhead rushed over and wrapped her arms around her. Several other women flinched as if suppressing an urge to gather around her and offer comfort as well. Regan clenched her fists at her sides, realizing that she'd stifled exactly the same impulse.

"Oh, my God, Syd, I had no idea you were in so much trouble. You should've called. I would've been there instantly." The redhead clung to Syd as the other women looked on.

Syd's face blanched. "Tina." She removed the woman's arms from her waist and stepped back. "Please have a seat."

The redhead's gushing smile turned into a pouty frown. Syd moved to the head of the table, and Regan watched a cascade of emotions wash over her face as she regarded each of her discarded lovers with a sort of reverence.

"I—" Her voice cracked. She cleared her throat and started over. "I really don't know what to say. 'I'm sorry' seems most appropriate, based on my past behavior. And 'thank you' seems so overused and inadequate for what you've done for me today. I'm not sure I deserve your help, but I am truly grateful each of you was willing to offer it." Tears glistened in the corners of her eyes. She started to leave but turned back to the group. "Thank you, really. You're all very special women."

With that the entire table cleared as the women swarmed Syd and enveloped her in a sea of hugs and reassurances. Regan marveled at the outpouring of emotion. Most of these women were mere acquaintances, but they still apparently felt a strong enough connection to support her. A deepened sense of respect swelled inside Regan as she recognized the courage it must have taken for Syd to face this gathering, especially under these circumstances. None of the women had been called upon, and it would have been easy for Syd to simply leave without further acknowledgment or comment. This was a side of her Regan had never seen, the side that faced difficulty head-on and took responsibility for herself and her actions. Regan made her way around the room toward the door and slipped out quietly, leaving Syd to experience the moment in private.

CHAPTER TWELVE

Syd almost dropped the stainless martini shaker she was twirling around her head when the insistent rapping started on her loft door. She'd chosen a quiet night at home over the noisy crowd at the Cop Out, but that didn't mean she'd abandoned civilization altogether. A cold dirty goose would help calm the frayed nerves caused by waiting for a verdict and seeing a roomful of her past flings. The stress would've sparked an all-night binge a few weeks ago, but she'd been content to come home and wait for the decision that could easily change the course of her life.

Placing the shaker on the counter, she glanced down in irritation at her crotch-length cut-off blue jeans and tank top with no bra. She'd intended to change while she waited for the phone call from Regan, then offer to meet her, either to celebrate or commiserate. Whoever was rude enough to try to tear her door off the hinges would have to accept being greeted by an underdressed woman. Syd wasn't expecting anyone. An image of the redhead flashed into her mind. She'd been reluctant to say good-bye when everyone left. Had she followed Syd home?

Frowning, Syd stalked over to the door and swung it open. "I said I didn't want company. I—"

She stopped mid-sentence. Regan stood rigid and startled, her hand poised. She was still dressed in her business slacks and blouse from court. The look on her face was fixed and unrevealing. Syd's heart sank.

"I guess you better come in. I don't want the whole complex to witness my meltdown when I hear your news." She stepped aside to allow Regan entry. "I assume you *do* have news."

When the door closed behind her, Regan grabbed Syd's hands like an eager child with a juicy secret to share. Emotion flooded her face. "Oh, yes, I have news. Maybe you should sit down. No, don't. Stand. Better yet, let's dance." Regan swung them around in small circles throughout the room until they collapsed on the sofa, Syd landing on top of her. Panting for breath, she finally screamed, "It's over. We won!"

Syd's heart stalled then galloped with another surge of adrenaline. She cupped Regan's face between her hands and kissed her on the mouth, fully and completely, allowing herself to feel the ecstasy of the moment and to relay it. She couldn't imagine that any kiss had ever been sweeter. When the euphoria over the news changed to aching physical arousal, Syd realized that the lips touching hers had suddenly stilled.

She opened her eyes and gazed into the deep swirling blue of Regan's stare. Regan made no attempt to free herself from her pinned position on the sofa. It was almost as if she'd tacitly submitted to Syd's will and was waiting for more. The situation was a reversal for Syd. While she usually controlled her seductions, she'd never actively taken charge. And Regan seemed a most unlikely candidate for topping. But their entire encounter so far was strange and unfamiliar. Syd wasn't used to feeling…joyful with a woman. There was something incredibly compelling about the feel of Regan beneath her and the sense that they were also on the same emotional plane.

"I should probably thank you," she whispered into Regan's ear, and lightly nibbled her lobe. She wedged her bare thigh between Regan's legs and felt her tremble.

"Don't you think we should stop and…" Regan made a feeble attempt to get up.

"No, I don't think we should start analyzing. You do way too much of that as it is. Just let me show my gratitude."

"You're doing an outstanding job so far." Regan relaxed onto the sofa. "Feel free to keep thanking me."

Syd ground her pelvis into Regan's and was rewarded with a throaty moan. "What did the judge say, Counselor? Spill it."

A stream of sexual current charged through her as Regan's groan of appreciation reverberated down her spine. This woman had fought for her professionally and now she was surrendering herself personally. Syd felt woefully unworthy but totally rewarded. She wanted desperately to give something back. This time it wasn't about her pleasure. It was about this gorgeous, intelligent, trusting woman beneath her.

Regan's breathing increased as Syd's rocking intensified between her legs. "All findings were in our favor. No negligence. No punitive damages. Payment of funeral costs."

"That's great." Syd hesitated. How could she possibly show her appreciation in a way that expressed what she was really feeling? Already her body was humming with arousal, close to the point of no return. But she didn't want Regan to misread her motives as purely sexual. Shifting to lessen the contact between their bodies, she said, "I should probably get up."

"Please don't. I need this and so do you." Regan pulled her back down and stopped further protest with a deep, penetrating kiss.

The pressure building inside Syd caught her by surprise. It was upon her so swiftly that she had no defense against it. She was unsure if it was the welcome news or Regan that sparked the spontaneous orgasm, but she was in the throes of release before she could warn her partner. She simply buried her head between Regan's breasts and sobbed as the climax rippled through her. She felt Regan shudder beneath her and wondered momentarily if she'd come as well, but dismissed the idea as too surreal.

After several minutes of silent crying, Syd regained her composure enough to say, "I'm sorry. I have no idea what that was about." She was thoroughly embarrassed by her lack of emotional and sexual control. This had never happened to her before, and she felt helpless and inept.

"Don't apologize. You've been emotionally shut down for months. Release was inevitable sooner or later." Regan put her finger under Syd's chin and raised her face so she could look into her eyes. "I'm just glad it happened with me. I'm bound by attorney-client privilege."

Syd appreciated Regan's attempt at humor, but she still felt she'd let her down. "So, what happens now?"

Regan's body telegraphed suppressed passion: her eyes lusty, her breath coming in short, labored bursts, and her skin flushed with desire. "Life returns to normal for both of us, I guess. You go back to patrol work, tomorrow if you want, and I return to the mundane cases of a municipal bureaucracy. Ho-hum."

"That's not exactly what I meant. What about *this*?" Syd sucked Regan's bottom lip and nuzzled a breast to emphasize her point.

Regan arched her back to meet the stimulation. "I see. We definitely have a situation. I find avoidance is not the best policy in cases like this."

Syd started unbuttoning Regan's blouse, teasing a trail between her breasts with her tongue. "I couldn't agree more. It's better to get it out of our system and move on." When Regan tentatively nodded in agreement, Syd said, "Come with me."

She pulled Regan from the sofa and led her toward the king-sized bed surrounded by uncovered windows overlooking the city. The uncustomary sensation of being in charge of a sexual interaction filled Syd with apprehension but also piqued her desire. Regan would allow her to do anything she wanted. And what a leap of faith that was, because Regan Desanto did not relinquish control easily.

Syd sat on the foot of the bed and motioned for Regan to come to her. When she reached for another of the covered buttons on Regan's blouse, her fingers trembled in anticipation. It seemed to take an eternity to release one of the fasteners and expose a small expanse of blushing pink flesh. She moved to the next button and had begun working it free when Regan grabbed her blouse on both sides, ripped the fasteners apart, and tossed it on the floor. Without further preamble, she removed her bra and slacks and, wearing only a thin black thong, stepped between Syd's legs.

The change from reluctance to commitment excited Syd even more. It was as if Regan had evaluated her situation in that instant between clothed and exposed and decided what she wanted. All hesitation vanished from her face as she offered her body for Syd's pleasure. But her eyes told another story. The crystal blue irises deepened into a stormy navy and seemed to beg for gentleness and patience.

"I'll take very good care of you." Syd kissed her softly and let her eyes relay the promise her words implied.

When Syd started to remove her own clothes, Regan stopped her. "Don't. I'd like you to take me with your clothes on. I want you to come in your jeans again."

The pounding flesh between Syd's legs responded to Regan's words as if she'd been licked. "Whatever you want."

She guided Regan backward onto the edge of the bed. Soft light from the streets below cast grayish shadows over the dips of Regan's toned body and highlighted the swell of her breasts. Syd knelt between her legs on the floor, caressing and teasing her way upward with her fingers, teeth, and tongue. The scent of Regan's arousal was heady and invigorating as she neared the join of her thighs. Her urge to satisfy her taste buds was powerful, but she knew it was too soon for Regan. Besides, she wasn't sure she could control her own body if she allowed herself just one sample. After all, she'd come earlier with much less stimulation. She couldn't risk that embarrassment again.

Reaching up to massage Regan's breasts, she reveled in the powerful transformation of the soft nursing tissue into a firm puckered mound of desire in her hands. She rose to her knees, leaned over Regan, and sucked a breast into her hungry mouth. Regan's body jerked in response and a slow moan escaped her tightly pressed lips. Syd humped against the side of the bed, trying to get closer. The seam of her jeans cut into her swollen lips. Without panties, the pleasure was too immediate and the pain too intense. She recoiled, clutched the crotch of her shorts, and jerked it away from her body. The early warning shards of orgasm threatened to overtake her again. She struggled to regulate her breathing and think of anything except the beautiful woman panting for release on her bed.

Syd was definitely in unfamiliar territory, her body shooting off with the slightest provocation. It was as if the wires connecting her emotional and sexual centers had been fused together and as one sparked, the other fired. Syd decided to enjoy the intensity of the sensation. It probably resulted from an overloaded stress level and this was her outlet. Tomorrow everything would return to normal; sex minus feelings equals fun.

"Are you okay?" Regan started to get up but Syd waved her off.

"I'm fine. I just need a minute." She'd never been so turned on before. Her former sexual partners always had to work hard to satisfy her, but without touching her, Regan had already solicited one spontaneous orgasm and Syd was on her way to a second. Had the element of control, the woman herself, or something else entirely heightened the experience? Right now Syd couldn't be sure of anything except that she wanted to please Regan.

She climbed beside her on the bed, needing the comfort and security of full contact. Regan's body called to hers with the power of the elements, and Syd brought their bodies together lengthwise, something she seldom desired or allowed with casual lovers. She kissed Regan's mouth, her face, and down the side of her neck, inhaling the flowery softness of her perfume and drinking it in like a drug.

Her eyes burned and she was surprised to taste the salty wetness of her own tears. When Regan seemed to notice her blinking, she said, "I'm sorry. I don't know what's wrong with me tonight. I guess I'm just so relieved and grateful."

Regan finger combed Syd's hair away from her face and kissed her forehead. "Nothing is wrong with you tonight. You're absolutely perfect."

The words sent a ripple of relief, appreciation, and passion through Syd. Regan knew how many women Syd had slept with, and still she reacted like they were each other's first lover. Syd kissed her again, licking and sucking her lips and tongue and pouring her entire being into this amazing woman. As their kiss deepened so did Syd's need. She nibbled her way down Regan's body, memorizing every curve and nuance until she reached the single patch of fabric separating them. Cupping her hand over Regan's sex, she squeezed the sheer thong material and found it soaked with the evidence of Regan's arousal. Teasing the garment aside, Syd gently stroked her engorged clit and was rewarded with a low humming moan that increased in direct proportion to her touches.

She tried to remember the last time she'd actually made love to anyone, not just traded orgasms. It had been too long. She'd almost forgotten what a powerful aphrodisiac it was to orchestrate the satisfaction of another woman, to pluck the strings of her physical body and make it sing like a finely tuned instrument. Somehow she'd known that Regan's body would be this responsive.

"Please, Syd. I need you."

The pleading request swirled through Syd like fever. She repositioned herself between Regan's legs, inhaling her scent and grinding her own pelvis into the mattress. The tiny patch of blondish hair glistened with moisture in the muted light. Syd licked Regan's protruding clit and teased her way down. Regan's legs tensed on either side of her.

"I want you inside me, now." The statement was almost inaudible but its intensity was palpable.

Syd lowered her mouth to Regan and simultaneously entered her with a possessive thrust a bit more forceful than she intended. Fearing she might've hurt her, she immediately started to withdraw.

"No, don't stop," Regan begged. "More."

As Regan's body responded to her pistoning fingers, Syd's lust swelled. The rough seam of her jeans rubbed painfully against her clit. Another explosion pending, she clamped her legs together against the sensation and concentrated all her energies on Regan.

It was as if Regan sensed her frustration and wanted no part of a one-sided exchange. "Don't hold back. Come with me. I know you want to."

Her words dissolved Syd's resistance. She allowed the tingling, stabbing excitement to consume her body and overpower her. Savoring and commanding Regan like a devouring beast, she humped the crumpled bed covers beneath her and let the climax possess her. As she tensed with the force of pending release, Regan's body quivered and convulsed beneath her. They clung to each other and Syd wondered about the joy she experienced each time Regan's muscles twitched against hers. Regan's pleasure had become her own, and she could hardly wait to have her again.

Syd lost track of time as they made love over and over through the night. When the first slivers of dawn crept through the cityscape into her windows, she watched the light play across Regan's features as she slept. Her soft curls of fine blond hair were tousled and moved slightly with each breath. Syd had never seen her so relaxed or so beautiful, her skin still flushed from their loving. The urge to take her in her sleep became almost overpowering, and Syd's body moistened in anticipation. She tucked her hand between her legs and considered a quick hand job but knew it would be totally unsatisfactory after last night's activities. Instead she gently kissed Regan's forehead and slid out of bed.

She scribbled several drafts of a note, left one on her pillow, grabbed a clean uniform, and headed to the station to shower and get back to work. Softly closing the door behind her, she realized this was the first time she'd spent the entire night with a lover. She was always gone long before first light. It was also the first time a woman had spent the night in her loft. She conducted all sexual encounters at someone else's home, in a vehicle, or some other neutral territory. Never, and there had been no exceptions until now, *never* at her place.

The thought dispatched a warm feeling through her system that soon changed to a knotted fist of anxiety. What had she done?

❖

Regan awakened slowly, her body alive with the cellular memory of recent sex. Her lips were swollen and her muscles ached from the containment and release of pleasure during orgasm. Her breasts were tender and the nipples puckered anew at the thought of Syd's mouth on them. Eyes closed and senses keenly alert, she replayed the evening's events and let the sensations wash over her. She wasn't ready to face the morning or Syd until she was certain she hadn't dreamed or imagined it all.

When she'd arrived at Syd's door, she'd intended to deliver the news about the verdict and leave. But when she saw Syd standing in front of her, barely clad in those jean shorts and tank top, her intentions had taken a sharp detour south. It was as if she no longer controlled her own mind or body. There was just something so sexually compelling about her that Regan felt defenseless. She wanted to blurt the news, celebrate their victory, and seduce Syd before she had time to object. And when Syd fell on top of her on the sofa, surrender seemed appropriate. They'd more or less agreed that they should spend the night working through their mutual attraction and then move on. It had been exquisite.

Regan knew without a doubt that she had been loved, not just sexually satisfied. Often with Martha she'd felt like a vessel into which her lover poured an occasional drop of affection to keep her appeased. For most of their relationship she hadn't felt intimately connected, and when she'd tried to assert her sexual needs, Martha only tightened her stranglehold on their rigid routines.

Was it any wonder that she'd been amazed when Syd experienced a spontaneous orgasm in her arms only moments after they'd physically connected? Such freedom of expression had been nonexistent in her life previously. And Syd's tears, regardless of their true cause, had shown Regan another side of this sensitive woman. Beneath the layered façade of cop attitude rested the heart of a passionate and caring person. Regan felt fortunate to have glimpsed her. That vulnerability had allowed her to surrender physically without reservation.

But Syd had surprised her in other ways as well. From what she'd seen and heard, Syd usually assumed the more submissive role during sex. Last night had been different. Without hesitation, Syd had become the initiator, almost as if it was something she *needed* to do. And Regan was more than willing to yield. There were none of the mental gymnastics that had inevitably accompanied a session with Martha. She'd been free to simply allow her body to feel, releasing all trepidation when Syd promised to take care of her. And Syd had kept her word, making love with a tenderness and passion that invited Regan to accept and let go, without thinking the whole encounter to death.

She brought her hand to her face and sniffed the musky fragrance of Syd that lingered there. She licked the remnants of her essence from the tips of her fingers and moaned in appreciation. Her body was suddenly fully awake and hungry. She rolled onto her side and stared at the pillow where Syd's head should've been.

"What the…" She lifted a piece of paper and squinted against the bright morning light as she read the message.

> *Last night was great. Very special. I'm glad we decided*
> *to get it out of our systems. Lock the door when you leave.*
> *Good luck.*
> *Syd*

Regan bolted upright in bed and looked around the loft. She called to Syd, unable to believe she'd left without even a good-bye. Disappointment flooded her. Of course Syd was gone. This was just a one-night thing. They'd agreed on it up front. Her anger made no sense. She knew who Syd was. She'd known that the moment this case was over their lives would return to normal. For Syd that meant no complications, and for Regan it meant victory and vindication. She'd faced her demons and stared them down. What more did she want?

As she searched the loft for her clothing scattered from the bed to the living room, she renewed the detachment that had served her so well through the years. Sydney Cabot had effectively neutralized her defense mechanisms in only one night, and for a few moments, before she finally fell into an exhausted sleep, Regan had allowed herself to imagine she could have more. But the only *more* she faced today was more vulnerability. She was about to walk back to her car holding a buttonless blouse together across her tender breasts. If she allowed anyone to see the freshly fucked look on her face, she would be humiliated.

Like the women in that conference room, she'd succumbed to the seductive powers of a proven gigolo. And, like them, she would be left with only the memory of an encounter that would be hard to match. Regan tore up the note and left the pieces scattered across the pillows. As she slammed the loft door behind her, she thought, *For an accomplished attorney you're not very smart.*

CHAPTER THIRTEEN

Syd shucked off her sweaty uniform and tossed it into the clothes hamper, thankful that her first day back on the job had kept her too busy to think. As she found fresh clothing, her eyes drifted to the still-ruffled bed. She'd avoided looking at it since entering her bedroom. She didn't want to start thinking about Regan again and wishing for the impossible. Her heart sped up when she saw shreds of paper clinging to the pillows. The note. She'd agonized over writing it, wanting to leave some kind of acknowledgment but fearful that Regan would feel pressured if she said anything sentimental. Her first several attempts were scrunched up in the trash.

Frowning, she pulled on a pair of baggy gym shorts and a T-shirt, opened the balcony doors, and let the cool evening breeze claim her overheated body. But she was horribly aware the torrid conditions that had plagued her all day had nothing to do with the weather. The entire surface of her skin chafed from the memory of Regan's touch, and a simple breeze would not ease her discomfort.

She headed into the kitchen for a much-needed martini and the return to sanity she hoped it would bring. As she walked through the loft she refused to look again at her bed or the sofa where she had fallen on top of Regan, knowing instinctively that they still bore the imprint of her body. That was the problem with having sex in your own place—reminders. It was easier to leave it all behind in someone else's home and pretend it never happened.

She took a sip of her drink and wished she could turn back the clock to last night. So much had happened and she understood so little of it now. Almost as if her wish had been granted, a knock sounded at the door. She rushed to answer it, her heart rate quickening in anticipation. Taking a deep breath, she swung the door open wide and motioned her visitor inside with a bold sweep of her arm. "Please, come in."

Jesse walked in with a knowing grin. "You were obviously expecting somebody else."

Syd did a double take and tried to hide her disappointment. "Not really. Just wishful thinking."

"You didn't come to the club after you got the ruling. I had to hear about it from your pals. So here I am. What gives? And don't try to bullshit me. I don't have the time, and I'm not in the mood to have smoke blown up my ass unless I'm getting sex afterward." Jesse walked around the loft, sniffing the air as she went. "Speaking of sex, you've had some in this very room, recently. That's unusual for you."

Syd couldn't suppress her smile. "Did you come here to talk to me or to talk at me? I haven't been able to get a word in edgewise since you walked in."

"Okay, give me a beer. Sounds like I'm going to need several." Jesse scrubbed her knuckles across the top of her head in a telltale sign of confusion and settled onto one end of the sofa. "I'm surprised," she said. "Why aren't you more excited? You'd normally be celebrating at the club with an entourage of women."

"I celebrated last night, sort of, with my attorney." As Syd made the statement, she wondered if she truly considered their night together just a celebratory fuck. Her next thought was even more troubling. What if that was all it had been for Regan? She handed Jesse a cold beer. Of course that's all it was. *What the hell's wrong with you, Cabot?*

"That tall, blond-haired butch type that dragged you out of the club last week? That attorney?"

"Yeah."

"Well, cowabunga. I knew I liked her."

Syd could feel Jesse's eyes following her every movement. She never tried to push. A well placed uh-huh or a knowing nod was all the encouragement needed. In the end, Syd told her everything anyway, so prying was unnecessary and a waste of energy.

"We made—had sex, here, in my bed." Syd paused, unsure what she could say to describe her time with Regan. Normally, that she'd hooked up with another woman was enough. The usual descriptors of quality, frequency, and varying positions followed later in the context of a running comparison to all the other women she'd bedded. But the experience with Regan had been different. It was unlike anything else. More intense, more open, just…more.

"And?"

Jesse's single-word question puzzled Syd. She was usually eager for the juicy details and bombarded her with inquisitive eyebrow raises, lavish lip-licking, and suggestive waggling of her teacup-sized breasts. But it was as if Jesse sensed a difference and knew subtlety was the best approach.

"And nothing. We had sex. I went to work. That's it."

"But you had sex *here*."

Syd chose not to respond to the implication that having sex in her home carried any particular significance.

"And you went to work? Did you at least give her a good-bye kiss?"

"I left a note." Suddenly what had seemed perfectly reasonable and appropriate this morning sounded cheap, cowardly, and cold. "It was my first day back on the job. I was in a hurry." *Not to mention that I didn't know how to face her.* "I wanted to let her sleep and—"

Jesse held up her hand. "You can stop. I don't need to hear anymore. You felt something for this woman and you didn't know how to handle it."

"Don't be—" The word "ridiculous" hung in her throat. Her gut demanded more. "Maybe. I'm not sure what I mean."

"Did she play your little come-and-get-me game?"

"Actually I was all over her. I don't understand what happened to me. One minute she was telling me we'd won the case and the next I was on top of her like an animal in season."

Jesse patted the sofa beside her and waited for Syd to join her. "And she let you? I mean, she was okay with everything?"

"That's just it, Jess. She didn't strike me as the submissive type and it didn't really feel like submission. It felt like she wanted to please me. At the same time, I had this definite feeling that she would be just as happy to take charge, if I'd let her. Does that make sense?"

"Perfect sense. She doesn't sound like your everyday lay. The woman's got class. So, how do you feel about her?"

There it was, the big F-word, the subject they avoided when

referring to her liaisons. It was like Jesse knew instinctively that Syd's sexcapades had nothing to do with feelings, other than avoiding them.

"It was great," she told Jesse. "And now it's over. We agreed up front to spend the night, fuck each other's brains out, and move on."

"I didn't ask what you *think* about it. I asked how you *feel*." Jesse eyed Syd with her no-bullshit stare and took the final slug of her beer.

How could she possibly answer Jesse truthfully? She had no idea what the truth was at this point. Her interaction with Regan hadn't been ordinary fare. Whatever the reason, she *had* felt a connection to her. And it wasn't until Syd embraced that gift that she realized her own susceptibility, her own desire to touch and be touched in that intimate, enduring way. It had been that sense of union that drove her from her own home the next morning without even a good-bye. She had no frame of reference for these feelings, and the idea of facing them and trying to figure out what they meant scared her more than staring down the barrel of a gun. She'd done the only thing she could do. Accepted the terms like an adult and walked away.

"Jess. I'm going through a lot right now, and I'm not sure what I feel about anything. Was it different? Yes. Would I do it again? Probably."

"That says a lot for you. But do me a favor and don't cut this one loose too quickly. Take your time and figure out what's really going on, now that the trial's over and you're not so preoccupied. Okay?"

Syd finished her martini and glanced toward the shreds of paper littering her bed. Syd didn't want Regan to feel anything more was expected of her. They'd had their celebration, and it was special, but they'd gone into it with no illusions. Maybe the note had given the wrong impression. Maybe Regan thought she had to send a stronger signal.

Syd was already plotting her strategy to avoid Regan in the future. She didn't understand why this particular woman stuck in her mind and made her deviate from her reliable methods of survival and pleasure. The question felt like a bomb ticking inside, foreign and dangerous. She had made the right decision to leave cleanly and quickly, she told herself again. Now she just had to stick with her plan. Obviously she wouldn't meet any resistance from Regan.

❖

Terry Blair leaned against Regan's desk. "We're getting calls."

"Calls?" Regan looked up at him blankly.

"Ever since the Cabot case. You've got some new fans out there."

"I just got lucky."

"Luck might've had something to do with it, but getting a judge to hear a potentially volatile wrongful-death case in a bench trial, then render a decision so quickly involved a lot more than luck. You don't give yourself enough credit." He flipped though a file. "Firms all across the state want to steal you away from us. Even some old law-school buddies of mine."

Regan tried to absorb what Terry was saying but her mind seemed blanketed in a fog of emotions that wouldn't dissolve. "I'm not sure I understand."

"The bottom line is that you're a hot commodity in the private sector again, Regan. You can pick and choose your next job, complete with any benefits package you want. Of course, I'm hoping you don't take the bait." He patted her on the shoulder and turned toward his office. "I'm proud of you. Excellent work."

After he left, Regan slumped into her comforting leather desk chair, her mind spinning. She'd spent the past week trying to process the tremendous shift in her life. It had taken days to move beyond the professional high from her victory in court and direct her attention to work, and she still hadn't found a way to put Sydney Cabot out of her mind. She seemed trapped in a permanent state of physical arousal, constantly plugged into her senses. Her body hummed like the wires along an electrical circuit, alive and energized from her lovemaking with Syd. But she felt more than sexually rekindled. She'd connected on an emotional level with Syd in a way she'd never experienced. Allowing herself to be completely vulnerable and available physically had opened a door to feelings she'd kept buried for years. It seemed inconceivable that one night of sex could produce such a profound change, and she kept waiting for the feelings to pass. But every nerve remained alert, as though at any moment Syd might walk in the door and tear off her clothes.

Regan had mastered the art of convincing herself that her emotional truth was the only one and protecting her overly sensitive heart from caring too much. It was easy to tell herself that Syd was only doing what came naturally. It was particularly easy to convince herself that she'd gone along with the plan willingly, because she had. But there didn't seem to be a magic button in her brain that could turn off the barrage of arousing sights, sounds, smells, and tastes that constantly reminded her of Syd.

She still couldn't understand why Syd had simply abandoned her with such insulting haste. She couldn't accept that the connection she'd experienced was one-sided. Syd had definitely enjoyed their lovemaking as much as she had. She'd described the encounter as "special." Was that what she told every woman? How could she just leave a three-sentence note that basically amounted to a callous dismissal? It was the highest form of insult and rejection.

Regan's emotional guardians sprang into place with the usual string of recriminations, guaranteed to successfully bolster her defenses. She knew Syd Cabot was a player the moment she saw her having sex in a public restroom. Her first impression had been correct. The string of ex-lovers willing to defend her even after they'd all made complaints behind her back should've been a warning to run the other way.

Regan knew better than most that any good player has a repertoire of readily available emotions to trick the weak and fool the unwise. She'd spent her childhood protecting herself and her brothers from the skilled ministrations of disengaged adults. But Syd's tears had seemed so genuine and heartfelt, Regan had simply allowed herself to fall for the oldest ruse in the book, a crying woman.

The memory of Syd with her head buried between Regan's breasts renewed a fresh round of desire. How had she been so easily duped? She wished she'd never met Sydney Cabot, never been assigned her case, and especially never made love with her. Only a desperate woman gave in as easily as she had that night. And she *had* given in, completely, another deviation from her normal behavior, another red light she'd ignored. She didn't understand what possessed her to disregard all the hazard signs and plunge headlong into this quicksand.

Shaking her head, Regan reverted to what she did best, her job. For the first time since she'd returned to the job a week earlier, she sorted the large stack of pink message slips in front of her. They were all from prominent law firms across the state. Her mood slowly lifted and she felt exhilarated about the possibility of a revitalized career in the private sector.

If getting Sydney Cabot off her mind wasn't possible, she'd do the next-best thing and remove herself from the situation completely. It wouldn't be the first time she'd relocated to forget a woman, and this one's talons were weak compared to fifteen years with Martha.

Shuffling through the messages, Regan came to the name of a woman she recognized and whose work she respected. She dialed the number, identified herself, and waited to be connected. A few minutes later she had a dinner appointment with Nancy Hyde to talk about a new job.

"There, I feel better," she said as she returned the phone to its cradle. A small, needling voice in the back of her mind replied, *Right*.

CHAPTER FOURTEEN

Syd yawned as she made the last tour of her patrol zone for the night. Since getting back on the job, she'd settled into the routines of shifts and lineups with a mixture of relief and deep contentment. She was back in command of her life, operating inside her comfort zone once more. Her work performance was nearing its all-time high, almost as if the shooting had never occurred. Life was returning to normal, with the notable and frustrating exception of her sexual adventures.

This past month was the longest dry spell she'd experienced in over a year, and it wasn't welcome. The rush of being back on the job satisfied an adrenaline need, but nothing assured her she was alive like frequent hot sex. She stopped by the club every night on her way home but no one sparked any interest. Jesse had even planned several singles nights to snap her out of the funk, but that hadn't worked.

While her body remained sexually inactive, her mind was out of control. Flashes of her night with Regan seemed trapped in a memory recall that tormented her over and over. She tried to rid herself of them by comparing their encounter with the numerous anonymous liaisons she'd had and telling herself there was really no difference, sex was sex. But each time she relived kissing, stroking, sucking, and filling Regan, or imagined herself responding to similar actions, her body disagreed. And if that wasn't enough, her traitorous mind had also begun a tormenting series of domestic scenarios starring her and Regan as the lesbian version of *Ozzie and Harriet*. She allowed herself to get caught up in the idea of a long-term relationship, sharing thoughts and feelings, building a life together, and making a home—things Syd had never thought about with any woman. Just as quickly as these fantasies rained down on her, striking her dumb with giddy possibility, they were gone, leaving her appalled at her pathetic clichéd predictability.

Despite recurring urges to sabotage her plan to avoid Regan Desanto, it seemed to be working out. She was careful to enter and leave the municipal building through the police-department entrance, which almost guaranteed no contact with other city employees. She hadn't seen Regan for more than a month, and the attorney had made no attempt to contact her. As they'd agreed, they had both moved on, and all Syd needed now was to return to her usual hedonistic pleasures, stimulated or not, and let nature take its course. The Priscilla incident had put her off her stride, but Syd was no longer trying to blot out pain with alcohol and sex. She wasn't taking stupid risks anymore, but it was time to jump back in the saddle. Once she turned on her come-hither charisma and her prey took the bait, the thrill of the tease would kick in and she'd be back in a game that felt comfortable.

Grinning at the thought, she headed toward the station to check off for the night. Just as she rounded the corner, a red convertible Mustang peeled out from the intersection, leaving a long streak of burned rubber in its wake. She sighed at the stupidity of the motoring public and flipped on her blue lights. The driver acknowledged her but didn't stop immediately. Syd followed the vehicle slowly into the back of a darkened parking lot on the next corner. After calling in the stop, she approached along the back of the vehicle and inched her way to the driver's door, pausing just shy of the jamb.

"Good evening, ma'am. May I see your license and registration, please?"

"I thought that would get your attention, Syd. Remember me?"

An attractive brunette slid her tall frame from the car and leaned against the side. The woman's well-defined upper body and thighs, accentuated by skimpy Soffe shorts and a tight sports bra, captured Syd's attention immediately. A familiar twitch between her legs caught her momentarily by surprise.

She struggled to recall a name, scanning the car for clues, and was rewarded when she saw a gym bag on the backseat.

"Dana, from the workout center, of course I remember you." She recalled her face from among those around the conference table the day of her trial.

"I've been trying to get in touch with you. You looked pretty stressed out in the lawyer's office."

Syd winced at the thought of *that* day, wishing she never had to remember it again—not the trial, not facing her exes, and especially not making love with Regan afterward. "Yeah, it was tough. How are you?"

The traffic stop had shifted to a social event, and Syd was anxious to redirect or end it altogether.

"How do I look?" Dana replied suggestively.

"Tempting as always." The reply was automatic.

With a glimmer in her eyes, Dana said, "Would you meet me at the club when you get off work? I'd like to get reacquainted." She reached between Syd's legs and squeezed.

Fabric and flesh rubbed together in a tantalizing sensation that caused Syd's breath to hitch in her throat. Her earlier resolution came to mind. Here was the perfect opportunity to get her sex life back on track. "Sounds like a great idea. I was just about to check out anyway. Give me thirty minutes."

Dana leaned in closer and grabbed Syd's rear with both hands, jerking their bodies together, scrubbing her pelvis against Syd's. "Any chance you could leave the uniform on? I really enjoyed peeling it off last time."

Syd struggled against the growing moisture in her crotch, reminding herself that she was still on duty. "That might be a bit risky." She backed reluctantly away from Dana, wanting to stay and let the familiar sensations overcome her. "But I'll be there shortly."

"I'll take you any way I can get you." Dana got back in her car, waved, and spun off, leaving another expensive patch of tire tread as she made a U-turn and headed toward the Cop Out.

"Perfect." Syd pumped the air with her fist as she got back in her patrol car and hurried through her check-off routine.

In less than twenty minutes, she was showered, dressed in capri pants with a camisole top, and walking into the club. Dana would've stood out in a crowd even without her lime-green workout shorts and matching sports bra. She was a couple of inches taller than most women in the place and considerably more buff, verging on too pumped for Syd. But desperate times and all. She needed to be reminded why she was here and was glad Dana hadn't bothered to change clothes. Nothing said sex like a scantily clad woman.

Dana flagged her over to a small table in the back where Jesse was just delivering two dirty martinis. She gave Syd a scathing look as she deposited the drinks with an unnecessarily loud thump. The precious cargo sloshed over the edges of the glasses and onto the table. "My bad. I'll get someone to clean that up just any day now." She stared at Dana's attire, rolled her eyes at Syd, and walked away mumbling about the dress code for a gym and a bar.

"I'm glad you came. I wasn't sure you would."

A part of Syd wanted to confess that she wasn't sure either, but the other part simply wanted to get laid so she could end a long dry spell and forget Regan Desanto. Neither seemed an appropriate thought to share. "It's good to see you again." She lied only marginally. She was sure it was *going* to be good. "You want to go to your place?"

"We just got our drinks. Don't I even deserve a pretend warm-up?" Dana's crooked smile said her words and her intent weren't the same.

"I've never known you to need one," Syd replied. "You look pretty hot in that outfit already. Let's just get out of here."

"You must be terribly horny. You know I like that." Dana leaned toward Syd and stared at her breasts with the eyes of an appreciative admirer. "Grab those drinks and follow me."

Syd liked to let her partners think they were in control, until they weren't. She walked behind Dana, enjoying her strut and the assertive set of her shoulders. Her red Mustang was parked behind the club in a dead-end alley surrounded by buildings, perfectly secluded. The vehicle was a little small, and the aroma of pizza from across the street was more likely to make her hungry than horny, but Syd had fucked women in less-appealing circumstances.

When they reached the car, she leaned against the side and handed Dana her martini. "Here's to getting reacquainted."

She downed her own in two gulps and threw the empty glass against the brick wall behind them. Dana's eyes sparked with excitement as she followed Syd's example.

"You're really on the edge tonight, aren't you? Let's don't waste time." She opened the car door, slid the front seats completely forward, folded them over, and waved Syd in. Once they were settled in the back, she kissed the side of Syd's neck and the sensitive lobes of her ears. She massaged her usually responsive inner thighs, ran her hand up the inside of Syd's camisole, and cupped her unencumbered breasts. "I love your tits. They're perfect. Perfect size, perfect nipples, perfect taste. Just perfect."

"I'm glad you approve," Syd lied convincingly. "Enjoy them all you want." She just wanted to feel that rush of excitement surge through her and take her away from the idly rambling thoughts of her wayward mind.

Dana stripped off her two-piece outfit with practiced ease, scooted Syd down on the seat, and knelt between her legs. "It makes me so hot when you say that. I'm already wet." She slid a finger between her legs and raised the slick, shiny appendage to prove her point. "See."

Syd closed her eyes and willed herself into the physicality of the moment. Dana's hands were rough against the smoothness of her breasts, not soft and worshipping like Regan's. She told herself she liked the contrast, but her body disagreed. Her nipples refused to pucker even slightly. She circled her hips and pelvis against Dana's thigh, hoping to stir the flame that always burned there. Dana raised Syd's garment and lowered her head to her breast. Her mouth was hot and inviting. Her tongue expertly stroked and teased, but still no response. Dana didn't seem to notice, her own excitement building.

"Oh, God, Syd. Will you touch me, please?"

Syd reminded herself that this was what she did. She loved driving women crazy until their need for her was so great that they begged for release. It was a powerful feeling of control and a most seductive aphrodisiac. But tonight her body refused to cooperate. No amount of foreplay or pleading from Dana could compel her into arousal. And Syd knew why. Her hands were not Regan's. Her mouth was not Regan's. Dana was not Regan, but that's who Syd kept seeing, as much as she hated to admit it. She wanted to go back to her perfectly normal sexual life before Regan Desanto, to anonymous liaisons for the pure pleasure of it, to no worries or regrets the morning after.

That one night with Regan, Syd had been emotionally weak, exhausted after the trial and overcome with joy at the victory. She'd simply needed a quick release and became the aggressor before Regan could resist. That uncharacteristic behavior would not happen again. Now she was stronger, back at work and in her element. She stared down at the young brunette worshiping at the altar of her breasts and knew it wasn't going to work. She had to get Regan out of her system once and for all. She needed to make Regan want her desperately, like all the others. Make her the aggressor without any power. Then she could relegate Regan to the status of her other sex partners; then she'd be free again.

"Stop." Syd eased back. "Dana, you need to stop."

"No, I don't. I'm almost there. Please."

As Syd worked herself to a seated position, her breast snapped out of Dana's mouth with a loud pop. "I'm sorry. I've got to go."

Dana stared at her with horrified eyes. "But I'm a mess. You can't leave me like this."

Syd straightened her clothes, opened the car door, and climbed out. "I'm sorry."

As Syd hurried toward the club, Dana peeled out of the parking lot, shouting something about her being a tease. Syd wasn't often on the frustrated end of a lover's emotions, and Dana's anger surprised her.

"You owe me two martini glasses," Jesse bellowed from behind the bar as Syd approached. "I draw the friendship line at stealing glassware."

Syd stood by the bar too confused and antsy to sit. "I'll pay for them. I'm sorry. I seem to be saying that a lot tonight."

Jesse's wrinkled brow said she was still annoyed, but concern won out. "What's the matter. Miss Tall Buff and Horny not do it for you tonight?"

"That's not even funny."

"I think it's hilarious. I could've told you that wasn't going to work."

"What makes you such an expert on what works or doesn't work for me?" Syd regretted the question immediately. She'd just given Jesse the opening she needed.

"Well, since you asked, let's get straight to the point. You're hung up on that attorney."

In spite of herself, Syd hesitated, wondering if that was even remotely possible.

Her silence was enough for Jesse. "See, I told you." The New York accent made her smugness sound even more pronounced.

"Don't be ridiculous. I'm not hung up on anybody."

Jesse retrieved a beer from the cooler beneath the bar, opened it, and slid it down the counter to a yelling customer without taking her eyes off Syd. "Let's review the evidence, shall we? How many times a week do you usually get laid?"

Syd wasn't in the mood for a walk down the corridor of her conquests, but she knew Jesse wouldn't let it go until she made her point, presuming she really had one. "It varies. If I'm seeing someone, it's…more."

"And when did you and Regan sleep together?"

"A month ago." Syd didn't need Jesse to do the math. "I've had a lot on my mind."

"That's never stopped you. How many times have you gotten laid since then, not counting failed attempts like tonight?"

"None."

"I'm sorry. I didn't hear that." She made a point of leaning closer, as if she'd suddenly gone deaf.

"None."

"I rest my case."

"You don't have a case. I've just been busy trying to get my feet back on the ground at work. It's not easy."

"I can see you need further convincing. How many times have I thrown singles nights so you could meet women in the last four weeks?"

Syd groaned.

"Right, and I've paraded women of every color, shape, size, culture, socioeconomic status, and sexual persuasion under your nose. You've hardly even taken a whiff. Face it, Syd, you're hung up on Regan and the old style isn't working for you anymore. You need to shed it."

"If you're going to pass out this shitty advice, you'd better get a shrink's license. And consider giving free drinks. It'll go down easier." Syd set her glass down. "I gotta go home."

The short walk to her loft seemed too long as Jesse's assessment of her situation spun through her head again. Damn it. She knew she hadn't had sex in a month. Anybody who stood within three feet of her could probably tell from the pent-up current whizzing around inside her. It was like dancing on top of an electric fence, and no self-help devices were helping.

She recalled the complete satiation she'd felt making love with Regan, like nothing she'd ever experienced. She'd always considered sex a purely physical act with entirely physical results. When she'd woken up next to Regan the following morning, her entire body was exhausted yet she was simultaneously ravenous to have her again. Watching Regan sleep, her heart and soul had ached with something so foreign and frightening that it had driven her from her home without a word. She'd written a note and bolted because she couldn't trust herself to stay and not tell Regan just how confused she felt.

If these *feelings* for Regan were so wonderful how could they be so terrifying at the same time? Syd knew the answer. She'd been out of her element and behaved in a way that was not comfortable for her. The next morning, when the lust wore off, she'd realized her mistake. Nothing had really changed for her. It had taken the past month to figure that out. Now that she understood why she'd behaved uncharacteristically she simply had to convince her body and heart that it was okay to enjoy Regan and then let go. Under less-stressful circumstances, she would discover the truth—that there was no special magic. She was still Syd Cabot and Regan was just another attractive woman. That's where her new plan would come into play—tease, seduce, and conquer.

Regan Desanto would be hers one final, purging time.

Regan parked across the street from the Thai restaurant and watched Syd walk toward the Cop Out in the next block. The sight of her dispatched flashes of heat through her body that were quickly replaced by cold chills. She wondered who Syd would liaise with tonight, but decided she really didn't want to know. Her former client's life was no longer any of her concern, personally or professionally. The case was over and they'd had their one night of passion. It was what they'd both agreed upon, so why did it still bother her that Syd had left that morning without a word?

Regan grimaced. She was upset because she wanted to believe she was different. In her fantasy she hoped that Syd would want more. But what did she really have to offer a woman who could have anyone she desired? Her own partner had found her unattractive and dumped her after fifteen years. Her sexual experience was mediocre at best and had probably been uninspiring, perhaps even boring for Syd.

But Syd's lovemaking had been anything but boring. It had physically released Regan to be adventurous. The memory of their passion burrowed deep into the cells of her body and throbbed like an incurable disease. Each night she tried to claw it out with her inadequate hands or some ineffective hunk of molded thermoplastic, but the ache persisted. Syd had satisfied her taste for Regan. It was over. But as many times as she'd told herself she was okay with it, Regan knew she was lying. She'd carefully reconstructed her emotional barriers and rationally accepted that a one-night stand was for the best. But the tiny hairline fractures that Syd had caused in her defenses would not heal. She'd seen glimpses of a gentler, more caring Syd and she *wanted* to believe they had a chance. She *had* to believe that what they shared was not only in her mind.

She watched Syd enter the club and physically ached at the visual absence of her. If she couldn't be with Syd, she'd have to be away from her completely. Seeing her by accident was not going to be an option. No one had ever affected her this way, making her crave and obsess. And this woman would not do it again either. She had to regain control.

Resisting the urge to chase Syd into the bar, Regan walked instead into the restaurant where she was meeting her old college friend and potential future boss. Nancy Hyde waved from the intimate window table and rose to greet her. She'd chosen a cozy spot out of the main flow of traffic but with a great view of the sunset.

They hugged and Regan smiled at her friend who never seemed to age.

Nancy had attended college late in life and specialized in child and family law. She was ten years older than Regan but looked like her contemporary. Her soft facial features and green eyes were accentuated by platinum blond hair in a tight gamine cut. She was the kind of exotically statuesque woman who could pull off short hair and look hot doing so.

"You look great." Regan assessed the fringed leather jacket, tweed pants, cashmere sweater, and ridiculously high-heeled Manolos and decided that family law paid very well. "How do you manage to never change?"

"Lots of strong drink and fast women. You look great, too. As usual."

Nancy Hyde was chasing women when Regan was still in grade school. They'd never acted on the occasional tug of attraction between them, content instead to appreciate each other. Regan smiled. "You're just the woman I need to talk to on several levels."

"One of the things I've always loved about you, Regan, is that you get right to the point. I thought being an attorney would squeeze that out of you. Is it work or personal?"

"Both." She'd never been able to lie to Nancy or even fool her for very long. She was too tired to try either at the moment.

"I've ordered a bottle of New Age white wine," Nancy said. "I know you don't drink but it's more like champagne. You'll have some and keep me company while I solve all your problems."

Spoken like a wonderfully loving Jewish mother. When Nancy set her mind on something it was hard to stop her. It was one of the things that made her a great attorney.

The waiter came, poured their wine, and hovered while Nancy tasted it. After he filled their glasses, she shooed him away and asked that he not return until their bottle was empty. They should be ready to order by then, she told him.

Without further preamble, Nancy launched into a succinct recap of her life since she'd last seen Regan, then they moved onto the Cabot case. "So you're ready to leave this cushy government job after only a year because you just won a big case? There's more to the story."

"I just need a change. This job isn't for me."

"Is it the nice salary you object to, or the substantial perks and benefits?"

Regan regarded her friend with a mixture of admiration and annoyance. The city had gone way over budget when they hired her, including in her contract a sizeable benefits package. "You really have been doing your homework, haven't you? Then you should know exactly why I need a change."

"If I had to guess, I'd say it was a woman." Nancy smoothed her platinum knot with a casual air belied by her intent stare. "Sydney Cabot. Am I close?"

"Too close."

"You're going to let another woman run you out of another town?"

The question struck Regan like a splash of ice-cold water. This wasn't the same thing at all. She'd left her family home because her parents were abusive and her mother was a selfish bitch. She moved from Nashville because Martha was fucking her boss and dumped her. She wanted to get out of High Point because... Dear God, Nancy was right. Her life sounded like a Jerry Springer rerun.

When Regan didn't answer, Nancy reached across the table and patted her hands. "I'm sorry. That was a little blunt even for me. Darling, you know I'll hire you tomorrow if that's what you want. You may need a couple of area-specific courses. That's easy to do while you work. I'll coach you through them. But a move won't solve the real problem, will it?"

Regan sipped the wine Nancy kept pouring into her glass and was starting to feel the effects on her empty stomach. A little light-headedness might be just what she needed to put a different spin on her situation. "I'm not even sure what the real problem is. It's not like we've been in a relationship for years or anything. We've only slept together once and—"

"Once?" Nancy shrieked, and heads all around the restaurant turned in their direction. Her vivid green eyes were huge with disbelief. "That must've been one hell of a fuck."

Regan jumped in her chair and jerkily set her wineglass down on the pristine tablecloth. The glass overturned and rolled onto the floor. "It was not a *fuck*."

The look in Nancy's eyes changed from startled to concerned. "My God, what has she done to you? Don't worry, darling. We'll figure something out."

A pair of waiters took care of the spill and replaced the table linen. Regan apologized before they drifted away. She caught a scornful glare only from the junior of the two men. No doubt the other guy had seen it all. He replenished her wine with an unruffled air.

Regan left the glass untouched after he walked away. "I'm really sorry, Nancy. I've been on edge for weeks now, like I'm crawling out of my skin. She woke up things in me I didn't even know were there. It sounds stupid."

"Tell me about her." Nancy's eyes were kind and encouraging, with no hint of judgment or disapproval.

"She's a lot like you, actually. She's extremely competent in her job, gorgeous, sexy as hell, and sleeps with whomever she wants whenever she wants. Her idea of a good time is sex with no strings."

"Ouch. I think I've just been insulted."

"I didn't mean it like that, but the two of you seem to be able to live without intimacy. I can't imagine life without that connection."

Nancy stared into her wineglass for several seconds, her eyes glistening with rare emotion. "Have you ever considered that some people experience intimacy through sex, not the other way around? That some women are just wired differently from you?"

As Nancy's words registered, Regan remembered her night with Syd. It *had* been intimate. Their connection had been real, so did it matter how they arrived at that mutual convergence of feeling? She knew only that when she was with Syd, she felt whole again. She deserved that. Syd wasn't perfect, but neither was she. Life was full of light and shadow. It took more courage to engage life's challenges than to cower on the periphery and merely accept whatever happened. If she walked away from Syd without exploring their potential, she'd never forgive herself.

Unsettled by her thoughts, Regan steered the conversation in a new direction. "Are you seeing anyone now?"

"Jean and I are still together, mostly. Apparently she finds enough redeeming qualities in me to keep coming back. She understands that I need flexible fences."

"Are you faithful to her?"

"When we're together."

"Do you love her?"

"Sure, at least by my definition. I'm not certain it would be yours." Nancy must have sensed Regan's unease because she quickly added, "And that's not relevant, since you and I are not in a relationship. Every couple has to define their love for themselves."

Regan sighed. "She felt connected to me. I'm sure of it. It's just not possible to experience something that amazing and intense if it's one-sided."

In her heart she knew Syd felt their connection. In her head she knew that feeling of connection had driven her away. The note left on the pillow made her intentions clear. Syd had spent a lifetime avoiding commitment and she intended to go on doing so. Regan could accept the evasive maneuvers and walk away, or she could fight for more. Was Syd even capable of doing something different?

Regan took a gulp of her wine. She would never find out if she simply accepted Syd's terms like all those other women. What did she really have to lose if she chose a different approach? As things stood, she was planning to give Syd and herself no chance at all. Whatever she did, the outcome couldn't be any worse.

"What do you intend to do, Regan?" Nancy asked.

"I'm going after what I want, finally. I'm not exactly sure how, but I'll figure it out as I go. Can I have a few days to think about the job?"

"Of course. It's yours if you want it. Take all the time you need. Unless I hear from you, I'll assume you've decided to stay on and ride this out." Nancy offered her a menu and a warm smile. "Would you like to order now?"

"If you don't mind, I need to go home. Thanks for meeting me. You're a good friend." She stood and gave Nancy a hug. "If you have a chance while you're in town go by and visit Izzy. I know she'd love to see you."

"How's she doing?"

"Really well, actually. I haven't been a very good granddaughter lately, with this case and everything else. Another of my many failures."

Nancy escorted Regan outside the restaurant and slid an arm around her waist. "Don't be so hard on yourself." She pulled Regan to her and kissed her gently on both cheeks. "Keep in touch," she called as Regan crossed the street to her car.

Settling behind the wheel, Regan debated going into the Cop Out. Maybe Syd would still be there and they could talk. A more likely scenario flashed through her mind. Maybe Syd would be in the restroom with another woman and Regan would only make a fool of herself by going there. Women who thought they could change a partner's behavior usually doomed themselves to disappointment. If Syd chose a different path and a different future, she had to make the decision for herself. All Regan could do was open the door.

With a soft groan, she leaned back in her seat. Syd had already slammed that door closed once. Why would she change her mind?

❖

Syd walked away from the Thai restaurant wishing she'd taken a different route home. After avoiding Regan for a month, she'd spotted her sitting at the front table with a gorgeous platinum blonde. The woman wore expensive clothes and gazed at Regan with the hunger of a sexual predator. The look made Syd nauseous. It hadn't taken Regan long to find someone else.

But why should she care? They'd spent one night having sex. Great sex, but just sex. And Syd was planning to seduce her again to get any residual urges out of her system. So let Regan have a night with another woman. It would be good for her to loosen up a little.

Tough words, she thought as she'd watched the two of them emerge from the restaurant. So why did she feel like someone was standing on her chest? And why did she want to run back and snatch Regan from the clutches of the platinum predator?

She hadn't waited around to watch them leave together. She didn't want to picture Regan naked, her head thrown back in ecstasy as she surrendered to the blonde's expert hands. The thought should have turned her on, but instead it haunted her like an apparition refusing to be exiled. Syd maneuvered an empty beer can away from the curb with her foot and soccer-kicked it all the way home.

CHAPTER FIFTEEN

Syd contemplated kissing the alarm clock when it beeped to life the next morning. Finally free of her dreams, she threw back her bedding and stalked into the bathroom. The plus side of waking up was that the images of Regan and that blond vixen stopped. On the negative side, she was horny as hell and had to go to work.

After a quick shower and a brisk walk, she was in the lineup room waiting for roll call before anyone else. The potential of losing her job had made it even more precious, so being early was Syd's token of gratitude. The other squad members started trickling in about two minutes before lineup with the enthusiasm of prisoners on death row. She tried to lighten things up, but they glared at her like she'd volunteered the team for overtime on Christmas.

"What's up, guys? You should be happy. I'm back to do all the work."

Harold Simmons, designated squad old-guy, said, "Sounds like you've been doing the *homework* too."

"What the hell does that mean?"

He shrugged. "Why don't you ask Brady?"

Syd looked around and realized that Gil wasn't there again. He hadn't been in lineup for the past few days and she hadn't heard from him. "Where is he anyway, on leave?"

"Transferred." The sergeant walked in, catching the end of their conversation. "Fall in."

"What do you mean transferred?" Syd glanced around at her

colleagues. No one would meet her gaze. Then it hit her with a gut-wrenching twist. Priscilla must've told Gil.

Her knees felt wobbly. Who could blame the guy for wanting a transfer after that kind of news? He probably never wanted to see her again, much less work with her on a daily basis. And the HPPD grapevine took care of the rest. Now everybody knew about it.

"You've been on the job twelve years, Cabot. You know what a damn transfer means. Fall in for inspection."

The remainder of lineup passed in a flurry of activity that she neither saw nor heard. As she checked her patrol car, Syd thought about the guys she worked with. They were like family. Everyone knew she was a lesbian, never talked about it, but seemed to accept it. They even invited the babe du jour, if there was one, to their cookouts with their wives and children. Now they couldn't look her in the eye. That's what happened to anyone who slept with a cop's wife. Never mind that she didn't know it at the time, her squad mates thought she was a home wrecker.

Syd felt sick. Technically she deserved whatever she got. It didn't matter if she was gay or straight. She knew each of these guys well enough to realize their disgust wasn't about that. She had violated the code of the brotherhood in the most personal way. Their objection was to the offense, not the offender. That fact didn't make it hurt any less. Just when things were getting back to normal after the trial, another thread from her past had come loose and threatened to unravel her life.

She thought about the decisions she'd made since the shooting, how she'd chosen to bury her feelings in drink and sex time after time without regard for the consequences. The personal and professional ramifications were finally becoming apparent. She'd used women in the most unflattering way and consequently had no real connection with anyone and a considerably lower opinion of herself. The resultant complaints could've been detrimental in her trial, but they had at least left an unfavorable blot on her record. She'd hurt people she didn't know and some she cared about, unknowingly but none the less painfully. Her behavior had probably also caused some of her fellow officers to question her abilities and decisions. The whole denial-and-avoidance scenario had only served to retard her recovery and growth. She needed to face her demons head-on, as she'd done with the women after trial, accept the consequences of her actions, and make smarter choices in the future.

Syd's head hurt thinking about it. Now was not the time to ponder all these heavy issues. She had a job to do, one of the jobs nobody wanted—working traffic for accidents. Today it seemed the guys were on top of their calls, leaving the crap to her. They were trying to make a point. She got it.

An hour before shift change Syd was at her favorite 7-Eleven checking on the new cashier and getting a free drink when she heard her call sign over the walkie-talkie. Dispatch wanted her to respond to a domestic disturbance. Great. Syd hated domestic calls, especially without an assist. Rule number one: never go in alone. They were statistically the most dangerous calls an officer responded to. You never knew what you were going to get. Some of her most serious injuries had occurred in these situations.

The call location was in a mid-income housing development. Most of the residents had lived in their homes since they were built and worked in the furniture business. But the recent economic downturn had hit this neighborhood hard. Several manufacturing companies closed, and where there were layoffs, stress and crime escalated.

Syd parked within two doors of the residence and walked up. She could hear raised voices as soon as she got out of her cruiser. She cased the area then climbed the porch steps and planted her left shoulder against the side of the door, leaving her gun hand free. Her pulse kicked up as the voices inside grew louder and more abusive. Adrenaline surged and her senses sharpened. She knocked on the door.

The yelling never stopped but the door flew open and a shirtless, pimple-faced teenager stood in the doorway. "What the fuck do you want?"

"Somebody called about a disturbance." Syd hated to state the obvious, but they were trained to tell folks why they'd been called.

"Ya think?"

"Jason, let the lady in so we can settle this," a female voice ordered from inside. The tone was calmer.

Syd stepped into the residence, feeling a little more comfortable. The room's furnishings were worn but clean, like the rest of the areas

Syd could see. The female appeared to be in her seventies, too old to be the boy's mother. She wore the uniform of a waitress at Henry James BBQ on Main Street and her name tag read Betty.

"I didn't do this and I ain't taking the blame." The kid resumed quarreling. "Talk to your lying husband."

"Don't talk about your daddy like that."

"He ain't my daddy and I ain't taking his shit no more." He ran into a back bedroom.

This was the reason going on domestics alone was a bad idea. One officer couldn't keep an eye on two upset subjects at once. "Are you okay here, ma'am," Syd asked.

"Sure, honey. Go talk some sense into him. There's three hundred dollars missing and I just want it back. He says he didn't take it."

"Why don't you have a seat in here and let me talk to him alone. I'll be right back." Syd inched along the hallway to the bedroom door where the teenager had gone. "Jason, can I come in and talk to you?"

"Sure cop-lady, come on in. I need a witness."

Syd didn't like the sound of that. Ambiguous statements from distraught people weren't usually a good sign. She turned the handle and pushed the door open with her foot while standing to the side. Jason stood at the foot of the bed holding a cocked .357 Magnum to his temple. His eyes were wide and he had the look of a caged animal, lost and hopeless.

"Oh, shit." Syd instinctively drew her weapon, dropped to the floor outside the bedroom, and peeked around the corner. Her Glock was trained on the boy's midsection. "Jesus. Jason, what are you doing?"

The boy's grandmother came running down the hallway.

"Ma'am, stay back. He's got a gun."

She started screaming. "Don't shoot my boy, please don't shoot him."

The woman tried to push her way past Syd, but another officer came through the front door just in time to intervene.

"Hal, keep her back. This kid's got a gun to his head. Call EMS and have them stage in the area."

"Got it, Syd." He ushered the frail, hysterical woman back to the front of the house.

"I didn't do anything wrong, lady," Jason screamed from the

bedroom. "Her worthless husband stole the money then said he'd beat me if I told. I can't take it anymore."

"Put the gun down and we'll talk about it. We'll get it straightened out."

"She always takes his word for everything. She don't care that he beats me."

Syd could see the terror in the boy's eyes and wanted desperately to help him. She ran through a list of possible things she could say but none seemed appropriate. She had to do something before the situation deteriorated. As if by the power of suggestion, Jason swiveled the gun from his head and turned it in Syd's direction.

"Don't do that, Jason, please. I don't want to hurt you."

Her weapon was still pointed center mass. In a flash of unwelcome memory she was back at the mall nine months ago when she shot Lee Nartey. This young man also had a gun pointed at her. Could she do it again? Could she kill another human being to save her own life, knowing what she'd have to go through afterward? Would it be justified? Was there any way she could alter the outcome without shooting him? All these questions bolted through her mind in a split second, a split second that could've gotten her killed if this boy was serious about harming someone.

"Jason, I know you don't want to hurt me or yourself. And I don't want to hurt you. Put the gun down." Her request was almost a plea. Her insides quivered and she hoped her hands were steady. Perspiration beaded on her forehead and under her vest as worst-case scenarios played out in her head.

What if she froze and Jason killed her? Would anyone miss her? Who would attend her funeral? Maybe a bevy of her bed friends, all throwing stones on her casket? How would she be remembered, as a home wrecker? What if his shot went astray and paralyzed her instead? Would anyone come to visit? Would they care about her at all if she was suddenly incapable of sex?

She shook her head to dislodge the disturbing thoughts. Now was not the time to lapse into what-ifs and self-pity. This young person was in trouble and she needed to figure out a way to help him. If she didn't, things could go south in a hurry. The boy's arm shook as he brought the gun back to his own head. She breathed a sigh of relief and took a chance.

"Jason, I'm going to put my gun down so we can talk."

From the front of the house, Syd heard Hal calling to her. "Are you fucking nuts, Cabot? Do *not* lower your weapon."

"Jason, listen to me. I'm lowering my weapon. Tell me what I can do to make this better for you. I'm not going to hurt you and I don't want to see you hurt yourself either. What can I do to fix this?"

He seemed to be considering her question. His gaze shifted from her around his room to the window and back. "Get me out of here."

"I can do that."

Her answer must not have been what he expected because his eyes widened in disbelief. Or maybe it was just that no one had ever tried to help him before. "You can?"

"Yes. How old are you, Jason?"

"Fifteen, I'll be sixteen next month."

"I can definitely help you. Put down the gun and we'll work it out. I promise." Jason would be of consensual age on his sixteenth birthday and able to make decisions about many things that affected his life. She was certain she could find him temporary housing for a month.

"Don't lie to me, lady. I've had enough of that."

"I'm not lying. We can make this happen, together."

The young man's hand shook as he slowly lowered the weapon away from his head. "Where should I put this? I just drop it, right?" He opened his hand and the cocked revolver seemed to float in slow motion to the hardwood floor.

"No, don't." Before the words left Syd's lips the gun hit the floor with a deafening explosion that reverberated throughout the house. A stabbing pain pierced her side. She looked down and saw a ragged tear in her uniform shirt. The black material grew sticky and wet. Cringing in agony and shock, she gasped, "Oh, God. I'm shot."

❖

Regan knew something was terribly wrong the moment she stepped off the elevator on her way out of the building. Officers huddled in the canteen were speaking in low, urgent tones. Their somber faces chilled her.

"Officers, I'm Assistant City Attorney Regan Desanto. What's happened?"

A young officer turned toward her. "One of our squad mates is involved in a standoff."

"What kind of standoff?"

"Some guy with a gun. It's been going on for a while now. Sounds pretty hairy."

"Which officer?" The question scraped across her dry tongue like sandpaper.

"Cabot."

She tried to control her voice so they wouldn't notice the tremble she felt inside. "Why aren't you out there?"

The officers looked at her like she'd committed blasphemy. An older officer spoke up. "We *would* be if the duty captain hadn't relieved us with night-shift guys. She's one of ours and we don't leave our folks. Hal's with her." He delivered his last statement like it should give them all comfort.

Regan walked away, managing not to breathe again until she was inside the elevator. When she did, energy followed the air out of her lungs and she clung to the sides of the car for support. Syd was involved in *another* potentially fatal situation and Regan's first thought was for her safety. She wanted to go to her, to make sure she was okay. She could drive to the scene and wait. A city attorney might be needed for legal advice on such a case. She would use any excuse just to make sure Syd wasn't hurt.

Regan rushed from the elevator to her car in the parking garage. Her first instinct was to *do* something. She climbed in and started to turn the ignition but stopped. Instead she clutched the steering wheel, trying to make a rational decision. What should she do? What *could* she do? Going to the scene would probably not be helpful, and if Syd saw her, it might even be distracting. Paralyzed by the duel of her logical thoughts and her illogical feelings, she pounded the seat beside her, cursing her inability to do *anything*.

In the midst of her helplessness, Regan wondered how she would feel if something happened to Syd. The short time they'd known each other had been rife with disagreement and challenge, hardly the foundation for a lasting friendship. Having represented Syd, she could find plenty of logical reasons for her apprehension. She was naturally worried for Syd's mental health. The possibility that she could choke in a similar scenario and get others hurt was also cause for concern. But none of these rationalizations rang true. The truth was she feared for Syd's safety because she cared about her. She cared enough that she was contemplating asking Syd to consider a relationship with her.

Regan stared at the car keys in her hand. If she drove away now and went home and waited to hear about the incident like any other member of the general public, she was making a choice. She would take the job with Nancy, and Syd would become history, a one-night stand that would eventually lose its potency in her imagination. The alternative was much riskier, the outcome uncertain. But playing it safe for the past fifteen years hadn't brought her happiness, and Regan had no one to blame for her dissatisfaction but herself. She should have left Martha long ago. Instead she'd settled. And whatever destiny might have in store for her, she wasn't going to do that again.

Regan got out of her car and went back into the police station, intent on waiting with the officers. But the canteen had emptied out. She approached one of the few men left in the room and asked, "Where are the officers who were here earlier?"

"At the hospital. We had an officer shot tonight."

Regan felt the blood rush from her face. "Shot?"

Her heart ached as if someone held it clenched in their fist. She tried to draw a full breath but her lungs labored under the pressure. *I should've gone. I could've been there for her. What if she's...* She couldn't complete the horrifying thought. Her legs almost collapsed under her. This couldn't be happening.

As she stumbled out of the room, she heard the officer call something after her, but all Regan could hear was her pulse rushing in her ears. She had to find Syd.

❖

The residence burst into a cacophony of activity. Hal was yelling that an officer was down. The sound of footsteps pounded toward her. Jason was crying in the corner of his bedroom. The grandmother was screaming for her little boy. More officers filled the hallway where she sat and edged toward Jason's bedroom.

"Don't hurt him. He didn't shoot me. It was an accident."

They looked at her skeptically and she repeated, "I mean it. Don't hurt him."

"We'll sort this out later, Cabot. Take her to the hospital," her sergeant told the EMS personnel.

Syd started laughing in the ambulance and couldn't stop. She knew it was partially all the adrenaline in her system but it was also the circumstances. The last time she'd fired her gun someone else went to the hospital but never came out. This time she chose not to shoot and felt pretty certain that she'd be okay. It might've been a stupid decision to some, but at least she was the only one who'd pay for it. Physical pain she could handle. The best part was that she hadn't hurt anyone else. That was something to celebrate. As they rolled into the hospital, Syd thought about Regan and wished she could share the news with her.

She felt lucky as the doctor examined her. The bullet had torn through her shirt, into the unprotected flesh of her left side, and exited cleanly. Her injury barely amounted to a deep gully scratch. She escaped the hospital with only half a dozen butterfly stitches, a pressure bandage, and a prescription for pain pills. Hal drove her home with a few attaboys for not getting killed and an aw-shit for lowering her weapon. At least he still cared.

Jesse stopped by not long after to mix a batch of martinis. "And no booze with your painkillers," she warned as an afterthought.

Syd laughed. "It's just a graze. Besides, I'm going to bed. It's been a long day." She didn't mention Gil's transfer. That was another conversation and she already knew what Jesse would say.

"I can stop by later, if you need anything."

"Just sleep." Syd shooed her out and then poured herself a dirty goose. One little pain pill and one little martini wouldn't do any harm. Besides, the doctor had told her to rest. She reclined gingerly on the sofa and after several minutes the residual adrenaline and fear seeped from her body as the cocktail took effect. In its wake came a tidal wave of repressed thoughts and feelings shaken loose by tonight's events.

She'd been in two officer-involved shootings in less than a year. That was more than most officers encountered in an entire career. Why didn't she handle the first one differently? Maybe she should've tried harder. Could she have talked Nartey into dropping his weapon like she did the young man tonight? Perhaps she was too quick to pull the trigger.

She remembered the fear that rolled up her throat that night, the sour taste of pending death. In that sickening moment she'd chosen to end another life. The deafening eruption as her weapon discharged, the brilliant muzzle flash, the sulfuric charcoal smell of gunpowder, and the horrid sight of exploding flesh as the bullet hit its mark, all returned with vivid clarity. Syd crumpled into herself, the searing pain that ripped through her injured side no match for the emotion that stormed her body. She tried to scream and release the pain, but her lungs filled with air and all that came out was a gasping sob. It felt as if her insides were trying to purge themselves all at once. And all she could do was cry about everything she'd done and everything she'd wasted since that night behind the mall.

She'd numbed the pain any way she could, and although her choices allowed her to feel alive, they were also poisons to intimacy. She could have shared her feelings with the departmental shrink, or with friends, but she'd buried them so well she had almost started to believe they didn't exist. Syd tried to remember the last time she felt emotionally connected to herself and another person simultaneously. The response was almost immediate—in this place, in almost this exact spot on her sofa, with Regan. That realization liberated another round of wrenching sobs as she recalled how she'd pushed Regan away. Their connection had threatened to force her back into the world of fully involved, fully functioning, fully accountable human beings. Syd hadn't been ready and had reacted out of fear. Regan made her feel vulnerable simply by trusting her and being so open and receptive despite her fears of being hurt again.

Syd curled up tighter, almost thankful for the pain of her injury. At least this time she had something to show, an external wound that legitimized her trauma. Tears flooded her eyes again and she didn't resist. She cried until she had nothing left and fell asleep.

❖

Regan didn't remember leaving the city building or driving to the hospital. Her next cognizant moment was standing in front of a receptionist demanding to know about Syd's condition and being told that HIPAA prohibited the release of any information. The flustered desk attendant went on to say that if she *really* was a city attorney, she'd know better than to ask.

Her last statement sobered Regan slightly. She apologized for her behavior and after much groveling was told that Syd had not been admitted. Regan breathed a little easier as she scoured the ER waiting bay for an officer who could provide a status report. The old derogatory adage about never having an officer when you need one came to mind. She vowed to review the department's staffing levels, which she suspected had contributed to this entire series of unacceptable events.

But Regan wasn't satisfied. She had to see Syd alive in person or she wouldn't be able to rest. She drove to her loft and vaulted the three flights of stairs two at a time. When she stood in front of the cold metal door, memories of the morning Syd left her briefly resurfaced, but she ignored her trepidation. She wasn't here to recriminate or judge Syd. She was here for that sensitive part of Syd that would need comfort and support when she acknowledged her deepest fears. And she was here for herself. She had to be sure Syd was physically safe.

Regan pressed her ear against the cold metal door for sounds of life and then knocked softly. No response. She tried again, still no answer. She dialed Syd's cell phone and listened once more but heard no ringing from inside. The call went to voice mail. Maybe the irritated hospital receptionist had just been trying to get rid of her. Perhaps Syd had gone to someone else's home to recuperate. The thought twisted her insides with disappointment and a noticeable dose of jealousy. Her last hope of news was Jesse. If Syd wasn't with her, she might at least be willing to give her an update on her condition.

❖

The Cop Out was packed with annoyingly friendly customers who wanted to chat and buy her drinks. But Regan waved them off on her direct course to the bar. She elbowed and apologized her way through without slowing down, but Jesse wasn't there. A blonde who looked barely old enough to drink herself was manning the station.

"Where's Jesse?" Regan asked over the din of festive voices.

"She's in the back." The girl nodded toward the rear of the club.

Regan tapped on a tri-fold screen with the word "office" scratched across the top. The makeshift door, which stretched across an opening no larger than a linen closet, wobbled from her touch.

"Angie, I told you I'm doing payroll. Give me a break."

Regan cleared her throat and said, "Excuse me, Jesse. It's Regan Desanto."

The rickety screen flattened against the side of the narrow entry with one whack from Jesse's hand as she exited. "Sorry. It's hard to get any work done in a bar. Everybody thinks you're here for their entertainment. They forget it's also a business." She studied Regan's face and her tone shifted. "But you're not here to be entertained, are you? Let's step outside where we can actually hear each other."

As soon as the door closed behind them, Regan asked, "Do you know where I can find Syd?"

Jesse gave her a quizzical look before responding. "Against my better judgment, I left her at home. She said she was going to bed."

"Was she really..." Regan couldn't bring herself to say the word. It was as if speaking it aloud would make it more real.

"Shot? Yeah, but it wasn't bad, only a flesh wound. It nicked her in the side where that stupid vest doesn't cover."

Regan expelled a captured breath and all the tension that had seized her body for the past two hours gushed out. She wobbled unsteadily and Jesse grabbed her arms, guiding her backward into a patio chair.

"Are you alright?"

Regan nodded and clasped her hands together where they rested in her lap. They kept trembling. "I'm glad she wasn't badly hurt. I've been trying to get some answers for the last two hours. Do you think she's okay alone?" Realizing the assumption she'd made, Regan quickly added, "If she is alone. I'm just concerned she might need something."

"She was alone when I left and pretty out of it on the pain meds they gave her at the hospital. I was planning to check on her when I leave here."

Silence grew between them. Neither spoke again until Regan composed herself enough to try to stand. "Well, then, I guess you've got everything under control."

"I don't know so much about that." Jesse held her gaze. "Can I get you a drink, a Coke or maybe something stronger tonight?"

"No, thanks. I'll be fine. I should go so you can get your work done."

"You really care about her, don't you?"

Regan wasn't sure why the question surprised her. After all, Jesse was Syd's best friend and her concern was certainly understandable. She considered avoidance or outright lying, but decided her actions had probably already given her away. "I'm not sure what my feelings are. But Syd's made her lack of interest in me very clear."

"Syd's had a rough year. I don't think she—"

"Please." Raising her hand to stop any further protests by Syd's friend, Regan said, "You don't need to defend her. Just tell her I asked about her. And thank you, Jesse. I can see why you're such a good friend."

She skirted around the side of the building and back to her car. Once she was safely inside, she buried her face in her hands and allowed the jumble of emotions free rein as they spilled out in uncontrollable sobs. She was relieved that Syd wasn't badly injured, worried that she might retreat farther into herself after this latest incident, disappointed that she wasn't able to see her, and horrified that she'd revealed so much to Jesse. The tears fell, and for the first time in over a year she didn't try to stop them.

CHAPTER SIXTEEN

The next morning Regan sprawled across her bed still dressed in work clothes from the day before. The reason for her come-apart at the Cop Out slammed into her memory. Syd had been shot and there wasn't a damn thing she could do. Her helplessness rattled her. Regan liked to feel that she could fix everything, but since Syd had entered her life, the rules had changed.

The morning sun streamed through the unadorned windows of her sparsely furnished bedroom, chafing at her groggy senses and tear-swollen eyes. She needed a hot shower, fresh clothes, and a diversion. A visit with Izzy seemed in order. Her grandmother was always the perfect blend of sage advice and frivolity. She could use some lightheartedness. Obsessing over Syd was fast becoming masochistic. She'd started to wonder if the shooting was a sign of some kind, warning her away from making a decision she would only regret. If she threw herself at Syd, only to be rejected again, she didn't know how she would handle the humiliation.

And there were worse possibilities. What if she and Syd tried to make something work, but Syd couldn't resist the temptation to stray? She'd spent fifteen years with a partner who used their home as a stopover between jaunts with her boss. Being alone didn't seem so bad if womanizing cheaters were her only alternative.

Regan decided Izzy would help straighten out her thinking. An hour later, with a dozen of her grandmother's favorite chocolate-glazed, custard-filled donuts, Regan stood at her door. She didn't have to knock.

"Somebody's holding out on me. Get in here with those donuts."

When Regan opened the door she stopped. Her once red-and-silver-haired grandmother had jet black hair cut into a short, spiky mullet. She wore a black T-shirt, boots, and black jeans with a studded black belt.

"Close your mouth, honey. There are flies in this place."

"Gram?" Regan placed the donuts on the small side table by the door and stared in shock. "What happened to you?"

"I'm Joan Jett."

"Of course you are. Wait right here." Regan looked around for the nurse, certain that her grandmother had mentally snapped. She didn't like leaving her in an assisted-living facility in the first place. It was what Izzy wanted. Now she had even more reason to take her home. "I'll be right back."

"Where are you going?" Izzy placed one hand on her hip and with the other reached up and snatched the black wig off her head. "I'm in costume for the dress-up birthday party."

It took a few seconds for Regan to adjust, then she burst into laughter. "You're a nut."

"I must've been pretty convincing, from the look on your face. It was a toss-up between Joan and Melissa. I thought black made more of a statement."

"It certainly did with me. You realize they're both into the lesbian thing, don't you?"

"That's why I chose them. Besides, who in this place is savvy enough to know that except you, me, and my costume assistant from last year?" Izzy flung the creature-looking hairpiece onto her bed, grabbed a donut from the box, and took a huge bite.

Regan hugged her and clung to her a bit longer than necessary. Izzy had a way of always making her feel better. She understood her on a level that no one ever had. When the rest of the family disowned her for being lesbian, Izzy was her only constant. And she often seemed a lot younger than her years.

"I love you."

"I love you too, honey. Now tell me why you're here so early on a Saturday morning, with a box full of bribes and looking like you cried all night."

One of the very things Regan so loved about her grandmother was also one of the most difficult to handle when she was upset, her directness. "Can't a girl visit her Gram without having aspersions cast on her character?"

"Don't pull that lawyer crap on me." Izzy took another bite of her donut. "I told you I had an experience with a woman once, didn't I?"

The donut in Regan's hand froze halfway to her mouth. "You most certainly did not."

"You got a problem with your mouth today, honey? The hinges are getting stuck in the open position." Izzy motioned to the twin rocking chairs next to her only window and they sat down. "I had a special female friend before I married your grandpa."

"Mother never told me."

"Do you think I would've told *her*?" Izzy's mouth twisted like her donut had soured. "Your mother was the most prejudiced, selfish person I ever knew. It's hard for me to believe she came from my loins. But we're getting off track."

"Are you making this up?" Regan was having difficulty believing Izzy's story. Was she experiencing some memory problems or drifting into delusions? Or was she just trying to make her feel better?

"Would I make something like that up just because I know my baby's got woman problems?" Izzy didn't wait for a reply before ambushing her. "Honey, don't try to sidestep. Who is she and what has she done?"

Star Trek wasn't the only place where resistance was futile; with Izzy the adage was especially true. "The woman I defended in the wrongful-death suit. I told you we won." She hesitated, trying to find a delicate way to explain that they'd had sex. "Well, afterward—"

"You slept with her, okay, go on. I swear, girl, sometimes I wonder which one of us is the old lady."

"Yes, we spent the night together. The next morning the only thing on her pillow was a note saying she'd had a great time and to lock the door on my way out. We haven't had any contact since." The contents of the note still stung each time she recalled them.

"Translation…you haven't called her, right?"

Regan stared at her grandmother like she hadn't heard a thing she said. "Of course I haven't called. I told you she brushed me off like the rest of her one-night stands. If she wants to talk to me, she knows where to find me."

Izzy rocked back and forth in her chair and appeared to be surveying the garden before she spoke again. "So the problem is, you want her to call and she hasn't. And you won't call her because you've never been any good at asserting yourself with women. Did I understand you?"

Regan began a feeble protest but recognized that she'd already lost that argument. Izzy had boiled the situation down to exactly the basic elements. Regan *did* want Syd to call. She *was* hurt that there hadn't been any contact since they had sex. And she hadn't contacted Syd first because she *was* scared of being rejected again. Even after deciding to seize the moment last night, she'd allowed her doubts to resurface. She should have broken Syd's door down, or at least asked to accompany Jesse after she closed the bar.

"You obviously care about this woman," Izzy said. "I haven't seen you this fired up since the night you told me about seeing those two carrying on in the restroom."

Regan's pulse kicked up slightly and her skin flushed with heat. The expression on Izzy's face said she'd noticed the reaction.

"Uh-oh."

"Yeah, Gram, I'm afraid so. I can really pick 'em, can't I?"

"Let me tell you about me and Peggy." Izzy's face took on a faraway look reminiscent of memories laced with love and pain. "I loved that woman, probably would've stayed with her forever. She was a hellcat when I met her, though. Chased anything in a skirt. But I saw something else in her and gave her all the freedom she needed."

"But how did you deal with that? I can't handle cheating again."

"I was patient and trusted her. In the end she came back to me."

"So why did you leave her?"

"I didn't, honey. She died in a car accident on her way to see me one night."

Regan's eyes stung with tears as she watched her grandmother's face flinch from trying to contain her sorrow. She took Izzy's hands in hers, brought them to her lips, and kissed them tenderly. "I'm so sorry, Gram. I didn't know."

Izzy flicked a tear from her cheek. "Of course you didn't. But my point is that you never know how much time you'll have with someone."

Her last statement struck home with Regan. How would she have felt if Syd had been killed? A pain too deep to name rose in the center of her chest. "She was hurt on her job last night. I was afraid that she might—" She couldn't make herself say it.

An emotion flickered across her grandmother's face, almost like recognition or a sudden awareness of something unspoken. "I know trust isn't one of your strong points, and with good reason. But if you want to trust this woman, you have to let her know that you accept her for who she is right now. Trust has to go both ways. Hold on to your pain and fear and that's all you'll have left someday. Why don't you give her and yourself a chance? If you don't, you'll always regret it."

Izzy was right. But Regan didn't know if she could learn to trust a woman who couldn't make a commitment to another person. Was the risk really worth it? There was only one way to find out.

She and Izzy spent two more hours talking, eating donuts, and preparing for the big costume birthday party that night. When she started to leave, Izzy kissed her on each cheek and stared into her eyes. "Honey, don't let this one get away. She's lit you up like a Roman candle."

"But you don't even know her, Gram. How can you say that?"

"Just call it an old woman's hunch. Besides I know my granddaughter. You're all twitchy. I'd say that's a first for you. Am I wrong?"

Regan fanned the blush that burned her cheeks. "I have no idea what you mean." She hugged her again. "Sometimes you're entirely too observant, Isadora Pearce."

"I know, but you love me anyway." Izzy grinned. "Come by about four and help me get back into my costume."

❖

When Syd stretched to relieve the cramps in her legs, the stitches in her left side reminded her why she was curled up on her sofa in the fetal position. Last night had been a nightmare and a blessing. Her body ached and throbbed from the physical challenges of the evening, and her eyes were puffy and unfocused from the emotional purging. In spite of it all, she felt surprisingly calm and alert.

She rose carefully from the sofa and walked out onto the balcony overlooking downtown. The domestic call, the encounter with Jason, and her subsequent injury replayed slowly in her mind. She remembered in perfect detail everything that happened and felt a rush of pride at how she'd handled the situation. Ever since the Lee Nartey shooting, she'd been uncertain that she could face another lethal-force incident and make the right decision. Her confidence had been shattered. But last night she'd trusted her instincts and utilized empathy instead of a weapon. It was the first time she'd trusted her feelings since the shooting, and the result was exhilarating.

Intuition had guided her throughout her career, but killing another person had destroyed her belief in her own instincts. Today things seemed to have shifted. She wasn't sure she could ever reconcile her personal beliefs with taking a life, but she felt closer to forgiving herself for what she had done. Maybe her crisis of conscience had passed.

She would probably still have to make adjustments, but she was more confident that she had a future in the job she loved. Jason's gratitude for being removed from an abusive home brought another smile to her lips. She wanted to share her experience with someone older and wiser who could help her put it all in context.

It was time to visit Izzy Pearce.

They'd met when Syd started volunteering in the assisted-living facility two years earlier. Izzy had a knack for seeing right to the meat of things, and Syd had missed a few of their regular visits since the shooting. She simply hadn't been able to face the thought-provoking, grandmotherly questions Izzy could ask. The answers would have been too painful, and she wasn't ready to make the tough decisions they would require.

After a cup of coffee, Syd picked up the phone. She had an apology planned, but Izzy didn't give her a chance.

Brushing aside Syd's excuses, Izzy said, "What are you doing later?"

"Nothing. I thought I could swing by."

"Good. I could use your help. Can you come this afternoon around four?"

"Sure. No problem."

"Do you think I look like Joan Jett?"

"What?" Syd felt a wave of sadness. Izzy had always seemed as sharp as a woman half her age, but perhaps she was slipping.

"I'll explain later," she said. "What's happening for you?"

"I got shot," Syd said. "No big deal. How about you?"

"I finally took your advice and told my granddaughter about Peggy."

"How did that go?"

"She coped. But once you're over sixty, no one thinks you understand passion."

Syd often wondered why relatives sent loved ones to live with strangers. If Izzy were her grandmother, she'd be living with her. Who wouldn't want such a bright, engaging woman close to them for as long as possible? She'd avoided discussing Izzy's family situation in case it was painful. She knew the granddaughter was important to her, and Izzy had been thrilled, a year earlier, when the young woman got a job in the area and moved here.

"Well, she'll relax once she's had time to think about it. You and your granddaughter seem close."

"Very. And it's not as though she's never heard of lesbians. She moved in with me after she finished high school and stayed until she met her girlfriend. They broke up last year."

"You never told me your granddaughter was gay. I've never even seen a picture of her."

"Oh, you haven't? Must've slipped my mind. So, tell me how you are really. Something seems different about you. Have you started letting go of those ghosts at last?"

That was exactly why Syd loved this little Irish lady so much. She exuded the perfect mixture of kindness and concern while getting straight to the point. "Actually, I think I have." She recapped last night's call, how she handled it, and her breakthrough afterward. "I think that helped with my confidence. Being able to make another choice, a better choice, and save someone's life sort of gave me permission to forgive myself for the other time. Does that make sense?"

"Of course it does. I'm so glad for you." Izzy's voice softened. "And there's more, isn't there?"

Syd wondered at Izzy's ability to see things in her that others missed. People who could do that were either blessed or cursed. Her thoughts strayed to Regan, another woman gifted with intuition. Several times during the trial preparations, she'd picked up on thoughts and feelings that Syd couldn't or wouldn't express.

Syd's sigh was a blend of resignation and hurt. She'd half-expected Regan to show up at the hospital or at the apartment. Maybe she hadn't heard the news. "You're right, as usual, my friend. There is something else. Last night I was thinking about how I've lived my life the past nine months, running from everything, hopping from bed to bed, hurting good people, pretty selfish, actually."

"We all do the best we can at the time, Syd. We use all types of defense mechanisms to help us through painful situations. And then we have breakdowns that always precede breakthroughs and start to create a different future for ourselves. That's just how life works. It's about change and having the faith to move forward no matter how scary it is."

"I'm just wondering how I can do that…move forward without dragging the past along with me," Syd admitted.

"Are you talking about making a fresh start?" Izzy asked.

"In a way." Syd hadn't thought about it in exactly those terms. She tried to explain. "I think people have an impression of me, when all they've seen is the side I've been showing…my worst side. I'm not sure how to get them to take a second look."

"People—?"

"At work," Syd said vaguely. "And…friends."

"Who is she?"

No beating around the bush, where Izzy was concerned. Syd started to protest, avoid, and deny, her usual responses to being found out, but diversions were ineffective. And for the first time in months she wanted to be open and honest. "The city attorney who handled my case."

"The one who didn't know what she was doing?"

Syd cringed. "I was upset when I phoned you that day. She was amazing. But I'm pretty sure she hates my guts. I've behaved badly."

"What do you like about her?" Izzy sounded enthralled, as always when romance was concerned.

"She's very sensitive and nurturing, majorly sexy, intelligent, assertive, and way too empathic. At times she seems to understand me even when I'm not sure I do."

"Did you get involved with her?"

"We slept together once and I left afterward without saying good-bye. I haven't had the nerve to call." The callousness of her departure hit Syd again. How could she have done that when she knew what

Regan had endured over her ex-partner's betrayal? Things like that left scars, and she'd just yanked the scab off without regard for Regan's feelings. The cruelty of her actions blazed through her like a scourge and she shivered in disbelief.

"Do you want to see her again?" Izzy asked.

"Yes, and I'd just decided I would sleep with her one more time when this happened." Izzy was silent for so long Syd asked, "Are you still there?"

"I was just thinking. Why do you want to sleep with her again… just once?"

"I felt a connection to her." Syd covered her heart with her hand. "It wasn't like anything I've ever experienced. It was amazing, but I think the circumstances had a lot to do with it."

"You hope it might be more…ordinary, next time?"

Was that really what she hoped for—a dulling of the power Regan exerted, an encounter that would break her hold? "It doesn't matter now, anyway. I changed my mind. She's already been hurt pretty badly and I don't have anything to offer her…anything she wants."

"How can you be sure about that?" Izzy asked. "I think you should ask her."

"I wish it was that simple, Izzy."

"It just might be. Call her."

"I'll think about it," Syd said.

The promise wasn't an idle one. She and Regan had some unfinished business. Syd wasn't looking forward to the conversation they needed to have, but she decided her discomfort was a good thing. Doing something different wasn't going to feel easy.

Syd had just showered and dressed for her visit when her three o'clock appointment arrived. She took a deep breath and let Gil Brady in. His phone call an hour earlier had been an unexpected shock. So was his appearance. His chiseled features and military haircut that usually gave him an attractive outdoors look today appeared strained and unkempt.

Syd tried not to show her anxiety. "Gil. It's good to see you."

He looked her up and down several times before his gaze settled on her midsection and the lumpy bandage under her fitted shirt. "How's it feeling?"

"Not bad." She struggled not to blurt out her apologies for having sex with his wife but decided it best to let Gil set his own pace. He had probably refined exactly what he wanted to say down to the smallest number of words. "You want to sit down? Something to drink?"

"No, this won't take long." The timbre of his voice was deeper and more strained than Syd remembered, making his Southern drawl sound almost like a growl. But considering what he'd been through, she could appreciate the need to growl. He shoved his hands into the pockets of his jeans, and Syd wondered if it was nerves or an attempt to keep from doing her bodily harm. "That shit with my wife was fucked up."

"I know." Syd wanted him to understand how important his friendship had become to her and that she'd never do anything to hurt him intentionally. She also wanted to tell him how confused and scared she'd been during that time of her life and that Priscilla helped her. But right now that didn't seem appropriate. "Gil, I—"

"Let me finish. We talked and I know you were going through a bad time. So was Priscilla. Killing screws people up. That don't make what you did right, but at least you were able to help each other." Gil moved to the center of the room while he talked. "She told me you didn't know she was married. Is that true?"

"Yes." Relief made her sound breathless. "I didn't even know her real name. I'd *never* get involved with a married woman, especially not a cop's wife. And certainly not yours. We were friends, Gil. I respect you."

He studied her for a few seconds. She'd seen the same intent stare many times when he was evaluating the statements of suspects. "I believe you. I'm just not sure we can be friends right now. Priscilla and I are trying to work things out. She still loves me and I'm glad she told me the truth."

"Me, too. Gil, I'm sorry."

"You didn't know." Pulling his hands out of his pockets, he walked toward the exit. As he opened the door he turned back to Syd. "I didn't tell anybody about this except Sarge. He must've blabbed it to everybody else. I sure didn't want it all over the PD. But I told the squad at the hospital last night to stay out of my business and to leave you alone. It's a private matter."

"Thanks, Gil."

"Be seeing you. Take care of that side and stop getting into gunfights." With that he softly closed the door behind him.

A wave of sadness mingled with hope swept through Syd's body. She felt like a kid watching her sandcastle being washed out to sea by the current: sad to see it go but hopeful that the fresh ground left behind would be more stable for building something new and better. If she was very lucky, the tide would eventually bring some of those original grains of sand back into her life and she, Gil, and Priscilla could be friends again.

CHAPTER SEVENTEEN

"Will you hold still, Izzy? I can't apply raccoon-eye mascara when you're talking and squirming all over the place."

Syd had shown up at the appointed hour to help Izzy prepare for her part as Joan Jett in the residents-only birthday party. She still didn't understand why this particular character. Most of the people who lived here had no idea who Joan Jett was, much less about her connections to the lesbian community. As far as she could see, Izzy's plan for shock value would go as limp as some of these men's…well that was too vivid an analogy.

She was just about to add the final touch around Izzy's left eye when the room door opened and a familiar voice behind her said, "Sorry I'm late, Gram," and Regan Desanto walked in.

"Oh, shit." The mascara applicator slid from Syd's hand and down Izzy's cheek, leaving a thick black streak.

Regan stood frozen, with her proverbial deer-in-the-headlights stare aimed directly at Syd. "What are you doing here?"

Syd was immediately drawn to the piercing blue of Regan's eyes and her body prickled as they caressed her. A month of avoidance had done nothing to soothe the gnawing hunger she felt for this woman. Regan looked deliciously casual in black jeans and a turquoise golf shirt with the collar flipped up, but her body language was unmistakably controlled. Her muscles appeared tense, her shoulders square, her posture totally erect as though she was trying to contain strong emotions through sheer willpower and physical limitation.

"Now, Regan, play nice. I believe the two of you have met." Izzy's mischievous grin was all the proof Syd needed that she'd arranged this "coincidence" and was quite proud of herself.

Regan's gaze danced from Syd to Izzy as she tried to connect two disjointed pieces of a puzzle. Her stunned expression slowly changed to a softer, more endearing look as she absorbed the scene in front of her, the two of them standing side by side like co-conspirators in some great plot. "Syd is the costume assistant you mentioned earlier?"

"Yeah, ain't it great? She searched all over the Triad to find my outfit last year."

There was still a hint of confusion in Regan's tone as she asked, "How long have you known each other?"

Izzy put her arm around Syd's neck and planted a kiss on her cheek. "About two years."

Syd felt Regan's gaze as she evaluated this information. The look warmed her and renewed a tingling sensation that had been missing since the last time they touched. She had to keep busy or she'd be mauling Regan right in front of her grandmother.

"It looks like your raccoon headed south in a hurry," she said, laughing gently at the sight of Izzy's running mascara. "Let me fix it."

Regan joined in the laughter as some of the tension lifted. Then she placed her hand on Syd's arm. "How are you feeling today?"

The sparks of attraction that shot up Syd's arm and weakened her knees made her forget last night's incident and its aftermath. "Huh?" Great. She was rendered monosyllabic.

"Your side, the injury?"

"Oh, it's fine, a flesh wound really. It was just my luck, again, that my vest was useless." Regan's look told her that she didn't understand. "Our flack jackets are basically two panels, front and back, no sides. This is the third time I've been injured in an area not protected."

"The third time?"

"Yeah. My abdomen and sides look like I've been used as the target dummy for a weapons course."

"What happened?" Regan asked, then remembered the last time she'd asked Syd to recount such an incident. "If you don't mind saying."

She listened in silence as Syd recounted the call that resulted in her injury and how she'd rescued a young man from an abusive home environment. Regan sniffed and coughed to conceal her tears until it became pointless and then let them fall freely. As Syd talked, Regan sensed a change in her. Something had shifted as a result of her experience, but she couldn't put her finger on what.

Izzy finished lacing up her black combat boots and said, "Honey, maybe you need to look for another line of work." She executed a slow turn, and asked, "Well?"

"You rock," Syd said.

Regan wiped her eyes and nodded. "To die for."

Izzy gave them each a parting hug. "Sorry you girls can't join me, but I'm sure you'll find something to keep yourselves busy. Besides, I might have company later and you need to be gone. Love you both."

She winked and left, with Syd and Regan yelling after her in unison, "TMI."

The small room seemed terribly quiet and entirely too intimate once the door swung shut. Regan looked at Syd and could've sworn the air around her crackled with sexual energy. She'd never wanted so desperately to kiss a woman and ravish her body as she did at that moment. Syd's emerald green eyes bored a path deep into her soul, igniting the yearning she'd fought hard to extinguish. Watching Syd with Izzy had only confirmed the tenderness and compassion Regan knew existed under her bravado. That knowledge unleashed a flood of arousal that rendered her weak. Syd moistened her lips with the tip of her tongue, and before Regan could stop herself, she was within inches of Syd, breathing in her musky fragrance.

"Can we—" Regan narrowly avoided completing the sentence the way she'd intended, with *have sex*, and substituted, "talk?"

"I'd like that because I really want to apologize."

"It's not necessary." Thinking about Syd day after day and being unable to control her urges had taken a toll. Struggling not to fondle her now was like trying to cage the wind, and she saw no reason to do so. If Syd only wanted sex, that was fine. Regan understood and accepted the boundaries. She just needed Syd prone and naked so she could feel the exquisite release that came from complete physical immersion. At a time like this words seemed so wasteful of air better spent on moans, sighs, and heavy breathing.

"I'm sorry…about the note and leaving you that way."

Syd's eyes held a level of sincerity Regan hadn't seen before, but her physical needs were interfering with her mental faculties and she couldn't verbally respond. Instead she took Syd's hands in hers and kissed the underside of her wrists. After each kiss, she trailed her tongue to Syd's palm and licked tiny circles on her skin.

"I need you again."

Surprise sparked in Syd's eyes but quickly blossomed into lust. "Let's go to my place."

As they walked out of Izzy's room and exited the building, Regan asked, "Will your side be okay?"

"You don't think I'm going to let a little thing like a gunshot wound stop me from making love with you, do you?"

"I really hope not." Regan almost exhaled her response after holding her breath in fear that Syd's injury might keep them apart even longer. She noted with interest Syd's reference to their making love instead of having sex. Semantics weren't important at this point as long as the hunger in her body was soon fed. But the words soothed a raw place in her.

The walk to Syd's loft seemed to take forever. Each step Regan took hardened the pulse point between her legs as she watched Syd's tight ass sway in fitted capri pants that caressed the shapeliness of her hips and thighs. She tried to make small talk but mumbled, imagining her face buried in the voluptuous cleavage peeking from Syd's ruffle-necked blouse. She'd never been so body-oriented or so certain of what she had to do.

Tonight she would give Syd what she seemed to want from her lovers, dominance and physical pleasure. And tonight Regan would take something she wanted as well, control and physical pleasure. She'd been suppressed and denied by Martha for so long that she'd forgotten what pleased her until her first night with Syd.

When they finally reached the loft, Syd opened the door and waited for her to enter. The moment they were inside, Regan backed her against the wall with a series of kisses intended to relay her objective. Syd's lips were soft, hot, and joined perfectly with hers, parting just enough to allow her tongue access. She slid into her slowly at first, tenderly exploring the sleek surfaces of her teeth, the ridges in the roof of her mouth, and the grainy texture of her tongue. Syd's fingers twisted into the short hair at the nape of Regan's neck, and she brought their mouths together more forcefully.

Regan's desire swallowed her in a flash of red. Splaying her hands against the wall on either side of Syd, she seared their bodies together with her heat. Her pelvis seemed to thrust and grind of its own accord, and her painfully hard nipples sought the cushiony softness of Syd's ample breasts. She felt like a clumsy teenage boy trying to get off for the first time, humping his girl against the bleachers, ready to squirt his premature load at any second. That was not how she wanted this night to be remembered.

She forced herself to back away from Syd, her mouth and body immediately protesting the separation. It felt as though life was being sucked from her as she withdrew. Syd reached for her, her color high, her lips red and waiting, her eyes liquid pools of desire. Regan offered her hand and led her to the sleeping area.

The room looked the same with its king-sized bed and bare windows with the city skyline as embellishment. Ambient light from the street below softly tinted the sheets. But this time Regan would not be offering herself like a dutiful lover. This time she would unbridle herself the way Syd seemed to, liberating her most primal physical urges. She would enjoy Syd as a purely sexual being without the usual voices in her head incessantly whispering of emotion.

Regan had never tried to separate her feelings from the sex act. This was different. Every move had to be intentional, every touch orchestrated to heighten Syd's arousal while governing her own. Her voice would be the first thing to betray her so she struggled to sound calm and controlled. "Take your clothes off."

Syd hesitated, her expression uncertain. The request was obviously not what she expected, but she complied, slowly unbuttoning her blouse and letting it fall from her shoulders. The white bra that cupped her generous breasts and the white palm-sized bandage on her left side clashed with her tanned skin. Regan flinched. She couldn't bear to think about the gaping invasion of her tender flesh. The urge to offer comfort briefly overtook her desire, and then she remembered her purpose and redirected. Stepping behind Syd, she released the hooks of her bra and tossed it aside.

"Touch your breasts for me." Regan knew she had to limit contact with Syd initially or she'd lose control. Already her body hummed and strained for release.

When Syd grabbed her breasts, her ass bucked into Regan's pelvis. She pressed back harder, gyrating her hips and groaning with pleasure. "Oh, God, Regan. I need your hands on me."

Regan's legs wobbled as blood rushed to her crotch, bringing with it the pain of restraint. She placed her hands on Syd's hips and guided them roughly against her until she was on the verge of climax. Then she disengaged from the too-enticing ass and ran a calming hand between her legs. "Keep rubbing your breasts," she panted over Syd's shoulder.

Syd tried to reach for her hand. She seemed confused and somewhat hesitant to comply. "But I'd like you to do this."

Her reluctance seemed out of character. Her performance in the restroom was all about being dominated and possessed, and Regan was giving her what she wanted but not allowing her to direct the encounter. She could easily fall to her knees like any other of Syd's lap girls and give her exactly what she was begging for, a top she could control, but then Syd would see her need, her weakness. Tonight she would be all about sex.

"Just do it." She put more authority in her voice than she intended, but stifled the urge to add a softer comment.

Stepping around Syd and facing her just beyond arm's length, she watched her palm the weight of her breasts and stroke her nipples with her thumbs. The taut extensions of flesh dimpled and puckered, and Regan wanted to suck them into her mouth. But Syd hadn't waited long enough, and when she had, Regan would make her wait longer. She edged her to the bed and instructed her to lie down on her back. Fully clothed, Regan knelt on the bed between her legs. She unzipped Syd's slacks and eased them down with seemingly inadvertent strokes.

Each carefully placed touch propelled Syd's hips to rise as she sought greater contact. "What are you doing to me, Regan?" Her voice was tight with urgency.

Regan was balancing precariously at the edge as well. It took all of her restraint not to answer. She'd had no idea how empowering and exciting sexual dominance could be. No wonder Martha had hoarded it for herself. She trailed her fingers up Syd's tanned legs to the inside of her thighs and stared in amazement as Syd's body opened for her. The evidence of her need glistened on the dark triangle of hair.

"Regan, please touch me."

Regan lowered herself as though she was going to give in to the request. Instead, she blew a light breath across Syd's clit and pulled back. But her withdrawal had not been as swift as she planned. Syd's skin was hot to the touch, begging to be cooled. Her center twitched with suppressed energy, offering itself for the ride, and the scent of her arousal drew Regan closer.

She pushed back from the brink just before she surrendered control. Hoping her fractured breathing wouldn't betray her, she said, "Touch yourself. I want to watch."

"Regan, please, I need to feel you. Come here."

It took every ounce of Regan's restraint not to cave. "Show and tell. What do you want me to do?"

Syd massaged her breasts with one hand as the other glided over the dip of abdomen to her pubic mound. She slid a finger between the moist folds of skin. "I want you to feel this. How hot and wet I am for you." Her fingers pulled long, slow motions between her legs, and each time she rose to meet them. "I want to feel you inside me. I want to look down and see you tonguing my clit. I want to watch you make me come."

As Syd fingered herself, thrashing and moaning from her own ministrations, Regan's body and mind were at war. She wanted to give Syd the pleasure she obviously needed and at the same time satisfy the lustful beast that coiled inside her. But she also wanted to tenderly explore this exquisite body without having to detach herself. She wanted to liberate her emotional desires for this woman, even though she knew the feelings threatened to render her powerless. She wondered why she kept denying herself for the sake of other women. With Martha she'd quashed her sexual needs for the emotional good of the relationship, or so she thought. Now she was smothering her feelings to indulge Syd's need for gratuitous sex. She'd thought she was doing something different, but she was simply on the flip side of the same old coin. As much as she wanted to believe she could compartmentalize, to do so was a rejection of her very nature.

Syd's movements had become more animated and her breathing more labored. Her entire body shifted on the bed into a shaft of moonlight. Regan froze, her eyes fixed on Syd's right side and upper abdomen. Etched across her copper-toned skin were two gnarly white scars, uneven and frighteningly misplaced on such a smooth, feminine surface. She stretched out her hand and slid it delicately over the vile invasions of perfection. "Do they hurt?"

Syd stilled and rose on her elbows, looking into Regan's eyes. "Not anymore."

"What happened?" Regan had to know. How had she not seen these before? But she remembered that Syd had remained clothed their first night together, at her request. Her insides bristled with outrage that any human being could inflict such harm on another. She felt a helpless fury that any situation could made a person believe such action was justified.

"Domestic calls. Those two were knives. Missed the vest again, got me." She leaned forward and cupped Regan's face. "Thank you for caring, but do we *have* to talk about this just now? In case you hadn't noticed, I'm in a pretty bad way here."

The feelings that Regan had tried so desperately to mask all evening came flooding to the surface. She wanted nothing more than to comfort, nurture, and protect this gorgeous creature, to show her that life was more than all the horror she saw daily. She wanted to express how proud she was of her professionally and of the choices she'd made. But more importantly, she longed to tell Syd that she cared for her and accepted her just the way she was. Syd's scars coupled with something in her eyes stabbed at Regan's heart and brought home the fragility of life and the absurdity of pretense and pride.

She eased Syd back on the bed and stretched her body lengthwise beside her, wedging her still-clothed leg between Syd's hot thighs. Unable to contain her desire to please Syd any longer, to demonstrate with her body what she seemed incapable of saying aloud, she allowed her emotions to engage. Cupping Syd's butt to bring her closer, she kissed the side of her neck, her ears, her cheek.

"Aren't you going to get undressed?" Syd's mumbled words seemed an afterthought to the undulating movements already starting on Regan's leg.

"Later." Finally allowing herself permission, Regan kissed those full waiting lips like she and Syd were true lovers too long parted. Her thighs burned and her center clenched spasmodically with the urge for release. She distanced her crotch from Syd's thigh, denying herself direct contact. Stalling this rush would not last much longer.

She buried her face between Syd's supple breasts, licking her way around the base. She savored each one like a scoop of ice cream with a rock-candy topping, delighting in the textural changes against her tongue, from yielding flesh to rigid tissue. Syd's moans as she writhed beneath Regan's hands and mouth were almost enough to send her over the edge, and she wanted desperately to feel her skin against Syd's. But she knew the second they were naked together, she would come spontaneously.

Sliding her hand between them and into the moisture that bathed Syd's sex, she said, "You are so wet." She separated the tender labia and teased Syd's erect clit with just enough pressure to elicit a responsive groan.

"For God's sake, Regan, I can't take much more."

"Yes, you can." Regan eased down the supple body, kissing and nipping moist tender skin as she descended, careful to avoid the fresh bandage that clung to her left side. She tongued her way past Syd's navel to her thighs and rested her face on the bedclothes between them.

Syd's neatly trimmed bush was awash with her fragrant juices. Regan allowed herself a few seconds of appreciation before permitting contact. Controlling her own orgasm at this stage would be extremely difficult. Drawing a shaky breath, she licked the sides of Syd's thighs and kissed a path to her sex, tending the swollen lips surrounding her clit. Syd rewarded her efforts with forward thrusts and sharp cries for more. Regan scooted lower and placed a hand between her own legs to stay the gathering sensations. Squeezing fabric and flesh together, she concentrated on Syd, letting her tongue dart back and forth across Syd's rigid pleasure point.

With each stroke they both seemed to tumble closer to the edge. Regan's clit throbbed painfully in her grip and moisture soaked her jeans as she tried to halt her pending orgasm. Syd clutched Regan's hair in her fists and held her firmly in place as she rode her tongue toward climax. Her breathing mingled with indecipherable phrases and finally exploded into words.

"Regan, I'm coming, Regan."

Regan greedily consumed the combination of sweet and salt that flowed from Syd's climaxing body, each lick and suck bringing her closer to her own end. She wanted to remember forever the telltales of Sydney Cabot's body as she came screaming *her* name. It would take a lifetime to expel the knowledge of Syd's reactions to *her* touch: breasts pliant in her hands, nipples rigid from her sucking, pelvis rising to meet the thrust of her tongue and crashing at its loss. Regan drew back to watch the expressions on Syd's face evolve from a concentrated near frown to anticipation, to joy, and finally that look of never-ending hunger in her eyes as she climaxed. Regan memorized every nuance, certain that no woman would ever scream her name so perfectly in the throes of orgasm.

Syd's gaze held hers and seemed to claw its way inside, searching for answers to the responses of her body. As Syd continued to buck and quiver beneath her, Regan gave herself permission to finally let go. She released the constricting grasp on her distended tissue and allowed it to purge. The tightly coiled bundle of nerves detonated instantly, and Regan bit her tongue to stop a scream that threatened to alert the neighborhood of their activities. Her body jerked and shuddered with a series of explosions so profound she thought they would alter her forever. Gasping, almost passing out, she collapsed between Syd's legs.

Regan couldn't move or speak. Time passed as the aftershocks faded and her heart rate slowed. She didn't open her eyes or stretch out her hand. At that moment, more than anything, she wanted to hug Syd and wallow in the physical connection they shared. She wanted to tell her how she felt and to describe in explicit detail everything she planned to do to her body next. But a strange panic gripped her, bringing with it all her doubts and fears. The voices in her head insisted that Sydney Cabot didn't do *next*. It was an anomaly that they'd slept together twice. The chance of a third time was practically nonexistent. Syd had apologized for that note and for her behavior, but she hadn't said anything about wanting a future. She wasn't sorry about the basis of their encounter, only the manner in which she ended it. Normally, Regan decided, she was better at hiding her indifference.

Picturing a gentler, more charming Syd offering a tender farewell instead of a callous brush-off, Regan knew she had to get out of this place or she would say things that should not be said. The power of Syd's sexual sorcery was strong and she had to escape.

She allowed herself a few more minutes of recovery, for her body to cool and her head to clear, then slid off the side of the bed and stood, straightening her sticky, wrinkled clothes.

"Not so fast," Syd objected in a soft, playful tone, as though she thought Regan was going to the bathroom or planning to undress properly and rejoin her. More seriously, she asked, "Please. Will you hold me?"

Regan avoided her irresistible stare. "I've got to go."

"Go?" Syd's voice rose with astonishment. "I don't understand." She seemed to struggle for something else to say. "Regan? What's wrong?"

Regan couldn't bear the plea in her voice. Before she lost her nerve and copped to every mushy, white-picket-fence domestic thought in her head, she had to get out of this apartment.

"I need to clear my head," she said as gently as she could.

"No...I mean, please...stay here." Syd elbowed herself up. "We can stop now and just...sit."

Regan imagined she could hear the wheels in Syd's head turning as she tried to figure out this bizarre turn of events. She paused, thinking, *Give me one good reason to stay.*

Syd was silent, her confusion obvious.

Regan started walking.

"Wait." Syd's voice summoned her.

Regan turned around a few feet from the door. Syd scrambled off the bed and walked toward her naked, as dangerous and beautiful as any predator. Her hungry stare held Regan in suspense, draining her will. She took a step back, knowing if she didn't keep her distance she would step into the arms Syd lifted slightly.

"Tell me what you want from me." Regan let the words flutter out.

"Stay and sleep with me." The soft invitation was edged with uncertainty. As though embarrassed by a weak moment, Syd immediately offered a sexy, taunting smile. "I'm not done with you yet."

"That's what I thought." Regan opened the door.

She could sense Syd's struggle for comprehension as she walked out, but this time she didn't look back. Even as she drove away she knew Syd was at her window, watching as she left her.

CHAPTER EIGHTEEN

S yd wrestled with sleep the remainder of the night. She tried to hold on to the sensations she'd experienced while Regan orchestrated her orgasm, the physical and emotional arousal that had saturated her like the rainy season. But a loneliness seemed to permeate her entire being as she thought about how much she'd really wanted Regan to stay. Syd ached for her physically and with a longing in her chest that felt clumsy and undefined.

At first light, she pulled a pair of sweats over a body still tender from Regan's touch and headed to her favorite place to think, the balcony's parapet. She'd just begun to recognize and cope with the residual emotions of the fatal shooting and subsequent trial. It felt like she'd opened the floodgates and every feeling she'd ever suppressed or denied had tumbled out. Fear, guilt, questions of self-worth, and morality plagued her.

Teetering along the low wall, she considered her life and how the domestic call rotated everything into a new shape, like looking through a kaleidoscope. Now, finally, some of the things the department's therapist had said began to make sense. Her guilt and her extreme behaviors were all a normal part of adjustment to killing another person. These were the reactions of a *normal* person to such a heinous task. Her coping mechanisms were temporary and need not be a permanent part of her life.

But where did Regan fit in? Syd tried to sort through the quagmire of her feelings and figure out what was going on between them. Her emotions had been in a vegetative state for so long, opening up felt like a bombardment. She knew the minute she saw Regan in Izzy's doorway that they would have sex. Perhaps it was the look Regan gave her or the sizzle that shot through her body when Regan touched her arm and asked about her injury in that soft, protective tone of hers.

Syd had intended to maintain control of the situation, not like their first encounter when she'd come at the first touch and cried like a woman in love. She'd been needy that night, and Regan's submission to her every desire, her total surrender and emotional exposure had allowed Syd to be vulnerable and to reclaim a part of herself that had seemed lost.

She was shocked by that, Syd recognized in retrospect, and afraid to admit that she'd felt great tenderness for Regan. Perhaps that was why she had walked away with such determination the next day even when something in her yearned to stay.

Last night, she'd planned to do things differently, to be more honest. She hadn't expected the total switch Regan had in mind, and was even annoyed at first when Regan managed the situation so completely. Yet being stripped of her usual mistress-in-charge persona and denied control of anything, including her own orgasm, had turned her on more than she could've imagined. At the same time she had needed more.

Syd was amazed by Regan's ability to deduce that and to show her what she was missing. Last night she'd given Syd exactly what she'd claimed she wanted, sex without sentimental complications. Nothing more. Regan had withheld the emotion that connected them the first time. Syd was still shocked at how that had felt. Being sexually joined to Regan again, but without the emotional component, was not only unacceptable, it was cruel. The sense of separation from Regan during those intimate moments showed her how much she needed the emotions missing from her dalliances.

Syd thought about the gap she hadn't been able to bridge, between the restrictions on her heart and the freedom with which she gave herself physically. Her passions over the past year had all been suspect. They had served as bandages to cover a wound. Sex was easy, but the giving of her heart had always been a separate issue. She'd questioned that intangible connection called intimacy and the passionate need to translate it into lovemaking. Now she found herself reevaluating the beliefs she'd taken for granted and the possibilities she'd rejected as unattainable. Intimacy, she decided, could be quite seductive, if her encounters with Regan were any indication.

The more she was with her, the more she wanted to be and the more she wanted to know about her: her likes, her favorite foods, how she looked completely nude, what spots on her body drove her wild when touched, what scared her, what could make her smile, and mostly what opened her heart and helped her feel safe. Everything about Regan contributed to a growing attraction that Syd couldn't control and increasingly didn't want to. If she gathered this information, she would start to share herself in return and the centurions guarding her heart would no longer be needed.

What did that mean exactly? *Am I in love with her?*

The thought caused Syd to wobble precariously on the wall, dizzy with the possibility. She quickly righted herself and hopped back down to the balcony floor. Just because a woman had invited her emotional and sexual feelings to coexist happily didn't mean she was in love with her.

Normally the very idea would have driven her out the door and straight to the Cop Out, convinced she was losing her mind. But Syd sank into a chair, letting the scary words skitter around in her mind. The truth of the matter was that she did care for Regan and was no longer willing to deny that fact. She didn't know if that caring rose to the level of love or was simply gratitude and newly freed emotions testing their wings. She wished Regan had stayed so she could find out.

Syd supposed it was about time she got a dose of her own medicine, but it hurt that Regan had just *fucked* her and left. She'd never had a problem with the idea of being used for sex, and using other women, but it sucked that Regan had decided to play by the same rules. Syd wasn't even sure if Regan got off. Why had she gone in such a hurry? Had Syd disappointed her in some all-important way?

She mashed a cushion under her head and lay back, finally noticing the deepening throb in her side. The pain gathered and Syd let it sweep her away, carrying her to a calmer place where she knew what to do. She could make the ache stop any time she wanted. Just take a pill. It wasn't so easy to remedy the pain in her heart. Syd smiled at the thought. At least she could feel it, and at least she knew its cause.

Regan Desanto.

The only question that remained was what to do about her.

❖

"Don't get up," Regan said, joining her grandmother by the window. The smell of freshly brewed coffee filled the small space. Izzy held a cup between both hands. "How was the birthday party?"

"Great, just great. Not a single damn soul knew I was Joan Jett, though. But it was a fun time. You know I love to party. How about you?"

"Me?"

"Yeah, you. Let me tell you about your evening." She paused, and when Regan didn't object she said, "You went home with Syd, had sex, and left. You've been walking around since probably about midnight or later and now you're here. How's that?"

"Jeez, are you psychic or just having me tailed? That's spooky."

"No, I recognize slept-in clothes when I see them and I'm old. That helps too." She subjected Regan to a lengthy visual inspection, then said, "Grab yourself a Diet Coke from the fridge, honey. It looks like you could use one."

They sat in silence for a while. Regan sipped her Diet Coke and swiped at beads of condensation as they formed on the can. She reviewed the night's events once more in her mind, trying to decide how much or how little she could explain. She'd left Syd's bed aching like she hadn't been satisfied in years. Hours of walking had done little to wear off the arousal that coursed through her. Each step only seemed to rekindle the passion Sydney Cabot sparked. What was there about this woman that drove her to such levels of physical distraction?

The question brought her to the root of the issue. "Gram, I think I'm in love with Syd." Izzy didn't respond immediately, as if she sensed there was more. "And it scares me to death."

Regan released a huge sigh and felt lighter for having stated her greatest fear out loud. Her eyes filled with tears and she fought to contain them. Izzy placed her coffee cup on the side table and moved the rocker so her knees were touching Regan's. She placed a hand on Regan's knee.

"Have you told her?"

What would've happened if she had? That one was easy. She was so emotionally raw and sexually psyched that if she'd stayed last night she would've blurted her feelings to Syd. And the end result would've been the same. Syd's parting words had said it all. She was only interested in the here and now. Sexual gratification, on her terms. They were terms Regan knew she could never accept.

She'd tried for sex—just sex—with Syd, but when she saw Syd's injuries her feelings rushed to the surface and her sexual tryst turned into lovemaking. Regan knew then that she would always want the surrender that came only with trust and true intimacy. She no longer wanted to pretend or hide her feelings. When had this happened? One minute she was floating blindly through her mundane life as a city attorney, comfortable in a relationship that had never met her needs; the next she was riding the razor-sharp edge of desire with a woman destined to break her heart. By then it was already too late for self-recrimination or turning back. She was firmly in the clutches of a force so pervasive that separation would surely be fatal.

Regan stared into eyes that reflected the blue intensity of her own and tried to explain. "I don't think she feels the same way."

"You won't know until you ask."

"I can't." Regan remembered the look on Syd's face when she started to leave, her confusion and struggle to say the right words and at the same time her determination to avoid committing herself. "We want different things."

"Oh, Regan. Life isn't about guarantees or certainties. It's full of mystery and ambiguity. Even when you think you know something, you often don't. That's what makes life worth living, the not-knowing. And that's hard for you, especially after Martha, but you have to give it another try. You owe it to yourself."

Regan smiled at her grandmother's wisdom. She had a way of getting to the root of the situation. But did she have the courage to face her fears and Syd's possible rejection? Her mind was reluctant, her body was already there.

Memories of last night triggered another wave of longing. The vivid recollection of their sex clung to the air in her nostrils like a whisper. She recalled images of Syd's body, beautiful and writhing with desire. Those images, like the flesh, were like grappling hooks in her brain, snagging and ripping through her feelings.

Regan wouldn't deny the truth. She had fallen hard for Syd. The passion she'd felt for her since their first night together never seemed to diminish or disappear, only to spark and spread. It was risky to care about someone with Syd's reputation and colorful past, but she'd seen her vulnerability and it was compelling. If given the chance of a relationship with Syd, she would take it. Syd was etched into her heart just as clearly as those knife and gunshot wounds were etched on Syd's body. And, like scars, the touches of some women never completely faded. Sydney Cabot was one of those women.

CHAPTER NINETEEN

Going to the same restaurant where she'd seen Regan with the platinum blonde gave Syd the heebie-jeebies. It had taken too long to choose her simple outfit of red blouse and beige cropped pants, and now she was running late. That would not make a good impression on a first date, if this could be considered a date. So far, the signs didn't appear to be in her favor for the perfect rendezvous, but she'd take whatever she could get.

She found Regan immediately, at the same table by the window that she'd shared with Blondie. Ugh. When Regan stood to greet her, the sight of her nearly took Syd's breath away. Her closely trimmed blond hair was immaculately roguish, the waves refusing to be tamed and a single curl spiraling down her forehead. She swaggered toward Syd in gray slacks that clung to her willowy frame and rested low on her hips. Her confidence and sexuality oozed from every pore like perspiration on a humid day. A pinstriped button-down shirt hugged her athletic breasts and plunged into the waistband of her pants, something Syd wished to do at that very moment.

As she approached, Regan tugged at an open leather vest that topped her shirt. The tips of her fingers brushed against her braless breasts and Syd almost groaned. "You look delicious."

The look in Regan's eyes showed her appreciation as they swept slowly up and down her body, pausing at her breasts. "I'm so glad you called."

She wrapped Syd in a hug that draped her in warmth and lingered. The flowery scent of jasmine wafted into Syd's nostrils like an aphrodisiac. "Me too."

Smooth, Cabot. You sound like a first-grader.

Regan's smile did nothing to soothe the turmoil that had consumed Syd since she'd made the phone call two days ago. It had taken all day Sunday and most of Monday to muster the courage to reach out, and then Regan put her off another whole day. The wait had been agony.

"I had to see you." *Now you sound desperate.* "I mean there's a lot to talk about, I think." *Stop while you're ahead.* Syd motioned to their table, realizing they were still standing in the center of the restaurant, still within each other's embrace. "Why don't we sit down?"

Regan held her chair as Syd eased into the seat, the coarse tweed upholstery brushing against an already sexually alert, tingling bottom. "I hope this place is okay."

Syd hesitated. "I saw you here with a blonde one night, very attractive. Are you dating her?" As soon as she spoke, she knew she sounded jealous. She was never inquisitive about other people's personal lives, but she realized that in matters concerning Regan Desanto, she wanted to know everything. "I'm sorry. That was out of line and absolutely none of my business."

"It's all right. You can ask me anything."

Regan's blue eyes bored into her without the slightest flicker and Syd knew she was speaking from the heart. It was amazing how much more attuned she was becoming to the feelings of others as she embraced her own. The thought of being so connected to Regan filled Syd with an appetite for something she couldn't name but that she needed as fundamentally as her next breath.

"And to answer your question, no, I'm not dating her. Nancy is a dear friend from college. She wants to hire me for her law firm."

"Good, I mean, not good that she wants to hire you, but good that you're not dating." Syd was saved from further babbling by the appearance of their waiter. "Are you interested in some wine?"

When Regan nodded, Syd made a selection and gave her order, then stared out the window trying to get her nerves and her horniness under control. Being in such close proximity to Regan generated images of climbing on the table and making love to her as the whole restaurant watched. So much for control. She squirmed like a kid on a wooden church pew halfway into a two-hour sermon. Regan looked amused, her eyes sparkling as if she was enjoying Syd's discomfort.

"You're not going to take another job, are you?" Syd asked.

Regan took several seconds too long to reply. "I haven't decided yet."

"Then I guess I'll just have to give you a reason to stay." Syd relaxed. Now that sounded more like her old confident, seductive self. "And I'm sure I can find one."

"I just bet you could, Officer Cabot. Tell me more. I'm intrigued."

"You're teasing me now. Don't you know it's not nice to torture a horny lesbian, especially in a public place? It can lead to unconventional behavior." The minute the statement was out of her mouth, Syd regretted it. Memories of her first encounter with Regan flashed back. The sparkle in Regan's eyes dulled as she seemed to be revisiting the same scenario. "I'm sorry. That was tacky."

"That was our beginning and, yes, it was tacky." There was no hint of judgment in Regan's voice, only the facts.

"Those days are over, trust me."

Regan seemed to consider Syd's comment, to sift through it in her mind like panning for gold, or the truth, which was often equally rare. "What makes you say that?"

"Because the need for that behavior is gone. I don't have to hide from my feelings anymore. And the only reason I'd want to take you in a public place is because I can hardly control myself when I'm around you. I want you that much, all the time."

Syd inhaled deeply, sure that she'd pass out if she didn't. Exposing her emotions was daunting because she had no idea how her admission would be received, but it was also exhilarating. She wanted Regan to know how she felt and to know that she could be trusted.

Regan's neck tinged with pink that crept across her face. She fumbled with the napkin in her lap. "I…don't know what to say, and I'm usually the talker."

"Then let me talk for a while. I've got a lot to say."

The waiter brought their wine, Syd tasted it, and he poured them each a glass. Syd raised hers in a toast. "To truth in advertising and relationships." They clicked glasses as Regan gave her a questioning look. "Because it feels a little bit like I'm selling myself here."

"You don't have to sell yourself to me. And you don't have to say anything you don't want to."

"It's not about want, it's what I *have* to do, for us. If there can ever be an us."

Regan took a tiny sip of wine and settled back into her seat. "Okay. I'm listening."

Neon light from across the street refracted through the window and cast a rainbow of color across Regan's ivory skin as Syd watched, captivated. Colors to represent the many phases and nuances of Regan's personality she had yet to discover. The possibility excited her emotionally and physically. She slid a hand up the inside of her thigh and pressed firmly against the fabric torturing her clit. A charge bolted through her as she realized how easy it would be to make herself come just sitting here looking at Regan. But now was not the time. Tonight was about expressing her feelings verbally, proving to Regan that she was sincere.

Syd summoned all her courage, realizing that this was the most important conversation she'd ever had. She wanted it to be perfect and to relay her feelings exactly. Such proclamations couldn't be rushed.

As if reading her mind, Regan smiled at her and said, "I've got all night. It'll probably take that long for me to finish this wine. I'm really not much of a drinker. So, take your time."

"I don't know how you do that, but I love it. Don't ever stop." She took another hefty breath. "The first night we spent together was amazing. At the time, I thought my reactions to you were about relief and gratitude over the case."

"And now?"

"Now I know it was about *you*, the person, and how incredibly safe, comfortable, and wanted you made me feel." A furrow forming across Regan's forehead made Syd stop. "Did I say something wrong?"

"You make me sound like somebody's mother."

Syd struggled with how to express what she felt. She'd had precious little experience doing that and was obviously botching it big-time. "Not at all. I didn't mean it like that. I've never felt that anyone cared about me that way, just for me."

The worried look lifted from Regan's brow and Syd tried again. "You saw the worst of me and weren't afraid. And God, do you turn me on. Couldn't you see that? I came almost as soon as I touched you that first time. It's like flipping a light switch whenever you enter a room. I'm on."

"That kind of talk can turn a girl's head, Cabot." Regan smiled and a mischievous glint twinkled in her eyes.

Syd had finally found the right words. If she could only keep that smile on Regan's face forever, she'd be happy. "While I'm on a roll I might as well go for it. I'm sorry again for leaving you alone in my loft with a kiss-off note. Not one of my finer moments."

"Why did you?"

Syd had a feeling Regan already knew the answer to her question. She seemed to understand Syd that well. But she needed to hear the words from her. "I was afraid. I woke up that morning beside you and never wanted to leave. That was a first for me and I didn't know how to handle it, so I ran."

"Are you saying it wasn't just about sex?"

Reaching across the table, Syd slid her fingers under Regan's and stroked the top of her hand with her thumb. Syd looked directly into her eyes, sensing that this question held the key to all Regan's concerns. "No, it was awesome but not everything. That night I allowed myself to *feel* for the first time in almost a year. It brought me to tears but it felt good at the same time. You helped me do that by being so open. Can you forgive me for acting like such a coward?"

Regan closed her fingers around Syd's, her eyes never leaving Syd's. "Done."

Syd shivered like tiny goose bumps were marching through her insides. One intense stare from Regan's eyes propelled her into a full-blown fantasy that she couldn't contain. "If you don't stop that, we'll have to skip dinner and go straight for dessert."

"Would that be such a terrible thing?"

"Not at all, but I need to ask a question first."

Over Regan's shoulder Syd spotted a well-dressed woman wobbling toward their table. She had wispy blond hair, the face of a cherub, and the body of a porn star, big tits, slender waist, and childbearing hips. She was the type who could lull a woman into a coma of safety with her eyes and fuck her until her bones turned to dust at the same time. Syd thought she looked vaguely familiar but couldn't make the connection.

The woman came to an unsteady stop beside Regan's chair and just stood, waiting to be acknowledged. The breath from her heavily painted red lips reeked of alcohol. When Regan looked up, her entire face blanched as white as their tablecloth. Her mouth opened but produced no sound. Already Syd didn't like this woman, whoever she was. Then it hit her. *God, no.*

"Well, what have we here? Aren't you going to ask me to sit down, Regan?"

Regan looked from the intruder to Syd, unable or unwilling to speak.

"What about you, Syd?" The woman asked. "May I join you?"

Syd could feel the tension from Regan's body across the table. She wanted to whisk her away from this place before the ax she felt hanging over them fell. Regan's face shifted and contorted as every conceivable emotion brushed across the pristine canvas. Shock followed by fear turned to annoyance, disbelief, and anger.

"You *know* each other?"

Before Syd had a chance to explain that she'd only seen this woman once years ago, if she actually was the woman Syd recalled, the interloper said, "Oh yes, we know each other in the biblical sense. Right, Syd?" With a contemptuous look at Regan, she added, "And I learned just tonight that your new friend here even fucked another officer's wife. Can you believe that?"

Syd sprang from her seat. Who was this vile creature and what dark corner of purgatory did she spring from, spewing all Syd's past transgressions? "Who the hell *are* you and what business of yours is it who I sleep with?"

Regan's skin turned deep red. "You've fucked *this woman*, too?" She spat the question at Syd through clenched teeth.

Syd's mind was spinning violently. Why was Regan's response so disproportionate? She knew Syd's past was littered with women who meant nothing. It was embarrassing to have one of them spoil their romantic dinner, but there was no reason to let the evening turn into a nightmare. They needed to take their discussion somewhere private. She reached for Regan's arm.

"Let's get out of here." As Regan jerked out of her grip, Syd said, "Regan, listen to me. I don't even remember this woman's name. It wasn't important."

Her comment seemed to affect Regan like a glass of cold water. She stepped within inches of Syd's face, eyes locked to hers. "Her name is *Martha*. And it was important to *me*. She's my ex-lover."

"Oh, shit." As Regan exited the restaurant, Syd felt as if she'd been gut punched. "Jesus, Mary, and Joseph."

"Yeah, small world, isn't it? Want to have a drink?" Martha asked.

If Syd were a violent person, she might've done her bodily harm. "You've *got* to be kidding."

She threw some cash down on the table and ran from the restaurant, desperate to find Regan and sort out this huge mess. She was too late. All she could do was watch the taillights of Regan's car as she sped away.

❖

Regan felt like her veins had been slashed open and the very essence of life drained from her. The only thing missing was a deranged scientist to collect her mutilated body and distribute it to the blood-thirsty undead. But that had always been Martha's job: draining her of joy, leaving her empty, and abandoning her. A full year later she'd done it again. What had started off as one of the most beautiful nights of Regan's life ended like a bad horror movie.

Martha and Syd. Kissing. Fondling. Sucking. Fucking and coming, together. The thought scorched her mind and curdled in her stomach. She stopped her car by the side of the road, leaned out the door, and vomited the bitter wine out of her system. It singed a raw path up her throat that only momentarily distracted her from the dark specter of betrayal that clutched her heart again.

God, how she wanted to believe Syd when she'd phoned to ask her on the date. She'd been so candid during that brief call, telling Regan that she wanted them to have a fresh start and get to know each other. That she wanted something different, something meaningful. Regan had even dared to hope that she was part of the change she could sense.

And tonight, Syd was so sincere, so genuinely in touch with her emotions that Regan had started to believe and hope. But the closer she got to Syd, the more skeletons fell out of her seemingly infinite closet. *She'd been fooled again.* When would she learn that no one could be trusted, especially in affairs of the heart?

Her old wounds festered as she drove out of town and for hours beyond. She had no idea where she was when she finally pulled off the shoulder of the winding road at an overlook. A small town blinked and twinkled its light display in the valley below as Regan leaned her head against the steering wheel and wept. No amount of crying would eradicate the vision of Martha and Syd's sweaty body parts entwined in an all-night comefest, and no rationalizations would alter the facts.

She could recite from memory every explicit and covert move in Martha's sexual repertoire. Syd would have been overpowered and perhaps she'd even enjoyed Martha's obsession for physical domination and sexual control. Regan couldn't stop the images of Martha's rough hands clawing Syd's supple skin or her philistine invasions of the feminine hills and valleys of Syd's body. Her stomach lurched again and she sat back against the seat and really looked at the rolling hills surrounding the small town below, at the cup-shaped valley and the glitter of lights like diamonds thrown on the ocean floor. Her emotions started to calm and cool in the presence of such a serene setting. When her life seemed most tumultuous, she often sought refuge in nature and the comfort of miracles too simple or too intricate to be explained. The chaotic perfection of nature helped her understand that some things were purely out of her control. It brought her back to basics.

Now, with that perspective came the realization that many other things *were* hers to command. One of those was her life and how she chose to live it. As Izzy used to say, "The truth is welcome in heaven." Regan dealt with some version of the truth every day practicing law. Now she needed to re-evaluate her truth in the cold, hard light of new information.

Martha was in town and she didn't know why. How had she found out about Regan's interest in Syd? Why did she feel the need to rub Regan's nose in some ancient liaison with Syd and to further expose Syd's affair with yet another woman? Where had she gotten that tidbit? What was her motivation for such an unkind revelation? Was Syd really as genuinely surprised by Martha's appearance as she seemed? Was there a logical, forgivable explanation for this whole fiasco?

Regan forced her emotions aside and came to the only logical conclusion. She needed more information. There were entirely too many questions for which she didn't have answers. She'd allowed Martha to destroy her life once. This time she refused to let it happen quite so easily. Why should she accept Martha's warped, self-serving statements as truth? Syd might not be the most emotionally tuned-in woman she'd ever met, but to Regan's knowledge she'd always been honest. If nothing else, she owed Syd a chance to explain. If not for Syd, then for herself. She couldn't release Syd without a fighting chance. It simply was not possible.

Her disgust with the idea of Syd and Martha together wasn't about her ex-partner. Who Martha slept with, fucked, or loved didn't concern her—as long as that person wasn't Syd. She had no feelings of love, jealousy, betrayal, or anger toward Martha. Any emotional connection she'd had to her ex was severed long ago. But the idea of Martha's or anyone else's hands on Syd's body provoked an entirely different array of emotions worthy of exploration.

She powered up her cell phone and checked messages: seven from Syd desperate to explain and one from Martha. Old business first. Regan started her car.

❖

Martha's suite in the downtown Radisson was indicative of the woman, needlessly extravagant. When she opened the door wearing a negligee, Regan wanted to deck her, on principle alone. Instead, she swept past her outstretched arms and crossed the room to stand at the balcony windows, as far away from her as possible.

"Don't be like that, baby."

"This is not a social call." Regan employed her courtroom voice, determined to remain objective and professional as she gathered the necessary information. "I need a few facts, if you're capable of distinguishing them from the continuous web of deceit you weave." Martha drifted toward her, sheer fabric floating behind her like wings. Her expression was that of a vamp intent on the seduction and consumption of another victim. "Why so hostile?"

Regan sidestepped her advance. "If you ever cared about me, please just answer a few questions. It won't take long." Regan knew it sounded like she was begging and she didn't care. She didn't care what Martha thought of her anymore because she'd do anything to find out what she needed to know.

Martha glared at her. "My God, I should've guessed this sooner. I thought you were coming by to talk about us. You're in love with this girl, aren't you?"

Hearing the words out loud thrilled Regan's heart and quickened her pulse, but hearing them from Martha made her want to slap her. She had no right to make assumptions about her life, especially since she'd tried to destroy it twice. "It's none of your business how I feel. What was that scene about tonight? Why are you here, Martha?"

Regan's question seemed to infuse Martha with fresh confidence. She captured Regan's hand and brought it to her overflowing breasts. "I was hoping for a reconciliation."

"Are you *crazy*?" Regan snatched her hand from the trap and backed away. "It's been a year. You don't love me, probably never did. I don't love you, and I could never trust you again. Do I need to go on?"

The bluntness of her rejection didn't seem to faze Martha at all. "Well, you can't blame a girl for trying." As quickly as she'd turned on the charm, it was gone. She sashayed to the minibar and retrieved a bottle of wine. "Care for a drink?"

"No, Martha, I don't want a drink. I want answers."

She motioned to the sofa, which Regan ignored and took a chair opposite. "No reason we can't be civil about this, is there?"

"If you answer my questions honestly, I'll be civil. Where did you hear about me and Syd? And how do you know about her partner's wife?"

"Some bar I stopped by tonight on my way into town, the Cop Out. Girls will tell you anything with enough drinks. You know that." She settled onto the sofa, wine bottle in hand, and crossed her legs. "Besides the trial was big news. It even made the Nashville paper."

"And Syd?"

"God, she is a sweet little thing, isn't she?" Martha rubbed a finger suggestively across her lips.

Regan fought an urge to flog her. Her face heated with anger and the suppression of rage at this vulgar and highly insensitive woman. What had she ever found attractive about her?

"I'm teasing you, baby. I know every emotion you ever had. You'd like to choke me right now, wouldn't you? But I made my point. You're in love with her."

"I'm going to if you don't tell me what I want to know."

"Okay, okay. I met her about three years ago at the same bar when Angie and I were in town for the women's ACC basketball tournament.

I bought her a few drinks and we went to my hotel room. I was totally into her but she wasn't feeling the love, if you get my drift. We did a little grab ass, then for some reason she turned chilly. I finally got off on her leg, fully dressed, as I recall. It wasn't one of my better performances. Afterward, she bolted."

Regan stared at her in disbelief, the heated image she'd carried of them together earlier bleeding from her mind. It was unlike Martha to reveal anything less than a report of stellar sexual performance, so her story had some credence. "Let me get this straight. You were with the woman you cheated on me with, and you were cheating on *her*? You took Syd back to the hotel room you were sharing with your mistress? And when she wasn't into you and wouldn't strip, you humped her leg? Does that about sum it up?"

Martha shifted uncomfortably on the sofa and took a swig straight from the wine bottle. "I wouldn't put it quite that indelicately, but the facts are accurate."

"Did you ever see Syd again?"

"No. As a matter of fact, when I was trying to explain why we needed to hurry, it inadvertently came out that I was in a relationship and *that's* when she went all cold on me."

"You are unbelievable." Regan rose from her chair and started toward the door.

She wanted to hate Martha for what she'd done to their life of fifteen years and for the pain she'd caused. But a preview of Martha's future flashed through her mind. It looked remarkably like her past. She would be forever chasing women, convinced that the next orgasm would be better than the last and the progressively younger elixir of life she sucked from her lovers would prolong her vitality. She would never be content. Before much longer the supply of willing young women would dwindle; Martha would be competing with younger, more appealing cheats. How pathetic.

As she closed the door, all Regan could feel for her was pity and sorrow.

CHAPTER TWENTY

Regan stared at Syd's loft door like it was the top of Pandora's Box, wondering if she really wanted to open it and realizing she had no choice. If she walked away now, she'd never know what might have happened, and that was unacceptable. She felt too much, wanted too much, not to explore the possibilities. Tentatively, she raised her hand and knocked. The door opened almost immediately and her heartbeat faltered as Syd stood in front of her.

Her eyes were red rimmed, her face splotchy, and her cherry silk blouse dotted with dark spots. "I've been so worried. Are you okay?" Her voice was high-pitched with stress and stuffy from crying.

"I needed to think." Regan controlled the urge to take Syd in her arms and comfort her. The pain in Syd's green eyes seemed to saturate her entire body. "May I come in?"

Syd stepped aside. "Of course, I'm sorry. So...you're..." Syd stopped as if she didn't have the right to speak. Her usually confident posture and enticing cockiness had disappeared. In their place was a sense of loss and despair.

"I think *I* need to ask the questions," Regan said.

"Of course, let's sit." Syd motioned toward the balcony. When they were seated in chairs facing each other, she asked, "What do you want to know?"

Regan's insides knotted with tension as she considered once again if she really wanted to hear what Syd had to say. Martha had admitted to a less-than-perfect seduction, which was totally against her self-serving nature. For that reason, Regan believed her story. What if the two versions differed? Who would she believe? Either way, she had to know.

"Tell me about your…whatever it was…with Martha. Everything."

Syd looked dismayed. "Are you sure?"

Regan nodded. "I need to know what happened."

"I've been trying to remember, and I think I've got it all straight. I met her at Jesse's place a few years ago, during the women's ACC tournament. We had a few drinks and I went back to her hotel. Something about the whole situation just didn't feel right…I remember that."

Regan struggled to keep her voice even and her tone unaffected by the jumble of emotions that rolled inside her. "Why? Wasn't she just another conquest?" It hurt to ask the question, and Syd's startled expression said she felt the sting as well.

"I can't explain it. Maybe just instinct. When we got back to her room, it was pretty obvious that two people were staying there. I asked and she said her boss was with her and not to worry because her partner was at home. That's when I made an exit as fast as possible."

"You didn't have sex with her?"

"No, we didn't even get undressed. She was rubbing up against me and I just left. I'm not a home wrecker."

"Except with your colleague's wife?" Regan didn't think a slap would've been as painful as she watched tears well in Syd's eyes. "I have to know, Syd." As if the simple statement could explain all the insecurities she felt and her need to have only the truth between them.

Syd nodded, and swiped at the tears. "It's all right. I don't want us to have any secrets."

Regan felt some of the tension leave her body. Syd's story had roughly approximated Martha's, and she didn't seem to be holding back any details. Her desire to clear the air appeared to be genuine.

"You saw me with her," Syd said with obvious difficulty. "That day…in the restroom. I thought her name was Lacy, but it's Priscilla."

Regan felt like someone reached in and squeezed the blood from her heart. Every agonizing statement from Syd's mouth was played out across her face. Her chin quivered and her voice wavered. The ache in Regan's chest grew with each honest line of confession.

"We met about the time of the Nartey shooting. She'd seen combat in Iraq and was as messed up as I was. We got each other in that sense,

I suppose…understood the toll that killing takes." Syd's affinity for this woman was apparent in the softness and reverence of her tone.

Regan was moved by her sincerity and her willingness to express the feelings that accompanied her revelations. She was also a little envious of this woman who'd been able to console Syd when she needed it most. "Go on."

"I didn't know she was married, much less to one of my squad mates. If I'd been aware of that, it wouldn't have happened between us. But I didn't."

Regan's mind replayed the scene she'd been unable to erase since that night. She could still see Syd's head thrown back in orgasm and the sinewy, mocha-skinned woman's hand thrust deep inside her. She clutched the arms of her chair, her entire being railing against the pictures in her head. Could she manage the jealousy they evoked and, more to the point, would she ever dislodge them from her mind? "Does her husband know about you?"

"Yes, she told him. I wanted to but she begged me to let her. She wanted to be honest with him so they could start over. They love each other very much, I think."

Regan ran out of questions and looked toward the city skyline, taking stock of her feelings about everything that had transpired the last several hours. She'd been exposed to more of Syd's colorful past than she wanted, but with it came another side of Sydney Cabot she wasn't used to, her free-flowing emotions and her willingness to share them. Syd hadn't offered excuses, only explanations, and Regan believed her when she said she'd wanted to face her lover's husband. She let out a long breath of relief that caught halfway up her throat. As far as Syd's integrity was concerned, she found nothing lacking, and she could see why Izzy had chosen a friendship with her. But, could she trust Syd with her heart? Was she ready for that level of responsibility and commitment?

She returned her attention to the woman seated across from her. Syd sat very still, hands clasped in her lap, waiting, Regan realized, for some response from her. She didn't have one. Maybe it was her own fear or the look in Syd's eyes that kept her from speaking. She needed something more from her.

As if sensing her reluctance, Syd slid from her chair, knelt in front of her, and placed her hands on Regan's knees. "I'm so sorry for everything I've put you through. I've been thinking about this a lot. From the minute we met, I've been nothing but a constant source of frustration and pain to you, and I'd do anything to change that."

The touch of Syd's hands combined with the genuine warmth of her words flooded Regan with emotion. Tears stung behind her eyes, and swallowed feelings spasmed in her chest. The desire to embrace Syd, to soothe her as she spoke almost overwhelmed her, but she knew instinctively that Syd needed to speak without her support.

"That first night in the club, my uncooperative attitude during the trial, coming on to you inappropriately while you were trying to defend me, bedding you then treating you like a one-night stand, and finally all this fresh hell tonight. I don't ever want to cause you pain again. I wouldn't blame you if you never spoke to me after tonight." Syd brought Regan's hands to her lips and kissed them lightly. Staring directly into her eyes, she said, "But before you decide, I have one more thing to say."

Regan tried to speak but words failed. She nodded, the warmth of Syd's kiss on her hands still tingling up her arms.

"I'm in love with you." Tears escaped the corners of Syd's eyes as she spoke.

A sharp intake of breath was Regan's initial response as her hands came to her chest. She stared open-mouthed for several seconds, unsure that she'd heard correctly.

"Yes, you heard me. I'm in love with you, Regan Desanto."

"Oh my God. You're—"

"In. Love. With. You. I'll say it as many times as you like, anytime, anywhere, to anyone."

Regan knew she needed to say something coherent soon or they would both die from sheer anticipation and anxiety. "How do you know?"

"I've never felt so completely discombobulated by a woman in my life."

Regan laughed, probably more from tension than anything else, but the emotional outlet was most welcome. "And is that a good thing, according to you?"

"Absolutely. There's never a dull moment with you. You were all kinds of professional and uptight in your job. Then when you let me seduce you, you surrendered your body like we'd been lovers for years.

That was so amazing. And the next time, when you left me begging for more…how could you?"

"You mean you weren't going to ask me to leave that night?"

"Leave? God no. I wanted you to stay the first night we spent together, but the second one I was in pain because I wanted you again so badly. I was trying to find a way to tell you without sounding like a horny sex slut."

Regan couldn't believe what she was hearing. She'd been wrong about Syd wanting her to leave. And all the hellaciously frustrating things she'd been through with Syd since the beginning had actually been endearing to her? Maybe in retrospect. She remembered Syd's confusion that night, and her tentative requests to be held and for Regan to stay.

"I should have given you more time that night," she said, half to herself. "I was afraid, too, Syd. I already cared too much and I couldn't risk waking up with you and—"

"Being discarded," Syd said sadly. "Regan, you've seen the absolute worst of me and yet here you are. You have no idea how that makes me feel. No one has ever had that much faith in me, except on the job. I can trust you with all of me."

Syd rested her head in Regan's lap and wrapped her arms around her waist. The simplicity and surrender of the action released all Regan's restrained emotions. Tears fell from her eyes and she didn't want to stop them. She finally knew that she could trust Syd on a basic level and that it was time to take a chance and trust her with her heart. Even Martha knew the truth. Time for her to face it as well. She'd waited forever to feel this comfortable in another woman's arms.

"I love you too, Syd."

The hug around Regan's waist tightened as Syd snuggled her way up, leaving kisses along the way. "Say it again, please."

"I love you."

When their lips came together, Regan experienced lightness in her heart that had never existed. She felt almost like they were floating off the ground. An army of endorphins vanquished any residual fears and everything became Syd-inspired. She was instantly wet, wiggling uncomfortably against her restrictive clothing. Their mouths and tongues sucked and probed. Their hands stroked, groped, and fondled every body part in reach.

Syd drew back from their kiss. "You make me so hot so fast." She lowered her head to Regan's lap again and ran her hands up the outside of her thighs. Burying her face in Regan's crotch she nuzzled against her jeans, sucking and blowing air against the fabric.

Regan almost came out of her chair as her hands went to the back of Syd's head, holding her in place. "Harder, please." She scooted to the edge of the seat to allow greater access but Syd pulled away and looked at her through lust-clouded eyes.

"Would it be a faux pas to ask for sex after just telling you I love you?"

"It would be a faux pas if you didn't." Regan stood, bringing Syd with her.

They'd shared Syd's bed twice before but somehow this felt different. This time Syd knew what she wanted from Regan and knew that she would continue to want it again and again. This was the person with whom she wanted to share her love and her life forever.

As Regan stood at the foot of the bed waiting expectantly, Syd said, "I don't want to have sex with you tonight. I want to make love with you."

Regan leaned into her. "You can do anything you want with me."

"The first thing I want is both of us naked…at the same time. That hasn't happened before." She shucked Regan's vest off her shoulders, threw it to the floor, and reached for the buttons of her shirt, then stopped. "Wait, I forgot something. Don't move."

She ran around the loft turning all the lights on and then lit candles throughout the bedroom area. When she returned, Regan was completely nude, sitting on the bed.

"I thought I told you not to move." Syd followed her lead and stripped quickly, leaving clothes scattered around the bed.

"I've always had a problem with authority figures. What's with all the lights?"

"I want to see every beautiful inch of you all the time we're making love. And, my God, you're more awesome than I remember."

Syd stood there amazed at the long loveliness of this woman. It was as if an artist had carved her from a mound of alabaster and breathed life into her. Her breasts, thighs, and lusciously tight ass were perfectly proportioned for Syd's tastes, feminine in an androgynous way. When she moved, taut muscles under her skin undulated as if beckoning Syd to join her.

Syd stretched out on the bed, extended her arms, and gave her a come-hither wave. Regan slid along side her and their bodies touched, skin to skin for the first time. Liquid fire poured over Syd as they made full contact. The muscles along Regan's frame flexed and straightened as she nestled into the softer dips and swells of Syd's body.

"I knew it," she whispered into Regan's ear as she tongued the rim. "I knew we'd fit like this." And the amazing thing to Syd was that she'd never actually thought about fitting together with someone physically. Now it seemed essential and so perfect that it was Regan.

She lightly traced Regan's face with the tips of her fingers, memorizing it visually and tactilely. Pausing at her lips, Syd outlined them with her middle digit and gently pressed inside. Regan sucked and tongued her finger while Syd watched. When she slid her finger out of Regan's mouth, she brought it to her own and licked the flavor of Regan from it. She ran her hands through Regan's wavy blond curls and brought their mouths together again. The light minty taste on her tongue mingled with hot breath from her nostrils, making her even more hungry and wet.

Regan's hands danced up her back and over her butt, shooting sparks of excitement through her. Then Regan was at her breasts, kneading and feasting. Her legs stiffened with building sexual tension as she straddled Syd's already soaked thigh. Syd had never been so acutely aware of the intricacies of her lover's body. It was a mental aphrodisiac as powerful as any physical stimulus she'd ever experienced. As Regan rocked her pelvis rhythmically, Syd watched every shifting muscle, every tiny change in her expression. She wanted desperately to prolong the moment as long as possible, but her body was beginning to take over.

"Roll over on your back," Syd said, and nudged Regan away from her.

Regan let a nipple slide from her mouth to protest. "Not yet."

"Yes, yet. I don't want either one of us to come right now and you're getting close."

Reluctantly disengaging, Regan looked up her. "How can you tell?"

"Body language, darling. Besides, I've always known you're a breast woman."

Regan blushed slightly and grinned with a mischievous glint. "And aren't you glad?"

"Extremely. Now lie down and let me have my way with you."

Regan flung her arms and legs open in surrender. "Please do."

Syd straddled Regan's body, absorbing the immense feelings of joy and gratitude that swept through her as Regan so readily splayed herself wide. "Are you okay?" Regan asked. "You look so far away. Are you having second thoughts?"

"Not at all. I just realized how incredibly lucky I am. I probably don't deserve you, but I'm going to have you anyway."

Regan kissed Syd and pulled her back down on top of her. "I love you and you deserve to be happy. Don't ever doubt that. Now make love to me before I explode."

Their kiss sent sweet ripples of desire through Syd's body and she bent low, rubbing her breasts back and forth across Regan's face. Her gaze followed Syd's breasts as they swung tantalizingly. She nipped at them with her mouth, trying to catch one.

"Cruel, you're so cruel."

After she'd had her fun, Syd let Regan capture a nipple in her hot, wet mouth. She sucked, tongued, and rolled the tender flesh, and the sensation rocketed Syd to the depths of her soul. Regan's mouth pulling on her breasts tweaked an invisible connection to her clitoris, which throbbed in pleasurable unison. Syd slid one hand between Regan's legs and cupped her soaking sex while using the other to tease her breasts. Then she let her crotch glide over Regan's stomach, lightly at first then grinding provocatively. With each gyration of her hips, she felt the pressure build. Against protests of more cruelty and deprivation, she worked her way down Regan's body with feather touches from her fingers and tongue.

Regan squirmed like the strokes were drenching rains and she the scorched desert. "I didn't know not touching could feel so damn good."

"You like that, baby?" Syd did a spider tickle in the soft curls between Regan's legs, careful to avoid direct contact with the part begging to be touched.

"Oh, yeah, I like everything you do to me."

Syd continued her tickling, teasing track down Regan's body and settled between her outstretched legs. Gripping Regan's thighs, she rubbed her face back and forth between them, blowing lightly across the swollen lips of her vulva. Moisture glistened on the blond hairs and the aroma of sexual need wafted to Syd's nostrils, kicking up her own desire.

Syd looked up into Regan's eyes, hooded with lust. "Soon, I promise."

"Yes, please. I need you, again."

Syd raised Regan's legs and positioned them over her shoulders. She watched Regan's face as she slid her middle finger into her mouth then lowered it. Regan's eyes were glazed and her stare frenzied as she lay exposed and expectant. Syd slithered her finger through the outer lips just enough to tease, then inched lower until she pressed against the slippery perineum. Regan's bottom lurched off the bed and then back against the pressure of Syd's touch.

"Oh. My. God. What was that? Again."

Syd complied and Regan bucked and collapsed against the force of Syd's finger until the bedding beneath her was soaked. Syd's clit pounded between her legs in direct response to Regan's arousal. She slid her finger up and nudged at Regan's opening. She couldn't hold out much longer. The tension in Regan's legs, combined with the husky moans deep in her throat, told Syd that she was on the edge as well.

"Please, Syd." Regan's voice was throaty and quivering with barely contained emotion.

"Do you want me inside you?"

"Yes, now." Regan humped to emphasize her point.

Syd inched her finger inside Regan's body, waited for the reflex thrust, and pulled back.

"Oh, nooo. Don't do this, Syd. I can't take it."

Lowering her head to kiss Regan's rigid clit, Syd smiled up at her. "Of course you can take it, baby. You're begging for it." She entered her again and felt Regan's insides contract around her, pulling and sucking her farther in. She withdrew.

Regan thrashed beneath her and reached out to force contact. "For God's sake. Lick me. Suck me. *Something*. I'm dying here. We'll do slow and easy later."

Syd smiled at the effect she was having. She would never have imagined Regan could be so passionate and demanding in her need. It was quite a change from the first time they'd had sex, when Regan had been submissive and her eyes had asked for patience. Now she knew her body and had no problems saying so.

"Okay, okay." Syd gave her what she wanted. She buried her finger deep inside and adapted to Regan's pace. Her lips captured Regan's clit and her tongue danced across the sensitive ridge of swollen flesh.

"Oh yeah, that's it. More tongue flicking," Regan said.

Syd's body burned and the sheet beneath her pelvis suddenly became an erotic stimulus as she rubbed against it.

"Come here, Syd. I need to feel you beside me when we come."

"But I can't do this," she licked slowly across Regan's clit, "if I come up there."

"Leave one finger inside and thumb my clit. I'm so close and I want to be holding you."

Syd reluctantly kissed the center of Regan's sex one last time and dipped her tongue into the opening before sliding on top of her, fingers still in place.

"Straddle my thigh. I want to feel you come on me."

"Oh, yeah." Syd moaned as she rode Regan's leg from her knee to the resting place against her crotch, then settled into Regan's thrusting rhythm. Regan flexed her quad muscle and Syd pumped hungrily against the firm, stimulating resistance as her clit twitched and strained toward orgasm. "Soon, baby."

"Me too, faster, please," Regan urged.

Syd nibbled the side of Regan's neck, her strong jaw, and eagerly found her mouth. They kissed and, connected at every point, humped, sucked, probed, and rubbed faster until they both gasped for air and Regan's coiled muscles started to release.

"Now, Syd, I'm coming now." She rocked her pelvis against Syd's hand and grabbed her ass to hang on. "Come with me, Syd."

A bolt of energy broke free inside Syd and spiraled throughout her body. Using her knee, she added pressure against the hand that worked Regan's clit. At the same time she pounded her aching flesh against Regan's thigh. "Oh yeah…now, baby, now."

Their bodies bucked and muscles quivered. Lusty moans of satisfied relief filled the room and the scent of their sex drifted in the air like a dense fog. Syd felt the cocoon of Regan's insides contract and release around her fingers in perfect time to the pulsing between her own legs. She rode the wave and marveled at the synchronicity of the moment.

When the physical sensations left them weak, they clung to each other, rocking, stroking, and soothing the heat from their skin. Regan reached down and pulled the sheet across them. Syd mumbled lazy thanks, unwilling to remove her fingers from Regan's body. She had never felt so connected to another woman, so comfortable in her arms, and so unwilling to be parted from her. Her heart ached with the beauty and perfection of the moment.

This is what love feels like, she told herself. She rested her head against Regan's chest and listened to the heartbeat that she knew from this day forward would be joined to hers. "I love you so much, Regan."

"I love you, too, baby." Regan barely attempted to move and asked, "Is it time for me to go?"

Syd could tell by the lilt of her voice that she was poking fun. "Don't even think about it." She wiggled her fingers still buried inside Regan and said, "And I've got just the method to restrain you, if necessary."

Regan settled deeper onto her hand and conceded, "I believe you do, Officer. Maybe I could learn to like authority figures after all, at least one of them." Then she moved away from Syd, seemed to consider her next statement, and said, "I hate to bring up a bad subject, but I do have one more question."

"Anything."

"Are there any more skeletons in your closet that I should know about?"

"Nope, you've seen them all. All the warts and all the mistakes. There's nothing else and nothing I'm hiding. I promise."

Regan rolled on top of Syd and captured her gaze, blue eyes sharp with sincerity and a sparkle of play. "Good, because after I finish ravishing your body, I plan to start on your soul. I want you, Syd, every part of you, inside and out."

"Take me. I'm all yours." Syd spoke those words for the first time in her life, and she meant them.

About the Author

VK Powell is a thirty-year veteran of a midsized police department. She was a police officer by necessity (it paid the bills) and a writer by desire (it didn't). Her career spanned numerous positions including beat officer, homicide detective, field sergeant, vice/narcotics lieutenant, district captain, and assistant chief of police. Now retired, she lives in central North Carolina and devotes her time to writing (though she still has trouble calling herself a "writer"), traveling, and volunteering.

VK is a member of the Golden Crown Literary Society and Romance Writers of America. She is the author of three erotic short stories published by Bold Strokes Books: "Toy with Me," in *Erotic Interludes 3: Lessons in Love*; "Dessert, Anyone?" in *Erotic Interludes 4: Extreme Passions*; and "One for the Road" in *Erotic Interludes 5: Road Games*. Her first novel, *To Protect and Serve*, was released in March 2008. *Fever*, VK's third book, will be set in Africa and is scheduled for release in 2010.